T0113642

Praise for
Shrouds of Holly

"Charming . . . Will provide warm holiday entertainment."
—*Publishers Weekly*

"Delightful . . . Starring an intrepid heroine."
—*Midwest Book Review*

"Well-crafted and surprising all the way to the last page, *Shrouds of Holly* is a pleasurable read that is sure to get you in the mood for the holidays!" —*The Romance Readers Connection*

"Likable characters, charming surroundings, and eclectic guests continue to make this an enjoyable series. Bravo, Kate Kingsbury . . . for making this a holiday tradition."
—MyShelf.com

Praise for
Slay Bells

"A pre–WWI whodunit in the classic style, furnished with amusing characters." —*Kirkus Reviews*

"The author draws as much from *Fawlty Towers* as she does from Agatha Christie, crafting a charming . . . cozy delicately flavored with period details of pre–WWI rural England." —**Publishers Weekly*

"A charming historical mystery. Its straightforward writing and tight plotting are reminiscent of Agatha Christie's books—with a dash of *Upstairs, Downstairs* mixed in."
—*Cozy Library*

"A true holiday gem." —*Mystery Scene*

DECKED WITH FOLLY

KATE KINGSBURY

BERKLEY PRIME CRIME, NEW YORK

THE BERKLEY PUBLISHING GROUP
Published by the Penguin Group
Penguin Group (USA) Inc.
375 Hudson Street, New York, New York 10014, USA
Penguin Group (Canada), 90 Eglinton Avenue East, Suite 700, Toronto, Ontario M4P 2Y3, Canada
(a division of Pearson Penguin Canada Inc.)
Penguin Books Ltd., 80 Strand, London WC2R 0RL, England
Penguin Group Ireland, 25 St. Stephen's Green, Dublin 2, Ireland (a division of Penguin Books Ltd.)
Penguin Group (Australia), 250 Camberwell Road, Camberwell, Victoria 3124, Australia
(a division of Pearson Australia Group Pty. Ltd.)
Penguin Books India Pvt. Ltd., 11 Community Centre, Panchsheel Park, New Delhi—110 017, India
Penguin Group (NZ), 67 Apollo Drive, Rosedale, North Shore 0632, New Zealand
(a division of Pearson New Zealand Ltd.)
Penguin Books (South Africa) (Pty.) Ltd., 24 Sturdee Avenue, Rosebank, Johannesburg 2196,
South Africa

Penguin Books Ltd., Registered Offices: 80 Strand, London WC2R 0RL, England

This book is an original publication of The Berkley Publishing Group.

FIRST EDITION: November 2009

Library of Congress Cataloging-in-Publication Data

Kingsbury, Kate.
    Decked with folly / Kate Kingsbury. — 1st ed.
        p.   cm.
    ISBN 978-0-425-23001-5
1. Christmas stories.   I. Title.
    PR9199.3.K44228D43   2009
    813'.54—dc22   2009027384

147429898

To Bill,
for believing in me when I sometimes
have trouble believing in myself.
Thank you, my love.
Without you,
I would simply cease to be.

ACKNOWLEDGMENTS

There are very few authors whose work cannot be greatly improved by a good editor, and I am fortunate to have one of the best. I sometimes think Sandra Harding knows my characters as well as I do. Thank you, Sandy, for another remarkable job.

My thanks to Paige Wheeler, my industrious and savvy agent, for her constant encouragement and enthusiasm. You never let me down and that means the world to me.

Many thanks also to Judith Murello and the incredible art department. My covers are a joy, and so beautifully rendered. I've loved every one of them.

Thanks to a dear friend, Ann Wraight, for sending me research clips and magazines all the way from England.

To my fans, who send me wonderful e-mails and give me so much pleasure with their warm wishes. The staff and guests of the Pennyfoot Hotel thrive on your praise. Thank you.

To a very special fan, Helen Gibson, who turned one hundred years old on June 28, 2009.

To my husband, for being the wind beneath my wings. Your understanding and faith in me give me the strength to persevere when the chips are down.

DECKED WITH
FOLLY

CHAPTER

🎠 1 🎠

The Christmas season was Cecily Sinclair Baxter's favorite time of the year. Or it would be, if it weren't for what had now become known as the Christmas curse.

Every year, it seemed, something quite dreadful happened to put a dampener on things. This year, Cecily fervently hoped there would be an exception.

After all, there was so much to look forward to with joyful anticipation. For one thing, her job as manager of the select country club situated on the quiet southeast coast of England afforded her scintillating company.

In the few short years since the turn of the century and Queen Victoria's demise, it seemed as if all of England were eager to celebrate with all the gusto they could muster. Her guests were no exception.

It was a time for music, dance, joyful laughter, and the consumption of vast culinary delights from her famed chef, Michel. The Pennyfoot wallowed in delicious aromas of spices and herbs emitting from the kitchen, while the halls were filled with the fragrance of pine and cedar, arranged by the clever hands of her best friend, Madeline Pengrath Prestwick.

Descending the curving staircase, beautifully draped with bright red ribbon and holly, Cecily absorbed the heartwarming sights and smells of Christmas with a sense of well-being. This year there would be no curse to spoil the celebrations. She was sure of it.

Her enthusiasm wavered a bit as she spotted the gentleman waiting for her at the foot of the stairs. Archibald Parker's stunted height and heavy girth caused him to wheeze, and his busy eyes constantly haunted the dark corners of the room as if he expected to see something undesirable lurking there.

His luxurious mustache apparently gave him some discomfort, since he twitched his nose at regular intervals while talking. Cecily found this all quite distracting, and had trouble following a conversation with the man, which is why she attempted to avoid him whenever possible.

Despite her best efforts, Archie, as he insisted upon being called, had managed to waylay her on several occasions over the past three days. It seemed that he had done so again, since his gaze remained fixed on her until she reached him.

"Mr. Parker!" She managed a polite smile. "You have risen early. It's not yet time for breakfast to be served. I trust all is well with you?"

DECKED WITH FOLLY

"Quite, quite, Mrs. B. Yes, indeed." Archie's twitching nose sent his mustache into a brief, lopsided angle. "I did want a word with you, however, if I may be so bold?"

Cecily suppressed a sigh. "Of course, Mr. Parker."

"Archie, please."

He looked so anxious she hurried to reassure him. "Archie, then. How may I be of assistance?"

His gaze switched to the corner where the grandfather clock resided. "Well, I was . . . er . . . wondering if you'd be interested in any of my wares. I'm a medical salesman, you know. In the great city of London." He coughed, bringing a pudgy hand to his mouth. "Yes, indeed."

Having been informed of that on more than one occasion, by Archie himself no less, Cecily had trouble hiding her irritation. "So you have mentioned. I believe I have already explained about my friend, Mrs. Prestwick? She is an herbalist, and supplies all my needs."

As on all the previous occasions when she had mentioned Madeline's penchant for herbal remedies, Archie managed to convey his disgust with a slight toss of his practically bald head. "Don't believe in all that weeds and herbs stuff myself. You never know what you're swallowing. Could be poison for all we know." He uttered a nervous laugh. "Now on the other hand, these little pills"—he withdrew a small bottle from his pocket—"best thing for the digestion you ever did see." He waved the bottle in her face.

"My digestion is in quite good order, thank you." Still holding on to her smile by sheer willpower, she started to move away, but Archie slithered in front of her again. "What about regularity? Have any problems with that?"

Cecily paused, her smile vanishing. "Mr. Parker, I really must insist that you not use this establishment for soliciting. If I find out that you have been harassing the guests with attempts to sell—"

"Oh, no, no, Mrs. B. You have my word you are the only one to whom I have mentioned my profession. Yes, indeed."

"Really. However did I manage to be so fortunate?"

Archie beamed. "Well, I just thought I could do you a favor or two, seeing as how you are always running about this building." He waved his arm in the air. "Pretty sizable building at that. Must be quite tiring at your age."

Cecily winced. While she was perhaps a little closer to fifty than forty, she did not consider herself in the least old, and to be reminded that she was no longer a sprightly young thing offended her greatly.

Archibald Parker was a guest of the club, however, and as such had to be treated with due respect. Even if the man was a complete and utter oaf. Moreover, he had arrived without a companion, and Cecily's kind heart compelled her to feel sympathy for anyone spending Christmas without a loved one by his side.

"I can assure you, I will enlighten you if I should feel the need for any of your medical remedies." She regained her smile, albeit with some difficulty. "In the meantime, perhaps you'd like to wait in the library for breakfast to be served?"

Archie glanced down the hallway. "Perhaps I will. Er . . . will your chief housemaid be serving breakfast this morning, by any chance?"

Taken aback, Cecily took a moment to answer. "You're referring to Mrs. McBride, perhaps?"

Archie nodded. "McBride. Gertie. Yes, that's her. I like her temperament. Spirited young woman, that." He attempted a wink, but his nose twitched at the same time, pulling his entire face into a grotesque grimace.

"I'm sure she would be most flattered by your comments," Cecily said, trying not to grit her teeth.

To her surprise, a look of alarm crossed Archie's flushed face. "Oh, please don't mention that I spoke of her." He shot a worried glance across the lobby. "Wouldn't want the young lady to get the wrong impression."

It was Cecily's considered opinion that her robust housemaid would waste no time in putting the objectionable man in his place. With considerable fervor if necessary. "Of course. You can rely on my discretion."

"Good, good." He thrust a hand in his pocket and came up with a large white handkerchief. Mopping his brow, he muttered, "Don't want to go putting ideas in young heads, now do we. Wouldn't do at all."

Cecily was about to answer when the front door flew open and a bulky man wearing overalls charged through it. Clive Russell was the club's maintenance man, and right now he appeared to be most disturbed.

His dark hair, usually neatly combed, looked as if he'd been fighting a strong wind, and he seemed to have trouble finding words, since his mouth opened and shut without a sound coming out of it.

Watching him stumble toward her, his hat crushed in his hands, Cecily felt a familiar sinking feeling in her stomach. "If you will excuse me, Mr. Parker," she murmured, and without waiting for his answer, hurried to meet the other man.

Clive halted as she reached him, his eyes wide with shock. "Dead body," he said hoarsely. "In the duck pond."

Cecily clutched her throat. For the past week she had fought the worry that something dreadful might occur, as it had so often during this time of year. Now it appeared her worst fears had been realized. It seemed they would never be rid of the dreaded Christmas curse.

"Oh, no, no." She drew a deep breath. "Tell me what happened."

Clive made an obvious effort to lower his voice as the sound of chatter warned of people descending the stairs. "Don't know exactly, m'm, though the bloke stinks of booze. I reckon he must have been drunk and fallen headfirst into the water. Looks like his head hit a rock or something."

"One of our guests?"

Clive shook his head, and Cecily swung around as someone spoke from behind her.

"Mrs. B.? Is anything wrong?" Archie peered up at her, his sharp gaze darting from her to Clive and back again. "Can I be of any assistance?"

"No, no, thank you." Cecily glanced at the grandfather clock. "Breakfast should be served any minute, Mr. Parker. I strongly suggest you make your way to the dining room. You don't want to be late for your meal."

The sight of guests filing down the stairs must have convinced the man. He gave Clive one hard stare, reluctantly nodded, and then ambled off after a small group of visitors heading for the dining room.

"Where is the body now?" Cecily demanded, drawing Clive out of earshot of the chattering guests.

"Still in the pond." He swallowed. "I didn't know what to do so I came straight here."

"All right. Find Samuel and ask him to help you get the body into the stable. Do it now while everyone is at breakfast and let's hope that no one sees you. Don't talk to anyone and don't answer any questions, is that clear?"

"Yes, m'm." Clive touched his forehead. "Right away, m'm." Instead of leaving, however, he hovered there, refusing to meet her gaze.

Her feeling of dread intensified. "What is it, Clive? What are you not telling me?"

For a moment she thought he wouldn't answer, but then he shoved his hat in his pocket and took a deep breath. "The dead man, m'm. I'm afraid it's someone with whom you're well acquainted."

She stared at him, her heart pounding so hard she was sure she would faint. "I thought you said it wasn't one of the guests."

"No, m'm. It's not."

The foyer appeared to tilt a little and she reached out a hand to steady herself on the hallstand nearby. "Not . . . not one of the staff?"

"No, m'm."

Drowning in relief, she grasped his sleeve and shook it. "Then for heaven's sake tell me. Who is it?"

"I'm afraid it's Mr. Ian Rossiter, m'm. Gertie McBride's ex-husband."

Stunned, she could only stand and stare at him. "*Ian?* But I thought he was in London. What is he doing here? Does Gertie know he's here?" She clapped a hand over her mouth.

"Oh, my goodness. *Gertie.* I shall have to tell her." She paused, leaning forward in her distress. "Unless you've already told her?"

"No, m'm." Clive shuffled his feet and looked away at the door. "I didn't tell anybody but you."

"Then I shall have to . . . oh, my Lord." She shook her head to clear the fog of disbelief. "Run along, Clive. Get Ian . . . get the body out of that pond and out of sight before someone else sees him. Then I want both you and Samuel to report back to me in my office."

"Yes, m'm." This time Clive shuffled off to the door, letting in a gust of cold wind as he opened it, then closed it behind him.

Cecily took a moment to collect herself. Ian dead. It didn't seem possible. She hadn't seen him in quite a while, but at one time he had been a trusted member of her staff. Until that dreadful affair when he'd married Gertie, neglecting to tell her he already had a wife in London.

He'd gone back to London after Gertie had found out the truth. Then a year ago he'd come back, demanding to see his twins. He'd even gone so far as attempting to kidnap Gertie's daughter, until Clive had caught up with him and saved the little girl.

Something had happened to Ian in those years after he'd left—something that had changed him into a hard, bitter man. Cecily uttered a deep sigh. Now he was lying dead outside, and once more her Christmas would be interrupted while she dealt with another death at the Pennyfoot.

*　　*　　*

DECKED WITH FOLLY

Downstairs in the kitchen, Mrs. Chubb wiped her brow as she leaned into the massive oven to retrieve a sizzling pan of sausages. With a tea towel wrapped around each hand, she grasped the pan and hauled it out to drop it on top of the stove. The tempting aroma of bacon and sausage reminded her she hadn't eaten her own breakfast yet. Nor, it seemed, would she have that luxury for at least another half hour.

Behind her, the clatter of dishes assured her the maids were loading up the dumbwaiter with covered silver platters of bacon, fried eggs, fried tomatoes, fried roes, and fried bread.

The fried herrings and poached haddock had already been sent up, and by now Gertie, Pansy, and the new maid, Mabel, hired for the Christmas rush, would be collecting dirty dishes to send down once the waiter had been unloaded.

It was all timed down to the second, and Mrs. Chubb, the Pennyfoot's competent housekeeper, took pride in seeing that everything was in the proper place at the proper time.

Even if it meant doing Michel's job, like getting sausages out of a hot oven. Glaring at the pantry door, she yelled, "Michel? What are you doing in there? I hope you're not sipping on that blinking brandy again!"

Mrs. Chubb rarely used questionable language unless she was really agitated. Apparently Michel must have noted her resentment, as he appeared in the doorway, his tall white hat bobbing back and forth as he wagged a finger at the housekeeper. "That ees no way to talk to a chef of such renown. I have not touched one single drop of ze brandy. *Non.*"

"Then what are you doing in there?" Mrs. Chubb slapped a cover on the sausages and carried the pan over to the dumbwaiter. One of the maids grabbed it from her and shoved it onto the pile of platters.

Waiting just long enough for the maid to haul on the rope and send the load up to the dining room, Mrs. Chubb spun around and came face-to-face with the chef.

"If you really must know," he said, his voice heavy with sarcasm, "I search for the jug of cream. I make the custard, and I must have the cream to put in it, *oui*? What is custard without ze cream, huh?"

"All right, you don't have to get all hoity-toity with me." Mrs. Chubb shoved past him and walked back to the large wooden table in the center of the room. "Next time, load the sausages before you look for the cream. I don't have time to do your job as well as mine."

Michel's face turned red, a sure sign he was about to indulge in his favorite pastime—rattling saucepans and lids just to establish his superiority to everyone within earshot. It was a completely wasted effort, since the staff was used to the noise and did their best to ignore him.

Mrs. Chubb winced as the first saucepan lid crashed to the floor. One of these days, she thought darkly, she'd bash one of Michel's saucepans right over his head. It was bad enough putting up with his fake French accent, which disappeared whenever he'd downed enough brandy to kill a cow—but his temper tantrums gave her a headache with all that crashing and banging.

She picked up her rolling pin, prepared to do some banging of her own, but just then the door swung open. Mrs. Chubb looked up, and dropped the rolling pin when she saw Mrs. Baxter walk in. Madam never visited the kitchen during mealtimes. She knew better than to disturb the staff during their busiest part of the day.

The housekeeper stared at her manager in dismay. Something had to be up for madam to come in during breakfast. Even Michel stopped banging the saucepans about, and the maids all stopped talking and stood huddled in the corner, apprehension written all over their faces.

Mrs. Chubb wiped her hands on her apron and waited.

Madam glanced around the kitchen, and her face looked pinched and white when she said, "I don't see Gertie. Is she upstairs?"

"Yes, m'm." Mrs. Chubb squared her shoulders. "What's she gone and done now, then?"

Madam blinked, as if she didn't understand the question. "Done? Oh, she hasn't done anything." She paused, and an odd expression crossed her face. Her voice sounded strange when she added, "Nothing that I'm aware of, at least. I do need to talk to her, however. Right away, in my office, if you please, Mrs. Chubb."

"Yes, m'm. Certainly, m'm." Her chest heavy with dread, the housekeeper beckoned to one of the maids. "Go and find Gertie. Tell her madam wants to see her in her office right away. After that, stay and help Pansy and Mabel until Gertie gets back."

Looking frightened, the maid dropped a nervous curtsey then fled out the door.

Madam passed a hand over her forehead. "I'm sorry, Mrs. Chubb. I know this is the worst possible time to drag your chief housemaid away, but it's imperative that I speak with her before—" She cut off her words abruptly and turned for the door. "I'll be as quick as possible," she called over her shoulder, then she was gone, the door silently swinging behind her.

Mrs. Chubb felt for the back of a chair and plopped down on it.

Michel whistled between his teeth. "What ze devil was all that about?"

"I don't know," Mrs. Chubb said slowly. "But I have a nasty feeling that whatever it is, Gertie is not going to like it."

CHAPTER

✿ 2 ✿

Standing in the entrance to the doorway, Gertie McBride dug her fists into her hips and, in a hoarse whisper, told the maid cowering in front of her, "I don't have bleeding time to go to madam's office now! Is she off her blinking rocker? I've got to get breakfast on the tables." Turning away, she grabbed a tray from the maid at the waiter.

"Madam said to tell you that it was important and to come right away."

Gertie paused. It wasn't like the frumpy little thing in front of her to stand her ground unless she was sure of herself. "So what does she want?"

"She didn't say." Looking close to tears, the maid raised her chin. "Mrs. Chubb said for me to help Pansy and Mabel until you get back."

Gertie glanced into the dining room and caught sight of Pansy, her second-in-command. The skinny young girl was heading toward her, balancing a pile of dirty dishes on each arm.

There was no time to dither about. It had to be important for Mrs. Chubb to send this little twerp to help them. Making up her mind, Gertie thrust the pan of sausages at the maid. "Here, take these in there and put them on the sideboard next to the eggs and bacon. And don't bleeding drop nothing neither, or you'll have to go back to the kitchen to get more."

"Yes, Mrs. McBride." The maid started to curtsey, thought better of it, grabbed hold of the tray, and scuttled into the dining room.

Pansy gave her a startled look as she scurried by, then lifted an eyebrow when she reached the door. "What's going on, then? Why is she serving?"

Gertie shrugged. "Dunno. Mrs. Chubb sent her up. I've got to go to madam's office. Just try and manage with her for now. I'll be back as soon as I can."

Pansy's face filled with concerned curiosity, but she nodded and carried the dishes to the dumbwaiter, where a maid took them from her.

Gertie waited just long enough to see Pansy take the last of the platters from the waiter. Satisfied, she turned and rushed down the hallway, frantically trying to recall whatever it was she'd done to earn a summons to the office.

Cecily looked up as the tap on the door disturbed her thoughts. Bracing herself for what she knew would be a difficult and emotional ordeal, she called out, "Come in!"

Gertie peered around the door, her face creased with worry. "It's me, m'm. You wanted to see me?"

"Yes, yes." Cecily beckoned her with an impatient hand. "Come in and take a seat."

Gertie slunk across the floor to a chair and plopped down on it. "Mrs. Chubb says it's important."

Cecily folded her hands on the desk and tried to collect her thoughts.

Leaning forward, Gertie blurted out, "I didn't do nothing wrong, did I, m'm? I haven't broken nothing, at least not in the last month or two, and I've tried to get the meals out on the tables on time. Course, it's bloody hard with a new maid what don't know her flipping right hand from her left and all, but I do try—"

"Gertie!"

Cecily had raised her voice to halt the torrent of words, and Gertie sat up as if she'd been stung. "Yes, m'm. Sorry, m'm. I'll shut up now."

Cecily drew a deep breath. "Gertie, I'm afraid I have some disturbing news."

The housemaid stared at her, her dark eyes widening in alarm. "Not me twins is it, m'm? They was all right when I left them this morning. Daisy's supposed to be taking care of them and she's a really good nanny, but sometimes—"

"Gertie! It's not the twins."

Gertie's shoulders sagged. "All right, then. You'd better tell me what it is and get it over with." She cleared her throat. "If you please, m'm."

"It's about Ian Rossiter."

The alarm leapt into Gertie's eyes again. "Ian? What's he been up to now? I hope he's not hanging around my twins again. I'll cut off his bleeding head if he . . ." She must have seen something in Cecily's face as her words trailed off, and she waited in uneasy silence.

"I'm afraid he's dead, Gertie," Cecily said, as gently as possible.

The housemaid slumped back, and her face was a mixture of emotions—shock, relief, and something Cecily hadn't expected to see. A distinct expression of guilt that was quickly extinguished.

"Bloody hell," Gertie muttered. "What happened to him, then?"

"We think he had been drinking, perhaps a little too much, and fell into the duck pond. He must have hit his head and drowned."

Gertie digested this news, then nodded. "I see. Well, like they say, everything comes to he what waits. I always knew he would come to a bad end one day. I'm sorry he's dead, but I can't say it's going to ruin my Christmas. Not after he tried to take away my babies." She flicked a wary glance at Cecily. "Does that make me a wicked woman, m'm?"

Cecily let out her breath on a sigh. "Of course not, Gertie. I know you've been living with the fear of losing your twins ever since Ian tried to kidnap little Lillian. I can understand how you feel, now that their father is no longer a threat."

Gertie sighed. "He should never have married me, knowing he was still married to his real wife. He should have been honest from the start."

"I think he felt obligated once he found out you were having his baby. He wanted to do the right thing."

"The right thing? By me or by his real wife?" Gertie rose, her face hard with bitterness. "He did neither one of us a favor. It was stupid of me to get in the family way before I was married, I admit that. But that didn't give him the right to pretend he was free to marry me when he had a wife sitting at home, did it. We went through that whole wedding in the church and everything. He was a cheat and a liar, and bloody dangerous at that. I'm not really sorry he's dead. I don't care if that does make me a wicked woman. I'm bleeding glad to be rid of him."

She rushed to the door, paused, and with a sob in her voice, muttered, "Excuse me, m'm. I must get back to the dining room." Without waiting for permission she dropped a stiff curtsey and flew outside.

The door closed sharply behind her and Cecily winced. She hadn't handled that well at all, but something about Gertie's attitude worried her.

It was no secret to anyone that the volatile housemaid had threatened to kill Ian on more than one occasion. Not that she didn't have good cause to hate the man. Some people, however, might get the notion that Gertie had something to do with Ian's untimely death.

Cecily shook her head, impatient with herself. It was an accident, nothing more. She was worrying about nothing. She had sent for Kevin Prestwick and he would be there soon. He would make it official, setting her fears to rest. She would just have to wait until then.

Gertie's headlong rush down the corridor almost ended in disaster as she rounded the corner. Since breakfast was still being served she hadn't expected to encounter anyone on her mad dash back to the dining room, but just as she reached the corner a man stepped out in front of her, then leapt back as she charged right into him.

"Strewth!" The man mopped his forehead, thrusting a thick lock of red hair out of his eyes. "I thought you were going to bowl me right over."

Having barely bumped him, Gertie tossed her head. "Sorry, sir. I didn't see you coming."

"Oh, that's all right, me ol' darlin'." The man winked at her. "I don't mind being bumped into by a beauty such as yourself."

Rolling her eyes, Gertie made to pass him by, but he laid a hand on her arm.

"Hold on a minute, what's yer blinking hurry? We were just getting acquainted. Let me introduce myself. I'm Sid Barrett—a gentleman and a scholar." He grinned. "I think my Christmas just took a turn for the better."

"If you'll excuse me, sir . . ." Gertie dragged her arm free of his grasp. "I'm needed in the dining room."

"Oh, right ho. Maybe later then." He tilted his head to one side. "P'raps you and me could have a pint or two down the old George and Dragon, eh?"

"I'm sorry, sir, but the servants are not allowed to mix with the guests."

Without waiting for his answer, she took off once more, shaking her head as Sid Barrett called out after her, "I'll try and catch you later, luv!"

"Not if I see you coming first," she muttered under her breath. Saucy blighter. Here she was, the mother of twins and all.

DECKED WITH FOLLY

Twins who now had no father.

The realization hit her under the ribs, making her gasp for breath. Not that Ian had been any kind of father to the twins. They hadn't known he existed until a year ago . . . and even now they had no idea he was their father. He hadn't set eyes on his kids until last Christmas, when he'd suddenly decided he wanted to take one of them back to London with him. Gertie still couldn't understand why he'd waited all these years, and why now. Not that it mattered. Ian was dead. She knew she should be sad about that, and in a way she was sorry he'd passed on at such an early age. But now she was free, and her kids were safe forever. That's all that mattered. And she was not going to let Ian Rossiter spoil another Christmas for her. Never again.

Reaching the door of the dining room, Gertie paused, her smile spreading over her face. She had Dan to keep her company now. In the short time she'd known him, he'd become more of a father figure to her little ones than Ian had ever been. Dan Perkins, who used to own Abbitson's butcher's shop, and who'd swept her off her feet with his ability to make her laugh out loud and his kindness to her children.

Her, Dan, Lillian, and James. They were like a family now, and even though Dan had never mentioned marriage to her, she nursed a strong hope that someday soon he'd ask her to be his wife. And that, she decided, would be worth all the bother she'd put up with from the late Mr. Ian Rossiter.

What's more, she had nothing to feel guilty about. Nothing at all.

*   *   *

19

Cecily looked up as the door swung open, half expecting to see Gertie standing there again. The tall, silver-haired man who entered, however, looked every bit as upset as her housemaid, if not more so.

"What the blazes is going on? I just saw Samuel and Clive in the stables and neither one of them will tell me what they're up to. They told me to ask you."

Cecily lifted a grave face to her husband. "I was just coming to tell you, dear. I'm afraid I have some rather bad news."

Baxter stared at her, his irritation turning to alarm. "Don't tell me . . . oh good Lord." He flipped his tails and sat down on the chair Gertie had vacated. "Who is it this time? One of the guests?"

"No, dear. It's not one of the guests. I'm afraid it's Ian Rossiter."

Baxter's eyes widened. "That scoundrel? What on earth was he doing here? What happened to him?"

"Apparently he fell into the duck pond and drowned."

Baxter pinched his lips. "Are you pulling my leg, because if so—"

"No, dear. I wouldn't joke about a dreadful tragedy such as this."

"The duck pond is less than two feet deep."

"Yes, dear, I am aware of that. Clive says the dead man smelled of spirits. He must have been drinking and fainted or something. It appears that he hit his head when he fell into the pond."

"Good Lord. Poor blighter. What in heaven's name was

he doing out by the duck pond?" Baxter shook his head. "For that matter, what was he doing here at the Pennyfoot? Did you know he was down here? I thought he was in London."

"Precisely the impression I had, as well."

"Have you sent for Prestwick and that fool policeman? I suppose we shall have to put up with his inept bungling as usual."

"Yes, I've sent for both Dr. Prestwick and P.C. Northcott." Cecily got up from her chair and rounded the desk to her husband's side. Placing a hand on his shoulder, she leaned over to murmur in his ear. "Do try to be civil to them both, Bax, dear. It is the season of good cheer, after all."

Baxter grunted. "Prestwick I can take, in small doses. That idiot constable, however, is another matter. I can't imagine how he keeps his job. Surely Inspector Cranshaw can see Northcott for the worthless twit he is?"

Cecily shuddered, as she always did at the mention of the inspector's name. The detestable man had sworn to close down the Pennyfoot years ago, when he suspected her of illegally running card rooms.

He had never been able to prove their existence, thanks to the well-hidden area beneath the floorboards of the wine cellar, and now that the Pennyfoot was a country club, her license allowed her to run the card games within the law.

Cranshaw, however, still bore a grudge, and was always on the lookout for any infraction that might lead to the closure of the club, and the banishment of what he considered a thorn in his side, namely Cecily Sinclair Baxter.

"Well," she said, dismissing the despised man from her mind, "since this is obviously an accident, Sam Northcott will have little to do but write a simple report. As for Kevin, he will remove the body and write his own report, and then we shall be done with the whole sad business."

She returned to her desk and sat down. "I just hope they get here soon so we get it over with."

"Amen." Baxter rose. "Shouldn't say this, but I can't say I'm sorry to see the back of that man. Nothing but trouble, that's all he was."

With her finger Cecily traced the Pennyfoot's name on the cover of the ledger in front of her. "I agree Ian caused poor Gertie a lot of heartache, but I can't forget what he was like when he worked here all those years ago. He was amusing, hardworking, and loyal. That's the Ian I like to remember and for that reason, I feel very sad that he's gone."

Baxter moved over to the desk and leaned his hands on the polished surface. "That young man departed a long time ago. He's not the same man who tried to kidnap our goddaughter and threatened Gertie on more than one occasion."

"No, indeed. I wonder what could have happened to him to change him so?" She looked up into her husband's face. "I wonder if there's someone we should notify of his death? He must have family somewhere."

Baxter shook his head. "Let Prestwick take care of all that. Try to put this out of your head, my precious. You have enough to worry about making sure your guests enjoy their Christmas. I don't want this to spoil your favorite time of year."

"I suppose so."

"By the way, how's that new footman, what's his name, getting along?"

Recognizing that he'd deliberately changed the subject, Cecily smiled. "Sidney Barrett? All right, I suppose. I haven't had any complaints. He seems a friendly young man, very eager to please. I was surprised how much he knew about the Pennyfoot's staff. He obviously did his homework before applying for a position here."

"Good." Baxter straightened. "It's hard to find good servants these days."

"It certainly is. We are so lucky to have good people to work for us." Cecily glanced at the door. "I wonder what's keeping those men. I told Clive to report back to me once they had hidden Ian's body in the stables."

Just as she spoke a light tap on the door answered her. At her summons the two men entered. Clive wore a worried frown that darkened his rugged features, while Samuel, her young stable manager, kept shaking his head, as if he still couldn't believe what had happened.

"That were a close one," Samuel said, scratching the back of his head. "Right after Mr. Baxter left, one of the guests came into the stables and started up his motorcar. One of the horses got spooked when the motor backfired and just missed giving Clive a nasty kick in the head."

Cecily looked at her maintenance man in alarm. "Clive! Are you all right?"

"Yes, m'm. Quite all right. Shook me up a bit, but more because I thought the bloke would see us hiding the corpse under the straw."

Hearing Ian referred to in such a callous way made Cecily

shudder. She still couldn't reconcile a lifeless body with the lively young man who had once been so much part of the Pennyfoot family.

It was a sad business, and couldn't have happened at a worse time. No matter how hard everyone tried to keep Ian's death a secret, she had no doubt that word would eventually get out. Once more she would be faced with the task of maintaining a cheerful, joyous atmosphere for the guests in the midst of tragedy.

Such was the Christmas curse of the Pennyfoot country club, and it had descended on them once more.

CHAPTER
❦ 3 ❦

"So what happened? Why did madam want to see you? Are you in trouble over something?" Pansy's eyes gleamed with speculation as she peered up at Gertie. "Go on, you might as well tell me, 'cos if you don't I'll ask Samuel. He knows everything what goes on here and he'll tell me."

Piling up the dirty dishes on the dumbwaiter, Gertie sniffed. "Don't be too bloody sure of that. How's that new maid, Mabel, working out, anyway?"

"Don't change the subject." Pansy balanced a tray of milk jugs on top of the dishes and tugged the rope. The waiter jerked, rattling the dishes, then descended out of sight to the kitchen below. "I want to know why madam sent for you."

"It's none of your bleeding business."

"I thought we was friends."

"We are, it's just . . ." Gertie paused to take a deep breath, then turned to the other girl. "If I tell you, will you promise to keep your flipping mouth shut and not tell a soul? Madam will have my hide if she thinks I blurted out the news all over the club."

Pansy's face lit up with excitement. "What news? Is it something good?"

Gertie shook her head, wiping the smile from Pansy's face. "What then? Tell me!"

Gertie leaned forward and whispered, "There's been an accident."

Now there was nothing but fear in Pansy's eyes. "An accident? Not Samuel, is it? Please . . ." She tugged at Gertie's sleeve. "Please tell me it's not Samuel."

Gertie puffed out her breath. "I don't know why you waste your feelings on that man. He treats you like dirt."

"He does not!" Pansy drew herself up, which wasn't very far. "He's a good man, our Samuel. He's just not . . . well, he's not . . ."

"Reliable?"

"Romantic!" Pansy glared at her. "What do you know, anyway? You've been going out with that Dan Perkins for more than a year and you still don't know if he's going to ask you to marry him."

Gertie tossed her head. "Who says I want to marry him, anyway?"

"Well, don't you?"

"It's none of your business."

"So did Samuel have an accident or not?"

"No. You can keep your bloody hair on. It wasn't Samuel."

"Well, who was it then?"

Gertie was about to tell her when Mabel staggered toward them, her tray loaded down with china tureens and bowls that looked as if they would all cascade to the floor and smash into smithereens at any minute.

"Bloody heck." Gertie rushed over and took the tray. Mabel had plenty of flesh on her but it was flabby, while Gertie's stocky build was toned by years of hard, physical work.

Carrying the tray over to the dumbwaiter, Gertie wondered, not for the first time, what kind of work Mabel had been doing before she got the job at the Pennyfoot. It couldn't have been housemaid work. She was much too soft and sluggish, and it puzzled Gertie why madam had hired someone like that at their busiest time of the year.

The shelf had been raised up again and Gertie dumped the tray on it. Pansy had already disappeared, having gone back to the dining room to finish clearing the tables. Mabel, however, stood staring down the hallway as if she was in a daydream.

Irritated, Gertie spoke sharply. "Have all the tables been cleared, then?"

Mabel started, her fearful eyes focusing on Gertie's face. Then she shook her head, reminding Gertie of a rabbit she once saw staring into the jaws of a cultivator.

The new maid's agitation only deepened Gertie's annoyance. "Well, get a bloody move on then! It'll be time to lay the tables again before we've got the blinking dishes washed up and put away!"

Mabel uttered a little whimper then scuttled away just as Pansy hurried back with another loaded tray. "Don't yell at her." She glared at Gertie. "She's not used to doing all this work. She told me she looked after her grandmother until she died, and then her nephew took all her money, leaving Mabel out in the cold. She's used to the finer things of life, not working her fingers to the bone like we do."

Gertie shrugged. "We all have our hard luck stories to tell. She'll have to get used to it if she wants to keep her bleeding job."

"Well, you don't have to be so nasty to her."

"You're just cross because I wouldn't tell you who had the accident."

Pansy dumped her tray on the waiter. "I don't care now, anyhow."

"All right, then I won't tell you."

Pansy shrugged, then as Gertie knew she would, turned to her. "Go on. You know you're dying to tell me."

Gertie leaned toward her. "It was Ian."

Pansy's eyes widened. "Your Ian?"

"Yeah. They found him in the duck pond. Drowned."

"How can he drown in the duck pond? It's not deep enough."

"I dunno. He just did. Hit his head or something."

Pansy stared at her. "You don't seem very upset."

"I'm not." Gertie turned her back on her and tugged the rope of the waiter to send a signal below. "And I don't want to talk about it anymore." She watched the dishes sink out of sight, trying not to envision Ian lying dead in the duck pond. She was done with him, once and for all. That was enough.

Cecily regarded the two men in front of her with a grave face. "I want to thank you both for your efforts this morning. I must ask you not to mention anything about this accident to anyone. The fewer people who know about this awful tragedy the better."

Clive rolled his hat around in his big hands. "What about Gertie, m'm? Who's going to tell her?"

"I've already told her, Clive. She took it . . ." Cecily paused, then added quietly, ". . . rather well, under the circumstances."

"Yes, m'm. I should imagine she would."

Samuel gave him a sharp look but said nothing.

"Very well, you can both return to your duties. Samuel, when Dr. Prestwick arrives, please show him where you . . . ah . . . laid the body. I'll try to keep the constable occupied until the doctor has finished his examination."

"Yes, m'm." Samuel touched his forehead with his fingers and turned to leave.

"And please see that no one else goes near it."

Samuel nodded and glanced once more at Clive with an odd expression Cecily couldn't interpret. Then, without another word, he left.

Clive turned to leave as well, and Cecily spoke quickly. "Clive, I trust you won't bother Gertie with this. She's had a nasty shock and won't want to discuss it anytime soon."

"Don't worry, m'm." Clive paused at the door and looked

back at her. "I wouldn't want to upset her any more than she is already."

Cecily smiled. "Thank you, Clive. I knew I could count on you."

Looking sheepish, Clive dragged the door open and charged out into the hallway. Seconds later a loud bump followed by a muttered curse brought Baxter's brows together.

"What the—?" He strode to the door and flung it open.

"You blithering idiot! Why don't you look where you're going!"

"Sorry, sir. Didn't see you." Clive's voice echoed down the corridor outside, fading into the distance as he added, "I'll watch out for you next time."

"Blasted clumsy clod," Northcott muttered, as he appeared in the doorway. "Knocked me 'elmet clean off, he did."

Considering he should have removed his helmet the minute he entered the club, Cecily could find little reason to sympathize. "Do come in, Sam." She nodded at Baxter, hoping he would interpret her meaningful look. "The doctor should have arrived by now, Baxter. Do be a dear and see if you can find him for me."

Baxter glanced from her to the constable, who was busily brushing imaginary dust from his helmet. "Right you are," he said, and gave her a slight nod that assured her he understood. Northcott had to be kept from interfering with the doctor until he had completed his examination.

He left the room, and Cecily waved a hand, indicating that the constable should sit.

He did so, still rubbing the narrow brim of his helmet.

"Good job he didn't put a dent in it," he muttered. "Or he'd have to cough up for a new one."

"Yes, quite." Cecily leaned back in her chair and linked her fingers in her lap. "Thank you for coming so promptly, Sam. This is all very distressing."

"Yes, it certainly is that." The constable pulled a tattered notebook from one chest pocket, then a stubby pencil from the other. Opening the notebook, he put on his officious tone. "Now then, Mrs. Baxter. Let h'us start at the beginning. When was the deceased found and by whom?"

"Earlier this morning, by Mr. Russell."

"Ah yes, the big baboon that barged into me just now." He licked the point of his pencil, then started scribbling. "Never did like that man. Too secretive if you ask me."

Cecily looked at him in surprise. "I didn't know you had many dealings with Clive."

The constable's expression took on a mysterious air. "I've 'ad reason to discuss a certain matter with 'im in the past. Before he came to work for you, that is."

Cecily's natural curiosity begged to know what sort of matter, but good manners kept her from asking. "I see. Well, in any case, Clive is of the opinion that Ian had been drinking and wandered into the duck pond."

"Where he decided to take a swim," Northcott said, chuckling at his own humor.

Cecily raised her chin. "I fail to see any amusement in the situation, Constable. A man is dead. A man, I might add, who once worked for me and for whom I still hold fond memories."

Northcott gave her a sly glance. "Quite right, Mrs. Baxter. My apologies. Though I have reason to believe he wasn't quite so welcome the last time he came around here."

Cecily sat up straight. As far as she knew, no one had mentioned to the police the incident that had taken place a year earlier, when Ian had insisted that since he was the twins' father, Gertie should relinquish one of them to him.

When Gertie had adamantly refused, Ian had tried to take Lillian by force, and only Clive's intervention had stopped him. Afer much discussion, and despite the urging of both Cecily and Mrs. Chubb, Gertie had decided not to involve the constabulary. She was afraid that Ian would wriggle out of it somehow, and become even more hostile toward her, making him even more dangerous. Or worse, that he might somehow prove that he had a right to be involved in the children's lives—something she would not tolerate.

Staring at Sam Northcott, Cecily wondered how he'd found out about the situation. Avoiding answering the comment, she said instead, "I have no idea why he was here this time. We didn't even know he was in Badgers End. The last we'd heard he had gone back to London, where, I believe, he still lives."

"I would imagine he came to see his babies." Northcott licked the point of his pencil and scribbled some more words in his notebook. "Been drinking, you say?"

"Clive smelled spirits on the body. We assume he had been heavily imbibing."

The constable nodded. "Well, h'I suppose I'd better go and see for meself. Where is the body then? Still in the pond, I hope?"

Cecily felt a stab of guilt. "Actually no, it's not. I didn't want any of the guests wandering by and seeing such a distressing sight. I had Samuel and Clive move the body. Since it was an accident—"

"Yes, well, we don't know that for certain, do we." Northcott heaved himself out of the chair and tucked his notebook back in his pocket. "I wish you hadn't moved the body, Mrs. Baxter. Deaths around here do 'ave a habit of turning out to be a matter for police investigation. I shall have to h'ascertain for myself that the death is accidental. For the record, you understand."

"I'm sure that won't be necessary." Cecily rose from her chair. "Dr. Prestwick will fill out a report. Besides, aren't you planning to leave for London shortly, for your annual Christmas visit to relatives there?"

Northcott beamed and nodded. "I am that, Mrs. Baxter. Nice that you remembered. I shall be leaving on the noon train tomorrow with my wife, so I shall have to close up this case right away."

Cecily smiled. "Well, then, why don't we let Dr. Prestwick take care of the details and you can attend to your records when you return in the New Year. I'm quite sure Mrs. Chubb will have some lovely mince pies and sausage rolls waiting for you in the kitchen."

She waited while the constable pitted his lust for Mrs. Chubb's baking against the need to follow proper procedure. After a moment or two he tucked his helmet under his arm and sighed. "You are quite right, Mrs. Baxter. It is Christmas, after all. I see no reason to h'attend immediately to the details. Wouldn't do to go rushing to the wrong conclusions, now would it."

His laughter sounded a little forced, but Cecily happily joined in. The last thing she needed was the constable poking around, asking questions, upsetting the guests, and generally disrupting everyone and everything, as he was wont to do in such circumstances.

"I'll be off to the kitchen, then," he announced, as he headed for the door. "Happy Christmas to you and yours, Mrs. Baxter."

"I'll certainly try to make it so," she answered, and let out her breath as the door closed behind him. Now, all she needed was for Kevin Prestwick to give her his report, and perhaps they could all put this tragic business behind them.

By the time Gertie could finally get back to the kitchen, the shock of Ian's death had begun to wear off. So much so that she felt guilty. She knew she ought to be feeling sorry for him. After all, he was still a young bloke and nobody should have to die when they're young.

Still, after everything he'd done to her and the twins, all she could feel was relief that she didn't have to worry about him ever again.

The thought put the smile back on her face, and she was still smiling when she shoved the kitchen door open and barged through it in her usual exuberant manner.

Coming face-to-face with Constable Northcott, however, wiped the smile from her face. It was the way he stared at her, those little pig eyes of his boring into her as if trying to guess what she was thinking.

"Well," he said, in the sarcastic voice she hated, "you don't seem to be that h'upset for a brand new widow."

"I ain't a widow." She walked over to the dumbwaiter and removed a tray of dishes, then carried them back to the sink. Dumping them down hard enough on the counter for the saucers to rattle, she added, "Me and Ian was never married legally. That means I'm not his bleeding widow. His real wife is the lucky woman, that's if he was still married to her, which I bloody doubt."

She heard Mrs. Chubb cough and glanced at her over her shoulder. Reading the warning in the housekeeper's eyes, she shrugged. She didn't care what the stupid policeman thought. She'd hated Ian Rossiter and she wasn't going to pretend to mourn his death.

"H'interesting," Northcott murmured.

Mrs. Chubb picked up a plate of mince pies and thrust it at him. "Here, Sam, take some of these with you. I know you must be in a hurry to be off, having to get ready for your visit to London and all."

Gertie turned back to the sink, but not before she caught the constable's thoughtful gaze on her. Her heart started beating a little too fast for comfort. Surely the stupid fool didn't think she'd shoved Ian in the pond.

"Thank you, Altheda. I'll be off then." The door creaked as the constable opened it. "Happy Christmas, all."

"Happy Christmas to you, Sam."

A strained silence followed, and Gertie knew Northcott was waiting for her to return the greeting. "Happy Christmas," she mumbled, without turning around.

She relaxed her shoulders when she heard the creak again and knew the door had swung closed. Bracing herself, she turned to face Mrs. Chubb.

The housekeeper stood by the table, her arms crossed, her plump face creased in a frown. There was no sign of Michel and the maids hadn't yet returned from the dining room, where they were still cleaning up.

Gertie drew a deep breath then blurted out, "If you're waiting for me to cry over Ian, then you're going to wait a bloody long time."

"I'm not expecting you to cry." Mrs. Chubb unfolded her arms and picked up a rolling pin. Slowly she began rolling it across the mound of pastry on the board in front of her. "I know it must have been a shock, though."

"A bloody pleasant one."

"Gertie!" Mrs. Chubb looked up. "That's a terrible thing to say."

"Yeah, well, Ian Rossiter did a terrible thing to me, trying to steal my daughter away."

"With that attitude you'd better not mention you saw Ian last night, then."

Gertie frowned. "Why not?"

"You was fighting with him, weren't you? That's probably why he got drunk. They could blame you for him falling into that pond."

Turning back to the sink, Gertie muttered, "It's not my fault if he can't bleeding look where he's going. Besides, I weren't the only one fighting with him. Like I told you last night, Clive ran him off the premises. He was a lot rougher on him than I was, and serve him bloody well right, that's what I say. What's more—" She broke off, thinking better of it.

The housekeeper narrowed her eyes. "What's more what?"

Marching over to the stove, Gertie grabbed the handles of a steaming cauldron. There was no need to tell Chubby everything. The less said the better, under the circumstances. "As far as I'm concerned," she said instead, "Ian Rossiter got what he bleeding deserved. Someone up there must have been watching over me and the kids."

She hauled the hot water over to the sink and tipped it. Blinking against the cloud of steam, she added, "Maybe it was my dead-and-gone husband, Ross, shoving Ian in the pond with an angel's hand."

"Angels don't kill people," Mrs. Chubb said, her rolling pin slapping back and forth across the pastry. "They save them."

"Yeah, well Ross was a real husband, and he loved my twins as if they were his own. He would protect them any way he could, even if it was all the way from heaven."

"Gertie McBride, you are talking nonsense." Mrs. Chubb sounded cross. "Sam Northcott told me Ian got drunk, wandered into the pond, and hit his head when he fell and drowned. Nobody pushed him. All I'm saying is there's no need to complicate matters by saying you had a row with him last night."

"Yeah, well, you can believe what you want and I'll believe what I want." Gertie grabbed a pile of the dishes and sank them into the hot soapy water. "Either way, Rossiter is out of my life for good, and I couldn't be happier. So, Happy Christmas to me and my babies."

Mrs. Chubb clicked her tongue in annoyance, but refrained from answering her.

Gertie swished the cloth over a large platter, wondering what Chubby would say if she knew that she'd seen Ian not once, but twice. In fact, there was a lot that the housekeeper didn't know, and Gertie saw no reason to enlighten her.

CHAPTER

4

Having answered a tap on her door, Cecily was delighted to see Madeline Pengrath Prestwick walk into her office. Madeline, as always, had dressed simply. She wore a simple peasant dress of pale yellow muslin, and in spite of the cold weather, a pair of gold sandals. She had forgone a hat and gloves, and her long dark hair flowed freely on her shoulders.

Without waiting for an invitation she drifted gracefully over to a chair. "I do believe it's stopped raining," she remarked, as she settled herself. "The sun is trying to peek through the clouds. I don't think we will have a white Christmas this year after all."

"Thank goodness." Cecily smiled at her friend. "The men always enjoy the Boxing Day hunt far more if they don't have to plow through a foot of snow."

"I'm sure the horses prefer it, too." Madeline gave her a grave look. "What's all this about Ian Rossiter drowning in the pond?"

Cecily sighed. "Another Christmas tragedy, I'm afraid. At least this time it was an accident. I know Ian was unpleasant and caused a lot of trouble, but I feel dreadful that he died in such a wretched way. So sad."

"Sad, indeed." Madeline's dark green eyes regarded her with speculation. "How is Gertie taking it?"

Cecily sighed. "As you would expect. More relieved than distressed, I suppose. Not that I can blame her."

Madeline nodded. "Unfortunate business for everyone."

Determined to change the subject, Cecily said brightly, "What plans do you and Kevin have for Christmas? You know you are more than welcome to join Baxter and me for dinner as we did last year. I simply cannot believe you have been married a whole year. It seems as if the wedding were only a few short weeks ago."

Madeline leaned back in her chair, her lovely features looking pensive. "In some ways it seems an eternity. It has been a difficult year at times."

Cecily nodded in sympathy. "The first year of marriage can be hard for most people, I suspect. I know mine wasn't all laughter and sunshine." She smiled. "But it's infinitely worth it for the later years."

"I certainly hope so." Madeline passed a hand across her forehead. "We are still at odds over my potions. Kevin refuses to believe in their power, even though he has acknowledged that modern medicine was originally derived from herbs and flowers. He is uncomfortable with what he calls witchcraft. Ridiculous man."

"Oh, I think he knows the worth of your potions. The problem is, as a doctor and scientist, he is unable to admit as much. He—" Cecily broke off as a sharp rap on the door announced the presence of yet another visitor.

Baxter entered the room first, followed by a handsome man in a light gray suit and blue cravat. Cecily rose to greet him, her hands extended in welcome.

"Kevin! How good to see you again. It has been much too long."

The doctor seized her hands and brought them, one at a time, to his lips. "Considering my profession, dear Cecily, I would say that is a blessing."

Baxter grunted his displeasure. He had never forgotten that Kevin Prestwick was at one time an avid admirer of Cecily, and might well have stolen her away had she been so inclined. "We've put the body into Prestwick's carriage," he said gruffly. "He's taking it to the morgue."

Cecily glanced at Madeline. "You must stay here with me, Madeline, until your husband has disposed of the body. I can't have you traveling with such grisly cargo."

Madeline's tinkling laugh rang out. "I assure you, dear Cecily, I have ridden with many a strange companion in my past, and compared to them, a dead body would be a decided improvement."

Cecily glanced at the doctor, who eyed his wife with faint disapproval. In all the years she had known Madeline, her friend had rarely spoken of her past and Cecily was under the impression she was the only one who knew the extent of it. She wondered if Madeline had shared all her secrets with her husband. Knowing Kevin as well as she did, she could imagine he would not have enjoyed learning the truth about his wife's early years.

"Cecily is right," Kevin said sharply. "I would rather take care of this matter without your company."

Madeline bowed her head, though a flash of defiance lit up her face. "As you wish. I shall enjoy visiting with Cecily. As she says, it has been much too long."

"Then it's settled." Kevin pulled a pocket watch from his vest pocket and peered at it. "I shall return for my wife as soon as possible."

"Wait, Kevin." Cecily raised a hand. "You haven't yet told us your conclusions concerning Ian's death."

"Ah . . . well, it seems quite obvious the man had consumed a vast amount of spirits. He reeked of it. I suspect his lungs are filled with water, but I'll know more after my examination at the morgue. It appears, however, that he lost his way and stumbled into the pond, hitting his head in the fall. Unfortunately for him, he fell in head first, otherwise he would probably have survived."

"So it was an accidental drowning, then?"

Kevin nodded. "That's what I'm expecting to put in my report."

Cecily let out her breath. She hadn't realized how worried she'd been until the doctor had settled her mind. It was a vast relief to know that for once she didn't have to worry about a fiendish murderer lurking in the halls of the Pennyfoot at Christmastime.

DECKED WITH FOLLY

Kevin had barely reached the door when Madeline spoke, her voice strangely soft and low. "You might do well to examine more carefully the wound on the dead man's head, my love."

Kevin paused, and without turning his head asked, "You know something, perhaps, that has escaped me?"

Madeline smiled. "Perhaps."

Kevin appeared to think about it, then gave a brief shake of his head, and left the room.

Madeline was silent until the door had closed behind both her husband and Baxter, then murmured, "For a doctor and a man of science, my husband can be remarkably obtuse."

Unsettled by the odd exchange between man and wife, Cecily felt concern once more niggling at her. "Why should he examine the wound? What exactly do you mean by that?"

"I mean that all is not as it seems."

Alarmed now, Cecily watched as her friend's face took on a look she knew well. Madeline's eyes seemed to glaze over, and her features grew slack and void of expression. In a voice low and husky, she muttered, "Dark nights invite dark deeds. I see danger lurking above a house of carcasses. You must beware the hand you cannot see."

Cecily had seen many of Madeline's trances, but rarely had she seen such apprehension in her friend's face as she regained her senses.

"Madeline! What is it that concerns you so?" Cecily rose and hurried over to her. "Tell me, what did you see?"

Madeline blinked up at her. "I don't know." Her voice shook and her cheeks seemed to pale. "Blood. Everywhere. Dead bodies. Many of them."

Cecily put an arm about her friend's shoulders. "It was just a vision, Madeline. You have had such visions before and nothing has come of them."

"They are a warning, Cecily. We should always heed the warning."

"Warning of what?"

Madeline sighed, and shook her head so that her hair swung about her shoulders. "That is the problem. I rarely know until I'm faced with the reality."

Cecily returned to her desk, her brow creased in worry. "You said many dead bodies. Are you predicting some kind of disaster?"

Madeline gave her an unhappy look. "I wish I knew, Cecily. I'm sorry. I just couldn't see."

"No matter." With a wave of her hand, Cecily did her best to dismiss the incident. "I imagine we shall find out soon enough if your warning proves to be accurate. In the meantime, let us wait for your husband's return in my suite, where we shall be a little more comfortable."

Madeline rose without a word and drifted over to the door. Following her, Cecily tried to forget the cryptic words her friend had uttered. Right now she had enough to worry about with Ian's death on the premises. All she could hope was that word of it had not reached her guests.

That hope was dashed a few minutes later when they encountered Archie Parker in the foyer. His sharp gaze took in Madeline's somewhat provincial appearance with one disparaging head-to-foot glance, then he ignored her, turning his attention to Cecily.

"I've been hearing rumors, Mrs. B. Nasty rumors at that. Something about a man drowning in one of your ponds?"

Cecily sent Madeline a swift warning glance, then said pleasantly, "I'm quite sure you are far too discriminating to take any notice of rumors, Mr. Parker."

Archie preened and smoothed the end of his mustache with thick fingers. "How astute of you, Mrs. B. Normally I would ignore them, but someone mentioned he saw two men carrying a third across the lawns a short while ago. I was wondering if the poor blighter was one of your guests?"

Inwardly cringing, Cecily managed a bright smile. "I'm sure whoever told you that was mistaken. A case of too much brandy, perhaps?"

Archie looked confused. "Well, it's a little early in the day for brandy, wouldn't you say?"

"Ah, but it is the Christmas season. Our guests are inclined to forgo the usual proprieties during the holidays." She waved a hand at Madeline, who had been standing silently, surveying the salesman with an odd expression.

"Mr. Parker. May I introduce my good friend, Mrs. Prestwick?"

Archie's brows raised in surprise, and he gave Madeline a closer look, as if doubting that Cecily would befriend such an unrefined creature. "Pleasure," he murmured.

"Madeline, this is Mr. Archibald Parker," Cecily said. "You two have something in common. Mr. Parker is a salesman of medical remedies."

"Really." Madeline's tone was decidedly cool as she surveyed the red-faced man.

"If you remember," Cecily said with relish, "I mentioned that Mrs. Prestwick is an accomplished herbalist. She is also the wife of our local physician."

Archie's nose twitched furiously, and his mustache danced in unison. "I . . . ah . . . no, I didn't . . . I had no idea . . ."

Cecily smiled. "If you will excuse us, Mr. Parker?"

"Oh, of course. Of course." Archie backed away, still staring at Madeline as if he were afraid she was about to bite him.

"Strange little man," Madeline murmured as she glided toward the stairs. "There's something odd about him, but I can't quite place it."

"Well, be prepared. He's likely to inquire after your digestive system, or something even more personal."

Madeline uttered a sound of contempt. "If that man has any medical knowledge at all, I'll give up making potions altogether."

Cecily was inclined to agree. It was one thing to sell remedies, quite another to understand how they worked.

"As a matter of fact," Madeline said, pausing at the foot of the staircase. "I would say that your Mr. Parker is a charlatan, and you would do well to avoid any of his bogus remedies."

Having come to a similar conclusion herself, Cecily gave her no argument. In any case, Archibald Parker was the least of her worries. What concerned her a great deal more was Madeline's suggestion that Kevin examine the wound on Ian's head, and her vision of dead bodies.

She considered pursuing the matter with her friend but just then Madeline uttered a sigh of annoyance and sped toward the front doors. At first Cecily thought she meant to go outside and was about to offer her a coat when Madeline halted in front of the hallstand, upon which sat a marvelous display of red and white candles wreathed in holly.

"Look at this," Madeline exclaimed. "Some blundering fool has disrupted my display." She started moving the candlesticks around, then paused. "I don't believe it."

Her concern growing, Cecily hurried over to her. "What is it?"

Madeline turned, her face stiff with outrage. "Someone has stolen one of these. Look at this." She picked up one of the candlesticks and thrust it at Cecily. "I had six of them and now there are only five. I can't believe—" She broke off, a strange expression creeping across her face.

Once more Cecily felt a stab of anxiety. "Madeline?"

Madeline blinked, shook her head and put the candlestick down on the hallstand. "My display is ruined, and now you have a thief in the Pennyfoot. Who would do such a thing?"

Cecily sighed in resignation. "It's all right. The candlesticks are not worth that much. They're made of lead, and merely silver-plated. That's why they're so heavy. Besides, the display still looks beautiful. I'm sure no one will notice the absence of one."

Madeline frowned. "Aren't you the least bit upset that someone stole one of them?"

"Well, yes, of course, but this is a hotel—at least," she hastily amended, "it was before my cousin turned it into a country club. Things go missing more than you'd think, and really I have far more important things to worry about."

"Then you are far more forgiving than I would be."

Madeline fussed with the display for several moments until she was satisfied it was as it should be, then stood back for a final critical scrutiny. "There, that will have to do."

"Good, then let us go up to my suite where we can relax for a while."

To Cecily's relief, Madeline sent one last look at the display then headed for the stairs. On the way up to the top floor, she seemed determined to put the subject of the theft out of her mind. She prattled on instead about a local villager who insisted one of her potions was making his hair grow back.

"Silly man," she said, laughing. "I gave him the potion to cure a cough. His hair is still as sparse as ever, but if he believes it's growing back, then who am I to dash his forlorn hopes."

Cecily smiled and nodded, though she didn't feel in the least like smiling. She knew quite well that her friend's chatter was an attempt to take her mind away from the events of the morning. It was a wasted effort. Madeline's comments earlier had thoroughly unsettled her, and now she had a deep sense of impending disaster.

Madeline was right. All was not as it seemed.

Mrs. Chubb paused to wipe the perspiration from her brow with a floury hand. All around her, maids hustled back and forth, carrying platters and tureens from the stove to the dumbwaiter. The smell of roast pork filled the kitchen, tempting her taste buds. It would be at least an hour or two before she could satisfy the pangs of hunger.

DECKED WITH FOLLY

She glanced at Michel, busy at the stove, his tall chef's cap bobbing as he danced from one side to the other, stirring, pouring, and piling food into the dishes. Mrs. Chubb shook her head. It never ceased to amaze her how much food a few dozen people could stuff into their mouths in one sitting. The day was an endless round of preparing meals, cleaning up, and then more preparing meals and cleaning up.

The clatter of dishes was giving her a headache, and she longed for her afternoon break, when she could put her feet up in her room and get on with her knitting. She still had to finish the mittens she was making for the twins for Christmas.

Shaking her head to dislodge the cobwebs, she picked up her rolling pin and smoothed out the lump of pastry in front of her into a large circle. Deftly she flipped the dough onto a pie plate, then picked up the bowl of raisin apple filling and tipped the lot onto the plate.

This was the last pie for the day. Get it in the oven and then she could slow down a bit and take a breather. It was hot in the kitchen, and a moment or two out in the backyard would cool her off nicely.

She looked for the last pie bird, but couldn't see it on the table. Someone must have moved it. More than likely picked it up with some dirty dishes. Clicking her tongue in annoyance, she walked over to the sink.

There was the pie bird, sitting on the counter. Relieved, she picked it up. Without that little porcelain funnel sitting in the center of her pie, there'd be nowhere for the steam to escape while the pie was cooking. Then she'd have a mess, all right. Burnt filling all around the edges. Madam wouldn't like that.

Out of habit, she glanced at the windowsill to make sure her ring was still there. She always took it off when she was making the pastry. If she didn't it ended up with pastry stuck in between all the little grooves, and it was a devil of a task to get it all cleaned out. So she left it on the windowsill until she was finished with the pies.

Only today, it wasn't there.

Mrs. Chubb paused, unable to believe her eyes. All the years she had been working at the Pennyfoot, and it had been far too many to remember, she had placed that ring on the windowsill and it had always been there when she came to get it. It had to be there.

With a little cry of dismay, drowned out by the din in the kitchen, she put down the pie bird and leaned across the sink for a better look. No, she wasn't seeing things. The ring was gone. It must have somehow been swept off the sill and into the sink.

Frantically she dug her fingers into the drain hole in some vain hope of finding it there. Behind her, she heard Michel call out above the racket of crashing pots and pans.

"Where the blazes is the pie? Sacre bleu! It should be halfway to cooked by now! Whatever are you doing over there in the sink?"

"Oh, go drink your brandy," Mrs. Chubb muttered, quiet enough so he wouldn't hear. Turning her head, she added more loudly, "My ring fell down the sink. It's gone!"

"We find it later." Michel waved a wooden spoon, dripping with gravy, in the air at her. "I must have that pie in the oven this minute."

"Oh, all right." With a last, searching gaze along the

windowsill, Mrs. Chubb turned and trotted back to the table. Staring at the pie, she couldn't think why she hadn't put the top crust on. Then she remembered the pie bird and had to go back for it, earning a scathing stream of curses from the irate chef.

Ignoring him, she took the pie bird back to the table and sat it in the middle of the apple filling. This had to be one of the worst days ever. Poor Ian lying dead in the duck pond and now her ring was lost. Mrs. Chubb slapped a second circle of pastry on top of the pie plate. What else was going to go wrong, for heaven's sake?

CHAPTER 5

The morning passed swiftly, and in no time, it seemed, Kevin returned to the Pennyfoot. Cecily had invited Madeline to join her and Baxter in the dining room for the midday meal, and Kevin arrived just as they were finishing the last crumbs of delicious apple dumplings with brandy sauce.

When Cecily offered to have a meal sent in for him, he declined, and instead asked that they adjourn to her office. "There is something of grave importance that we must discuss," he said, filling her once more with cold dread.

She rose at once, signaling Madeline and Baxter to follow her and together they made their way to her office. As Baxter closed the door, she let out a long sigh. "It's bad news, isn't it."

Kevin waited for the women to seat themselves before following suit. "I'm afraid so." He paused, waiting for Baxter to also take a seat.

Unable to wait a moment longer, Cecily blurted out, "Ian's death wasn't an accident after all?"

Baxter looked startled, while Madeline merely nodded.

Kevin glanced at his wife, then folded his hands across his chest. "I decided to take my wife's advice for once. I examined the wound on the victim's head. It couldn't have been caused by a rock. It had a distinct shape. A hexagon, obviously the result of being struck by a heavy object."

"A candlestick," Madeline said.

Both men stared at her, while Cecily, realizing at once what was coming, sank back in her chair.

"Candlestick?" Kevin's voice was sharp again. "How do you know that?"

"There's one missing," Madeline said calmly. "Out there on the hallstand. It was part of my display and someone has removed it. I think it might have been used for a much more malicious purpose."

She gave Cecily a look of apology. "I didn't want to say anything until I was sure, but when Kevin mentioned the hexagon-shaped wound I knew it had to be the candlestick. I sensed the aura of malice when I touched them, and besides, they have a six-sided base."

"Good Lord." Baxter leaned forward, his jaw tense with shock. "Are you telling me someone murdered Rossiter?"

"It would appear that way." Madeline sighed. "I'm so sorry. I know this must be a shock to you both."

"Why?" Cecily covered her face with her hands for a moment. "Why here? Why now?"

Baxter groaned. "Not again."

Kevin got up from his chair and pulled a watch from his vest pocket. "If the candlestick was used as a weapon, then we should try to find it."

"It's such a beautiful Christmas candlestick," Madeline said mournfully. "I do hope you get it back."

The loss of the candlestick did not concern Cecily at all. Nor was she as shocked as Madeline might think. Ever since Clive had burst into the lobby with the news, she'd had an uneasy feeling that Ian's death might not have been an accident.

What's more, she was thinking about Gertie's reaction when she told her that Ian had died. It hadn't been the first time Gertie had threatened dire harm to Ian if he didn't leave her and the twins alone. Not only that, Gertie hadn't seemed in the least surprised that Ian had returned to Badgers End. Which suggested she already knew that he was in the vicinity.

She needed to have a word with that young lady, Cecily decided. As soon as possible.

Gertie pushed the sweeper back and forth across the carpet, angling in between the dining room tables to get underneath them. Pansy was across the room polishing the sideboard, and Gertie had to raise her voice above the squeaking wheels of the sweeper.

"Where's that Mabel got to? She's supposed to be in here helping us."

Pansy shrugged. "Dunno. She went down to the kitchen and she hasn't come back yet."

"Bleeding useless, that girl." Gertie dragged a chair out of her way. "You'll never guess what she did last night. Lit all the flipping candles on the Christmas tree."

Pansy spun around. "Go on! What'd she do that for?"

"She said she's never seen candles lit on a Christmas tree and wanted to know what they looked like." Gertie paused to get her breath. "Can you imagine what madam would have done if she'd seen them? Ever since that year when the tree caught fire and nearly burned down the hotel she's never lit another candle on there. I could have screamed when I saw them all flickering away like that."

"Did you make her blow them all out?"

"You bet I did. I bloody helped her, too." Gertie shook her head. "It's a bloody good job it was after nine o'clock and madam had gone to her suite. I told that little twit she'd better not tell anyone what she done or she'd be out on her ear. If I hadn't seen the flickering light under the library door and gone in there gawd knows what might have happened."

Pansy's eyes opened wide. "She could have burned down the hotel!"

"Well, she didn't, so don't say nothing. She might not be much of a worker, but we need her help and it's too late to hire anyone else for the Christmas season now."

Pansy turned back to her polishing. "I won't say nothing, but I just hope she doesn't do anything else stupid."

"Yeah, me, too." Gertie started sweeping again. "So how

are you and Samuel getting along now? Is he still not talking to you?"

Pansy shrugged. "I haven't seen much of him lately. He's been busy with the horses and the motorcars, what with all the guests coming in for Christmas."

"You two are always arguing." Gertie pulled another chair out of the way and shoved the sweeper under the table. "I don't know why you bother."

"I like Samuel. And he likes me. He just doesn't want what I want, that's all."

"You mean he doesn't want to get married."

"He keeps saying I'm too young to know me own mind." Pansy spun around to face her again, scrunching up the polishing cloth in between her hands. "He won't believe me when I say I know down deep in me heart he's the one for me."

Gertie leaned on the handle of the sweeper. She felt sorry for the young girl, but someone needed to tell her the truth. It would be better coming from a friend, than for her to find out the hard way. "It's just an excuse, Pansy. Find someone else. Someone what will bleeding appreciate you. Stop wasting your time on Samuel. The truth is, he'll never marry you, no matter how old you get. His heart belongs to someone else."

Pansy's face crumpled. "But I love Samuel. He's the only one I want. I can make him forget his old girlfriend, I know I can. Doris is in London now and I'm right here."

"Doris might be in London but her twin sister is still here in the Pennyfoot. Daisy has to remind Samuel of Doris every time he sees her."

"I know that. I wish she'd gone to London with her sister. I really do."

Gertie sighed. "I'm sorry, Pansy, but Daisy is a good nanny and I'd hate to lose her. I'd never find another one to live in a room in a country club and look after the twins the way she does."

Pansy dabbed at her eyes with her sleeve. "I know. I just don't know what to do."

Gertie sighed. "Men. Who'd have 'em. I've had more than my share of 'em and, I tell you, half the time they're not worth the trouble."

"Well, what about Dan, then? I thought you were really sweet on him."

"Dan's all right. But he's another one what's bleeding afraid of getting married. Can't say as I blame him, though. Taking on another man's kids is not everyone's cup of tea. The twins can be a handful at times, and it's hard to tell them off when they're not yours."

"But Dan loves James and Lillian. You said so."

"Yeah, well, loving them and taking care of them is two different things, ain't it."

"It's a shame." Pansy turned back to her polishing. "Children should have a father to take care of them."

"Yeah, well, my kids haven't had much bloody luck in that department, have they. They never really knew their real father."

Pansy shook her head. "I still can't believe Ian's dead. I only met him once, but you've talked about him so much I feel like I knew him. He—" She broke off as a voice spoke from the doorway.

" 'Allo, then! Look who's here! If it ain't the bold and beautiful Gertie McBride."

Gertie froze. She'd know that voice anywhere. It was that bloke she bumped into earlier that morning. Sid Barrett, that was it.

Pansy was staring across the room at him, but Gertie refused to turn around. She jumped when his voice sounded right behind her, almost in her ear.

"How about that pint at the pub, then?"

"I told you, sir, I'm not supposed to be mixing with the guests."

"He's not a guest," Pansy piped up. "He's one of the footmen madam hired for the Christmas season."

Gertie swung around to face Sid, eyes blazing. "Why the bleeding heck didn't you tell me that?"

He shook his head. "Tut, tut. Such language from a lady. You didn't ask me, luv. Besides, I liked the way you called me sir."

"Don't you luv me, you lying bugger." She frowned at him. "How'd you know my name, anyhow?"

Sid grinned. "Made it my business to, didn't I." He tapped his nose. "I can find out anything I want if I really put my mind to it."

Pansy giggled, and Sid winked at her, then set his gaze firmly on Gertie.

He made her nervous. Gertie gripped the sweeper's handle. Something about his eyes. Shifty, that's what he was. "I have to get on with my work," she said stiffly. "So bugger off. You're not supposed to be in here anyhow."

"Right." He glanced at Pansy then, who was staring at him all starry-eyed. "So how about you, then, luv? You'll have a pint with me, won't you?"

Giggling again behind her hand, Pansy nodded.

"No she won't," Gertie said, sending Pansy a warning look. "She's already got a boyfriend."

Looking back at Gertie, Sid tilted his head to one side. "Well, I really just came in to say I'm sorry for the loss of your husband."

Gertie stared at him. "You knew Ross?"

Something flickered in Sid's eyes. He seemed at a loss for words for a moment, then said slowly, "I thought she said his name was Ian Rossiter." He nodded his head at Pansy. "I thought I heard her say as how he'd died and that he was the father of your twins. Sorry if I was mistaken."

Gertie took a moment to collect her thoughts. How long had the bloke been standing there listening to their private conversation? No wonder he had shifty eyes. He was a bleeding Peeping Tom. "Ian Rossiter did die last night, but he was never my husband," she said shortly.

"But he was the father of your twins, right?"

Gertie tossed her head. "Not that it's any of your bloody business."

"Ah well, anyway, I'm sorry." Sid laid a hand on her shoulder. "That's a terrible tragedy, to lose your husband. Especially when you've got two little ones to look after."

Gertie shook off his hand and moved farther away from him, putting the sweeper between them. "You needn't feel sorry for me. I'm glad he's dead. So there. He never was no good so good bleeding riddance to him, that's what I say."

She was hoping to shock the man into leaving her alone, but Sid seemed unaffected by her bitter outburst. He looked about to say something, but another voice interrupted from the doorway. A gruff voice, with an officious tone that Gertie knew well.

"Well, well," P.C. Northcott said, moving into the room. "I find that h'interesting. Very h'interesting indeed."

Gertie sighed as she turned to face the constable, but it was Sid Barrett's reaction that surprised her. With a muttered "Strewth!" he darted past the constable and practically ran from the room.

If she wasn't so upset by the man's rudeness she would have laughed. Constable Northcott was the last person on earth to reprimand anyone for annoying one of the servants. The only servant the constable had any time for was Mrs. Chubb, and that was because he enjoyed the sweets she gave him every time he visited her in the kitchen.

As for the rest of them, they was dirt under the constable's feet, not worth any consideration. Which was a laugh, since he weren't no better himself, having been brought up by a dustman and a wife what took in laundry to keep food on the table.

One of these days, Gertie thought fiercely, she'd let him know she knew about his humble beginnings. That would put an end to his preening about with his fancy talk and all.

"I was looking for Mrs. Baxter," Northcott said, puffing out his chest. "I 'ave urgent business with her. She's not in her h'office, so where is she?"

Gertie raised her chin. "I don't know where madam is.

I'm not her bleeding keeper. She's probably in her suite and won't want to be disturbed."

The constable's eyes narrowed. "There's no need to take that tone with me. Kindly go to her at once and tell her I need to speak with her. I'll wait in the lobby." He twisted around so fast he almost lost his balance.

Gertie waited until he was out of earshot then poked out her tongue. "Bloomin' ninny he is," she muttered. "Thinks he's so clever. I wonder what he'd say if he knew everyone laughs at him behind his back."

"Well, I hope you're not the one to tell him that," Pansy said, looking nervous. "It doesn't do to upset the bobbies. You never know what they might do."

Gertie uttered a short laugh. "That silly fool don't know how to keep his helmet on straight. I'm not afraid of him." She picked up the sweeper and tucked it under her arm. "I'd better go and tell madam he's here, before he eats all the tarts Mrs. Chubb made for supper. I never seen a man with a sweet tooth like that one."

"Give me the sweeper." Pansy held out her hand. "I'll finish in here for you."

Pleasantly surprised, Gertie beamed at her. "That's blinking good of you, Pansy. Ta ever so!"

Pansy gave her a weak smile and took the sweeper from her. "I ain't got nothing else to do until we get ready for supper, so I might as well do the carpets."

Gertie felt another twinge of sympathy. "You're not seeing Samuel, then?"

"Nah." Pansy's shoulders sagged. "He said he was going to be busy this afternoon."

"Well, look. Wait until I get back and then we'll go for a walk with the twins. It's their nanny's day off so I promised to take them and I'll be glad of the company."

Pansy brightened. "Really? I'd love to go for a walk. I haven't been out walking in ages."

"Good. I'll be back in half a mo." Hurrying off, Gertie cursed Samuel under her breath. What was the matter with men that they couldn't make up their minds what they wanted?

Samuel should do the right thing and tell Pansy he was never going to marry her, instead of stringing the poor girl along with hopes and dreams that weren't ever going to come true. *Men.* The world would be a lot happier place without them. Even Dan. She never knew where she was with him.

One day she'd be thinking he really did love her and want to be with her, then he'd go and say something that would make her think he regretted ever coming back to Badgers End.

Maybe he should have stayed in London. Then he wouldn't have raised her hopes again, just when she was starting to get over him. He'd been back a year, and never a word about his plans for the future. Their future. Or maybe there was no future for either of them. At least not together.

Thoroughly disgruntled, she stomped up the stairs to madam's suite and rapped on the door. Mr. Baxter answered, and he didn't look too happy, neither.

"Yes, what is it?"

Gertie pinched her lips together. Usually when he spoke like that he was arguing with madam. Which meant she'd better be bloody careful what she said to him.

"Excuse me, sir," she said, bobbing a curtsey, "I'm sorry to disturb you but P.C. Northcott is here and he says he has urgent business with madam. He's waiting in the lobby."

Mr. Baxter gave her a curt nod. "Thank you, Gertie. I'll inform Mrs. Baxter. Please tell the constable she'll be down in a moment or two."

"Yes, sir." Relieved to have escaped without incurring the master's wrath, Gertie fled down the hall to the stairs. Next time she came back, she vowed silently, she'd come back as a man. So help her, she would.

CHAPTER
✿ 6 ✿

Following her husband down the stairs, Cecily tried to regain her composure. She'd very much wanted to speak to Gertie before the constable arrived, but her argument with Baxter after Kevin left had taken up far too much time. Now it was too late to question her chief housemaid. It would have to wait until after her meeting with the constable—which no doubt would be unproductive.

She was not in the best of moods to deal with his illogical rambling. Her argument with Baxter had been intense and familiar. Her husband, perhaps rightly so, had expressed his supreme displeasure at her becoming involved in yet another murder.

He'd even gone so far as to forbid her to take any part in the investigation, which did not sit well with her at all.

DECKED WITH FOLLY

Had it not been for the fact that Ian was known to them, they might well have come to an impasse, resulting in a very unfortunate atmosphere for the Christmas season. Baxter, however, had finally conceded that having known Ian intimately, at least in his younger years, Cecily was better equipped to find out who would have wanted him dead and why.

Cecily was also fairly certain that Baxter harbored the same fears she did, about Gertie being somehow involved, which was perhaps another reason why he had agreed not to stand in her way. Yet he did issue a host of dire warnings and extracted a promise that she would keep him informed of her every move. That was something she had found almost impossible to do in the past and no doubt it would prove equally difficult in this case.

Deep in her dark thoughts, she almost passed by the constable, who hovered at the foot of the stairs, clutching his helmet under his arm.

"I knew it!" he exclaimed, as she greeted him. "I knew it would turn up as a murder, the minute I heard he'd drowned in two feet of water."

"Hush!" Cecily glanced around the lobby in alarm. "We don't want to upset the guests."

"Oh, of course not. Sorry, Mrs. Baxter. Wasn't thinking, was I."

Baxter rolled his eyes, his face clearly expressing his displeasure.

"Let us go to my office," Cecily said hurriedly, sensing her husband's imminent explosion of wrath. "We can talk freely there."

She led the way, keeping up a cheerful conversation about the holly wreaths on the walls, and how Madeline had woven them herself. "It's really a shame you don't spend your Christmas in Badgers End," she said, as she opened the door. "You could have attended our Christmas pantomime. Phoebe Carter-Holmes Fortescue has worked very hard on this year's presentation. It promises to be quite lovely."

She couldn't blame the skeptical look on the constable's face as he murmured an answer. Phoebe's presentations, largely consisting of ill-conceived performances by her unwieldy dance group, were more often than not a total disaster.

The fact that Cecily's audiences enjoyed them, at least those who did not sit close enough to be wounded by flying objects, was based more on their anticipation of a fiasco than on appreciating the nonexistent artistic talent.

Having closed the door, Baxter ushered Northcott to a chair while Cecily took her seat behind the desk. The lack of space in the tiny room, which held little more than her desk, four chairs, and a filing cabinet, always made her feel somewhat constricted when there was more than one person in there with her.

Never was that feeling more pronounced than when Sam Northcott was present. She assumed it was because more often than not he was either the bearer of bad news, or she was in the unfortunate position of having to impart unpleasant news herself.

Sitting back in her chair, she tried to calm her thoughts by clasping her hands together. "Well, Sam, I'm afraid we are dealing with yet another troublesome problem."

"We are, indeed, m'm." Northcott stole a glance at Baxter. "Please accept my condolences. I know you were fond of the deceased."

"He was once one of my favorite servants," Cecily agreed carefully.

Baxter cleared his throat and she sent him a warning glance. He had agreed not to interfere with her discussion with the constable, and she knew he had set himself an almost impossible task.

"Yes, indeed." Northcott withdrew his notebook, then took out a pencil and licked it with disgusting relish. "Now then, I think it is safe to say that this h'is an open-and-shut case, so to speak."

Cecily raised her eyebrows. "I beg your pardon?"

Northcott scribbled something down then raised his head. "Well, I think it's obvious who done Ian in." He coughed. "I mean who perpetrated the crime. It had to be his ex-wife what murdered him—Gertie McBride."

Baxter made a strangled sound in his throat, while Cecily could only stare at the constable's round, flushed face, searching for words that would not come.

Northcott nodded. "I have it on good authority from an h'eyewitness what 'eard the suspect say she was going to kill him. In fact, according to my source, Gertie McBride took a knife to the deceased on the very night he died and threatened to slit his throat."

Cecily felt as if all the air had rushed out of her lungs. She gripped the edge of the desk and struggled to sound calm as she forced out the words. "Who told you that?"

Northcott shook his head. "I'm afraid I'm not at liberty to say, m'm."

"Good Lord, man!" Apparently unable to keep his promise, Baxter rose from his chair and loomed over the wary constable. "You can't possibly believe that Gertie McBride would do such a thing?"

"Besides," Cecily said quickly, "Ian didn't die from a knife wound. We believe he was hit over the head with one of my candlesticks. I told you that when I rang you."

"A candlestick, which, I believe, was standing on your 'allstand in the hall."

"And could have been picked up by anyone in this hotel," Baxter put in.

"Have you heard anyone else threaten to slit the victim's throat with a knife?" Northcott preened when neither one of them answered. "H'I rest my case."

Actually, Cecily thought, she had heard more than one person threaten Ian in the past. Clive for one, when he had come to the rescue when Ian had tried to abduct little Lillian. And Gertie's boyfriend, Dan, when he'd heard what Ian had tried to do. Why, even Baxter had threatened to thrash the man within an inch of his life for terrifying his precious goddaughter.

For that matter, Madeline had once threatened to turn Ian into something quite nasty, which might or might not have been an empty threat. But it was a measure of how many people wished Ian Rossiter ill will.

She could hardly relate all that to the constable, however. Not in detail, anyway. "I have heard several people make various threats at times," she said firmly. "None of which, I haven't the slightest doubt, were meant to be taken seriously.

Gertie's included. You can't accuse someone of murder based on such flimsy evidence."

"From what I understand," Northcott said, still scribbling in his notebook, "there have been many an occasion when your housemaid has made similar threats. What's more, she was the last one to see the victim alive last night. Right here on these premises. I think that's quite enough reason to take her down to the station for questioning."

Cecily swallowed, while Baxter seemed at a loss for words. His eyes held a desperate look, signaling her to do something. The problem was, right then and there, she had no idea what to do. All she could think of was Gertie's voice, low and full of bitter venom. *I'm not really sorry he's dead. I'm not.*

The constable was right. Gertie had threatened Ian on more than one occasion. Had she finally endured more than she could bear and struck back? If so, Cecily thought with a pang of desperation, there was little she could do to save her. Gertie would be doomed to spend the rest of her life in prison, and two children would have to grow up without a mother or a father. It just didn't bear thinking about.

Cecily took a deep breath. No. She could not, would not believe Gertie McBride was a killer. "Sam," she said, silently cursing the tremor in her voice, "I know you are in a great hurry to begin your Christmas holiday. Arresting Gertie and questioning her will take time. All the paperwork, for instance. What's more, Gertie has the afternoon off. I believe she has taken the twins out for a walk. She won't be back for at least another hour or two."

She leaned forward, giving him her warmest smile. "Can't this wait until you get back? That way you can start off your holiday without upsetting your wife, whom I know must be anxiously waiting for you right now."

Northcott wavered, uncertainty all over his face. "Well, it's not proper procedure, is it."

"We could make absolutely certain that once Gertie returns to the hotel, she will not be allowed to leave again until you return." Cecily glanced at Baxter, who finally found his tongue.

"House arrest." He nodded to emphasize his words. "That's what we'll do. We'll hold Gertie under house arrest. She won't make a move without us knowing it."

Hope crept across Northcott's ruddy features. "Well . . . if you think . . ."

"Absolutely." Baxter thrust out his hand. "You have my solemn word on it. Gertie will be under our care until you can arrest her properly."

Cecily made a small sound of protest but Baxter frowned at her, warning her to keep silent.

"All right, then." Northcott folded his notebook and tucked it in the vest pocket of his uniform. "In that case, I'll be off."

Heaving a huge sigh of relief, Cecily rose from her chair. "Thank you, Sam. We do appreciate your understanding."

Northcott struggled to his feet and wagged a finger at her. "Mark my words, Mrs. Baxter. If I come back to find Gertie has scarpered, I shall come down on you very hard." He leaned forward to make his point. "Very 'ard indeed."

Longing to bite the finger pointed at her, Cecily nodded. "I understand. Happy Christmas, Sam."

Northcott nodded, then turned to Baxter. "I hold you entirely responsible for the prisoner until I get back. I hope that's understood."

"Have no fear my good man." Baxter slapped him on the shoulder so hard the constable stumbled forward. "We will take good care of her."

Coughing, Northcott glared at him. "Make sure you do." He reached the door and looked back over his shoulder. "Happy Christmas all."

The door closed behind him, and Cecily sank weakly onto the chair. "Goodness, that was a close shave. I had visions of Gertie spending Christmas all alone in that miserable jail. Can you imagine those poor babies if their mother wasn't there for Christmas morning?" She shuddered. "I just can't stand the thought of it."

"It's not over yet," Baxter said grimly. "What did Northcott mean about Gertie being the last person to see Ian alive?"

"I don't know. But I'm certainly going to find out." Cecily leaned back and grasped the bell rope behind her. Giving it a sharp tug, she added, "I had no idea Gertie had seen Ian, or even knew he had come down to Badgers End."

"I thought you said Gertie had gone for a walk with the twins."

"So she will be." Cecily smiled. "But not for another hour."

Baxter shook his head. "Devious." He stuck his thumbs into his trouser pockets and rocked back on his heels. "You don't think that Gertie might have—"

"No," Cecily said, cutting him off before he could say the words. "I don't."

"Well, neither do I, of course, but I have heard her threaten to kill him if he came near the twins again."

"You have also heard me say I'd divorce you if you kept ordering me about."

His wry expression was comical and she smiled. "You know full well I'd never carry out that threat."

"Well, yes, but that's a little different."

Her smile faded. "Gertie didn't kill Ian. She can be abrasive at times, and a little too belligerent for her own good, but she is simply not capable of taking another life. I'd stake my own life on it."

"Well, let's hope you don't have to do that." Baxter rose as a tap on the door disturbed them. "I'll let you talk to her alone. She'll be less intimidated if I'm not here."

Cecily had to smile at the idea of Gertie being intimidated by anyone. "Good idea, darling."

"You'd better inform her she's to be a virtual prisoner until Northcott gets back." He pulled a face. "That's not going to go down well. Frankly, though, I'm surprised Northcott agreed to hold off arresting her. Usually he's in his element when he can take someone into custody."

"Which just goes to show he's not confident about his judgement."

A second tap on the door sounded louder than the first. Cecily nodded at Baxter then called out, "Come in!"

Gertie's anxious face appeared in the gap. "You rang for me, m'm?"

"Yes, come in, Gertie. Mr. Baxter was just leaving, weren't you dear?"

Baxter hesitated for one second longer, then strode out the door, shutting it firmly behind him.

Gertie still looked uneasy as she took the chair opposite Cecily. "Mr. Baxter didn't look none too pleased. I didn't do nothing wrong, did I?"

It was the second time she'd asked that. Realizing that gave Cecily cause to worry. Praying that she'd been right to defend her housemaid, she said quietly, "Why didn't you tell me you saw Ian last night?"

Gertie's shoulders jerked in surprise. "I didn't think to, m'm. It weren't no secret. I'd have told you if you'd asked me."

She must have seen something in Cecily's face since she leaned forward, a frown furrowing her brow. "You don't think I had anything to do with him dying, do you? He was drunk. The doc said so, didn't he? He fell into the pond and drowned. I wasn't even there. I didn't know—"

"Gertie." Cecily paused, then said carefully, "We believe that someone hit Ian over the head with one of the Christmas candlesticks. We won't know for certain until after the autopsy if the blow to the head killed Ian, or if it simply knocked him out and he drowned, but either way, it appears that the head wound was responsible for his death."

Gertie's face had paled considerably as she'd talked. She seemed to have trouble getting her tongue to work, and finally blurted out, "S-someone deliberately killed Ian?"

Cecily sighed. "We don't know if the assailant intended to kill him, but at this point P.C. Northcott is anxious to arrest someone for murder."

Gertie might not have had the benefit of a formal education, but she was astute enough to grasp the implication behind Cecily's words. "So he wants to bloody arrest me," she stated flatly.

"Gertie—"

"I didn't kill him, m'm."

"I know you didn't, Gertie. Unfortunately, someone told the constable you threatened Ian with a knife. Tell me, is that true?"

Gertie hung her head. "Yes, m'm. I did." She looked up again. "Just to frighten him off, though. I would never have used it, m'm. Never. Not even on *him*."

"I believe you." Cecily sighed. "This all seems very unfortunate at the moment, but I promise you Mr. Baxter and I will do everything in our power to find out who was responsible for Ian's death before the constable returns from his Christmas holiday."

Hope crept into Gertie's eyes. "He's not going to arrest me today?"

"No." Cecily got up from her chair and walked around to pat Gertie's broad shoulder. "We promised that you would not leave the hotel until he got back, however."

Gertie's chin shot up. "But what about me twins? They was looking forward to a walk on the seafront. It's Daisy's day off, and I promised to take them. I'm supposed to meet Dan down there in half an hour."

Cecily wavered.

Gertie's dark eyes pleaded with her. "They've been so good I hate to disappoint them. Pansy's coming with me and all, and they love to see her."

Cecily let out her breath on another sigh. "Oh, well, in that case, I shall hold Pansy responsible for seeing that you return."

A weak smile flashed across Gertie's face. "I've got to come back, don't I. I'm not going to leave me twins behind. Besides, it's Christmas. How can I miss Christmas at the Pennyfoot?"

Her voice broke, and Cecily thought she saw a tear glistening in her housemaid's eye. A rare event indeed. "Try not to worry." She gave the young woman another comforting pat. "I promise you we'll all do our very best to get all this sorted out."

Gertie sniffed and rubbed her nose with the back of her hand. "I bleeding hope so." She glanced up at Cecily's face. "Sorry, m'm. I shouldn't be using them bad words in front of you."

"It's quite all right. Quite understandable under the circumstances." Cecily returned to her chair. "Now, if I'm going to help you, you must tell me what happened last night between you and Ian." She gave her chief housemaid a hard stare. "And Gertie, if you don't want to be sent to prison for something you didn't do, I suggest you tell me every single word that was spoken."

CHAPTER

❈ 7 ❈

Gertie stared down at her hands for a long moment, then drew a shuddering breath. "I was in the kitchen. Must have been about six. Mrs. Chubb was in the laundry room. Michel had gone home and the maids were all in the dining room cleaning up. So I was all alone in there."

She paused, and Cecily leaned forward. "Is that when you saw Ian?"

"Yeah. He knocked on the back door. I thought it was Dan knocking and I rushed to let him in. Gave me a really nasty jolt to see Ian flipping standing there. I thought he was still in London."

"So did we all. What happened then?"

"Not a lot. I told him he couldn't come in. He started arguing. Said he'd come to see the twins and nobody was going to stop him. I could tell he'd been drinking, I could smell it on him. I told him if he didn't leave I'd call Clive." Gertie flashed a look at Cecily. "He's afraid of Clive." She gulped. "I mean he was."

Cecily nodded. It wasn't hard to see why Ian was intimidated by her maintenance man. Ian was not a tall man and his body was quite frail, whereas Clive's impressive height, broad shoulders, and barrel chest made him look like a giant in comparison. "Go on, Gertie. I'm assuming he didn't leave right away?"

Gertie shrugged. "No, he didn't. He started coming in through the door and I backed up to the table. Mrs. Chubb had left a roast on the table for supper. The carving knife was lying next to it so I picked it up. Just to scare him, I swear. I yelled at him to get out before I did something really, really bad to him, like slitting his bleeding throat." She coughed behind her hand. "Sorry again, m'm."

"And he left?"

Gertie chewed on her bottom lip for a moment, then shook her head. "He just stood there, arguing back at me. Then all of a sudden Clive appeared in the doorway. He dragged him out and I heard them shouting at each other, then it all went quiet." Gertie looked up again. "I didn't hear nothing after that. Clive looked in and asked if I was all right, and I said yes and then he was gone."

"I see." Cecily frowned at the ledger in front of her. "And you were quite alone with Ian until Clive arrived on the scene?"

"Yes, m'm."

"That's strange."

Gertie looked puzzled. "What is?"

Cecily smiled at her. "P.C. Northcott said someone told him you had threatened Ian with a knife. He wouldn't tell me who it was, but I can't imagine Clive would say anything to him."

"No, m'm. Clive would never say nothing that would get me in trouble. I'd swear on it."

"Well, then, in that case, someone else must have heard you, unless—" She broke off as someone rapped on the door.

Gertie looked scared and hunched her shoulders as if bracing for a blow.

Cecily muttered an irritable, "What now?" Then louder, "Yes? Who is it?"

The door flew open and a young woman stepped into the room. She wore a fashionable skirt under a coat trimmed with fox fur, and silk ribbons adorned the wide brim of her hat.

Her face looked vaguely familiar and Cecily frowned. It was customary for one of the footmen to escort a visitor to her office and make an official announcement of her name. This sudden invasion was most unsettling.

Before she could speak, however, Gertie shot to her feet. "Oh, my gawd, it's Gloria."

Cecily stared at Gertie, then back at the visitor. "You two know each other? But how—?"

The woman glared at Gertie and walked farther into the room. Scowling at Cecily she said in a low, fierce voice, "I want to know where Robert is hiding."

Cecily raised her eyebrows. "Robert? I don't think I know—"

"She means Ian." Gertie had a look on her face that suggested she was about to be sick. "Remember? That's Ian's real name. Robert Johnson. He changed it to Ian Rossiter when he came to work for you so she wouldn't find him. This is Gloria Johnson. Ian's real wife."

"Oh, goodness." Cecily rose from her chair. "Of course. I thought you seemed familiar but it's been a good many years and I had forgotten—"

"Where is he, Mrs. Sinclair? Where's my Robert?"

Cecily swallowed. "Actually, it's Mrs. Baxter now. I . . . ah . . . perhaps you'd better sit down." She glanced at Gertie, who still stared at Gloria as if she were looking at a hungry lion about to charge. "You, too, Gertie. Unless you'd prefer to leave?"

With a look of sheer relief, Gertie nodded, took another sidelong glance at Gloria, then fled out the door.

Out on the Esplanade, Gertie let the full force of the cold wind blow in her face. After the horrible morning she'd had, she needed something to clear out the tangle of thoughts in her head. Heedless of the wisps of hair escaping from the pins, she stood at the railing and watched the angry waves churning onto the wet sand in a tide of froth and spray.

Maybe she should have told madam everything. Maybe she should have told her how she'd seen Clive later the night Ian died, long after he should have gone home, and how he was soaking wet, as if he'd been out in the snow for a while.

She should have told her what really happened, and she might have done, if Gloria hadn't barged in on her.

A tiny hand crept into hers and a voice struggled to be heard above the crashing ocean. "Mummy? What's the matter? Are you all right?"

Looking down at her daughter, Gertie found the strength to smile. "Course I am. It's Christmas, isn't it. Everything's always all right at Christmas."

Lillian's rosy-cheeked face glowed with the bite of the wind. "Is Father Christmas coming soon?"

"Soon." Gertie gripped the small hand tighter. "As long as you and James behave yourself, that is." She looked down the Esplanade to where Pansy stood throwing a ball for James to catch. A wave of panic almost made her cry out.

What would she do if the constable arrested her and put her in jail? What would happen to her children? Who would look after them? She couldn't expect Daisy to take care of them until they were grown. Daisy was only a nanny, and she'd made it clear she wouldn't be around once the twins were old enough to take care of themselves.

Madam and Mr. Baxter had to find out who killed Ian. They just had to, and quick. Because if they didn't, it was very likely she could end up in prison or swinging from a rope for something she didn't do. Gertie closed her eyes and prayed as she'd never prayed before.

"Mummy?"

A tug on her hand opened her eyes. Gertie blinked tears away and smiled at her daughter. "I'm all right, luv. Honest. I just got a little bit of sand in me eyes and it made them water a bit, that's all."

Lillian's worried frown vanished, and she pointed down

the Esplanade to where a tall figure of a man strode toward them. "Look! There's Uncle Dan!"

James had already seen him coming and was tearing down the Esplanade toward him, with Pansy running hard to keep up with the little boy.

Gertie pulled in a deep breath. "Come on." She took hold of Lillian's hand. "Let's go and meet him."

Hurrying along beside her eager daughter, Gertie rehearsed how she would tell Dan everything that had happened. He'd be shocked, just like she was. She could only hope it didn't ruin his Christmas.

She wasn't going to let it ruin hers. Ian Rossiter had done enough damage to her and the twins, and no matter what happened afterward, she wasn't about to let him spoil their Christmas. Somehow she'd get through it, and somehow madam would find out who did it and she'd be in the clear.

As for Gloria, well she felt sorry for her. It wasn't going to be easy for her to hear Ian had been killed, even if he had been a rotten husband.

In fact, it amazed Gertie that they were still together. After Gloria had found out he'd gone through a fake wedding and all, Gertie was sure Gloria would have had nothing more to do with him.

They must have patched things up somehow.

But now Ian was dead and Gloria was all alone. They didn't have no kids, Gertie had learned that much when Ian had tried to take Lillian away. Maybe it was just as well.

Gloria hated her. She'd seen the venom in Gloria's eyes

when she'd come in madam's office. Not that Gertie could blame her for that. It must have really hurt to find out your husband had secretly married someone else.

Sighing, she put away the bad thoughts. She was close enough now to see Dan's welcoming smile, and right then that was all that mattered to her. The rest of it could wait until she got back. Right now she was going to enjoy the next hour or two with the man she loved and her kids. Pansy, too. For a little while, life was good again.

Cecily folded her hands in her lap, reluctant to look at the silent woman seated in front of her. For the second time that day she had to tell a woman that the man she'd loved had died.

She'd had no idea that Gloria was still married to Ian—or Robert, if that was his real name. In fact, she was beginning to think she had never known Ian at all. After all that had happened, she could find nothing to equate the hard, bitter man who had just died with the bright young lad who had served her so well in the past.

"You know where he is, don't you."

With a start, Cecily looked up as Gloria broke the tense silence. "Yes, I'm afraid I do." She cleared her throat. "Gloria, I am so very sorry. Ian . . . your husband was found in the duck pond this morning. I'm afraid he's dead."

Gloria's expression remained stoic, though tears stole out from her eyes and coursed down her cheeks. "I suppose he was drunk?"

Her voice was accusing, as if this were all Cecily's fault. She flinched, but met Gloria's hard gaze steadily. "Yes, it appears that he might well have been enjoying a little too much spirits, but that was not the cause of his death. Not directly, anyway."

Gloria's eyes held a flicker of uneasiness. "So what did he die of then?"

"He . . . we think someone attacked him."

It had sounded brutal, put like that, and Cecily wished she could have found a better way to say it.

Gloria, however, seemed to bear the brunt of it with remarkable fortitude. Although there was a distinct tremor in her voice when she asked, "So, do you know who it was that hit him, then?"

"Not at present, no, but we are endeavoring to find whoever killed your husband and bring him to justice."

Gloria pulled a handkerchief from her pocket and dabbed at her eyes. After a long, difficult moment of silence, she muttered, "I thought, when he didn't come home last night, that he might be over here."

"I'm sorry." Cecily fidgeted on her chair. There had to be something she could say other than that, but right then, she couldn't think of a single thing.

After another long pause, Gloria spoke again. "Robert was always talking about the twins, and how he'd like to see more of them. I never thought, when he left to go down the pub last night, that it would be the last time I saw him. I went right to bed after he left, and I thought he'd be there when I woke up, but he wasn't and I . . ." A slight sob escaped, and she blew her nose hard.

"I'm so sorry." Cecily leaned forward. "Can I get you something? A cup of tea, perhaps?"

Gloria shook her head. "I bet it was someone at the pub. Robert was always getting into fights. I didn't like some of the people he kept company with, neither, but he was always telling me I worry too much." She dabbed at her eyes again.

At a loss as to how to comfort the grieving woman, Cecily said awkwardly, "Perhaps you'd feel better if you were at home. I'll have someone drive you—"

"No!"

The woman's vehemence startled Cecily and she raised her eyebrows.

Before she could speak, however, Gloria spoke, her words tumbling out so fast she stumbled over them. "I can't go back there now. I really can't. I'll never go back to that place. Never!"

Concerned, Cecily quickly tried to reassure her. "It's quite all right, Mrs. . . ." She hesitated, having forgotten Ian's real last name.

"Gloria." The widow looked up at her, and Cecily saw a moment of intense fear flash across her face before she composed herself again. "It's just that I don't know what I'm going to do now. We've been living in the flat over Abbitson's, the butcher's shop in the High Street. It was free all the time Robert was working in the shop. I can't stay there now that he's gone."

"You were living here in Badgers End?"

"Yes, m'm. Robert wanted to move down here to be closer to his children. I didn't want to leave London but he said he'd come without me if I didn't go with him."

Cecily wondered if Gertie had known that Ian was living in Badgers End and how she would have reacted to the news.

It seemed they had all escaped what could have been a very difficult situation, though she would have wished a better solution to the problem than Ian's death. Much as she despised the treacherous thought, it seemed that someone had done Gertie an enormous favor.

She watched the other woman tuck her handkerchief back in her pocket. "Do you have relatives in London? Perhaps someone you can stay with until you can decide what you want to do?"

Gloria shook her head so violently a couple of hairpins flew out of her hair and skidded across the desk. "I can't go back there. Really I can't. I don't have nowhere to go. There was just me and my mum. My dad took off when I was little and my mum died two years ago."

"Oh, I'm sorry."

Gloria squeezed her eyes shut and opened them again. "Robert was all I had left and now he's gone, too. He didn't have no one, either. What am I going to do? I have to take care of burying him and everything, and I don't know what to do about that and . . ." Again her voice broke into a sob.

Cecily made up her mind. After all, it was Christmas, and she couldn't bear the thought of this poor woman all alone and helpless. "You must stay here at the Pennyfoot," she said, rising to her feet. "We will help you see to Ian's funeral and burial."

"Oh, I couldn't." Gloria jumped up from her chair. "Now that my husband's gone I couldn't afford—"

"Free of charge." Cecily smiled at the other woman's expression. Surprise, relief, and something else she couldn't quite read flashed across Gloria's face. "Just until you get everything settled and find something more suitable for your needs," she added hurriedly. "No one should have to spend Christmas alone at a time like this."

Gloria looked as if she would burst into real tears. "I don't know what to say." She spread out her hands in a gesture of helplessness. "All I can think of is—thank you."

"There's nothing else to say." Cecily tugged on her bell rope. "I'll have Samuel take you back to the flat to fetch your belongings, and then when you return one of the maids can show you to your room. I'm afraid it's rather small, tucked next to the attic on the top floor. We usually keep it free for children, but we have no child guests at present so you are welcome to occupy it for as long as you need it."

"That is most generous of you, Mrs. Baxter. Thank you."

"Not at all. I feel we owe you that much, since your husband died on our premises."

Gloria's expression changed to one of sadness. "I'll miss him. He wasn't much of a husband, but he was mine. I'd like to know who did this to him."

"We'll find out in due time." Cecily looked up when she heard a knock on the door. "Come in!"

Pansy stood in the doorway, her face full of curiosity as she glanced at Gloria. Obviously Gertie had told her the identity of their visitor.

"Pansy, please tell Samuel I need him to take Mrs. Johnson to the High Street to fetch her luggage. When she returns I'll need someone to show her to room number one."

Pansy looked surprised, but said nothing as she dipped her knees.

"Thank you again," Gloria said, a little breathlessly, "I'll try not to get in anyone's way."

"I hope you will join the guests for meals," Cecily said, as the widow hurried to the door. "Especially the Christmas dinner. Michel always outdoes himself at Christmas."

"I would like that. Most kind of you." Tears glistened in Gloria's eyes once more as she bowed her head, then followed Pansy into the hallway.

Cecily sank onto her chair. She wasn't at all sure she'd done the right thing. There was bound to be animosity between Gloria and Gertie. Perhaps the two of them would find a way to avoid each other. Gertie would have to understand that she couldn't turn the poor thing out into the cold, after losing her husband in such a tragic way and with nowhere else to go. All she could hope now was that Gloria's presence in the Pennyfoot wouldn't cause more trouble.

CHAPTER

8

"I really enjoyed that walk this afternoon." Leaning across one of the dining room tables, Pansy laid a folded white linen serviette on the left of the place setting. "Your twins are really fun to be with."

Gertie twisted her mouth in a wry smile. That was easy for Pansy to say. She didn't have to clean up after them, or make them behave when they got into mischief. "They're fun if they're in a good mood and not scrapping with each other. They get bloody overexcited this time of year. They drive me blinking loopy wanting to know when Father Christmas is going to get here."

Pansy laughed. "You're lucky to have them. I wish I had little ones like that." Her face sobered. "Don't look as if I'll ever have 'em, though, at this rate."

Gertie snorted. "Watcha talking about? You're only a young kid. You've got lots of time to find a husband."

"I don't want just any husband. I want Samuel."

"Yeah, well, I wouldn't hold your breath waiting for that one." Gertie picked up a crystal glass and polished the rim with a corner of her apron. "How many times have I told you to look for someone else?"

"Well, if I can't have Samuel, I want someone just like your Dan. I think he's smashing."

Gertie grinned. "Yeah, he is. He's so good with James and Lillian."

"He is that." Pansy lifted the pile of serviettes and moved to the next table. "He was a lot of fun to be with today. He made me and the twins laugh. I like that."

"Me, too. I don't think I ever laughed as much as I do with my Dan."

"He looked tired, though. Like he'd been up all night. How'd he get that graze on his cheek? It looks nasty."

"Had an accident in his motorcar, didn't he." Gertie followed her, resting the tray of wineglasses against her hip. "He told me someone stepped out in front of him and he had to swerve to miss him. He hit another motorcar coming the other way."

"Goodness!" Pansy looked at her in dismay. "He could have been killed."

"Nah, he wasn't going fast enough."

"Don't you get scared when you go out riding in that motorcar with him?"

Gertie shook her head. "Dan's a good driver. He's taking me out in it this evening. They're having a Christmas party down at the pub, with dancing and everything."

Pansy sighed, her face taking on a dreamy expression. "Oh, it must be lovely to have someone take you out dancing. I can't imagine Samuel ever doing that."

Gertie felt like shaking her. Here she was having to sneak out tonight to be with Dan and risk getting into big trouble, while Pansy was too timid to go after what she wanted. "Then find someone who will."

Pansy made a face. "Not that easy is it. I don't get out much, and when I do I don't go to places where there's single blokes."

"Well, we've got a couple of single blokes staying here for Christmas. How about that Archie Parker? He's here all on his own. He'd probably jump at the chance of taking out a gorgeous young woman like you."

Pansy made a gurgling noise of disgust. "A fat old medicine man. I can do better than that." She tilted her chin up and looked thoughtful. "Now, that Sid Barrett. I wouldn't mind taking a turn around the Esplanade with that one. He can make me laugh, too. He knows how to treat a lady, and make her feel special, all right."

Gertie's smile vanished. "You'd better stay away from that one. He's trouble. I can sense it a mile off."

"You're just worried he'll fancy me instead of you."

Gertie snorted. "What me? No, thanks. I wouldn't touch him with a lamplighter pole. You can bleeding have him if that's what you want."

"He fancies you, though. He's always following you around."

"Yeah, well he's out of luck. I wouldn't have nothing to do with him if he was dripping in diamonds."

Pouting, Pansy slapped a serviette down on the table. "Well, you don't have to, do you. You've got Dan."

Gertie sighed. She wasn't too sure about that. It was nice to have someone to go out with, and she really enjoyed being with Dan, but she couldn't help wondering if she should take her own advice and give up on the idea of him ever asking her to marry him.

Then again, she wasn't getting any younger, and with the twins and all, her prospects weren't too bright. If Dan didn't want a ready-made family it was unlikely anyone else would, even if she did meet another bloke.

She might just as well enjoy what she had and stop worrying about whether or not Dan would ever propose. The thought of giving up her dream made her heart ache, but dreams were for young kids, and she wasn't a kid no more.

"I wonder why that Mrs. Johnson is staying here," Pansy said, breaking into her thoughts.

For a minute Gertie thought she hadn't heard right. "Mrs. Johnson? You mean Ian Rossiter's wife?"

Pansy nodded. "Actually, she's his widow now, isn't she. I don't know if I'd want to stay in the place where my husband was killed."

"Gloria is staying here?" Gertie shook her head. "I don't bloody believe it."

"She's in room number one. I took her up there myself about an hour ago."

"Why would she want to stay here?"

"I dunno, but she had a lot of luggage with her. Samuel had to go and fetch it from the High Street."

"What was it doing in the High Street?"

"Samuel said she and Ian was living in a flat over Abbitson's, the butcher's shop. Just think, if Dan still owned it, he'd be her landlord."

"Flipping heck." Having placed the last wineglass on the table, Gertie swung the tray down by her side. "That's it. I've had enough surprises for one day. I'm going back to the kitchen. It's almost time to start dishing up the supper, anyhow."

"I'm not finished yet." Pansy dropped another serviette on the table in front of her. "I have to go and ring the dinner bell in a minute."

"I'll ring it for you." Gertie headed for the door. "You get finished up in here." She waved away Pansy's thanks and stepped out into the hallway.

After the bright light of the chandeliers in the dining room, the tiny flickering gas lamps on the walls were dim by comparison, and she blinked to adjust her sight.

Gloria here, in the Pennyfoot, right under her nose. It didn't seem possible. All she could hope was that they didn't bump into each other. The less she saw of Ian's widow, the better.

She had taken just a few steps when she saw a movement outside the library door near the other end of the hallway. Two people stood close together, as if deep in a private conversation.

As she approached one of them broke away and sped off in the direction of the lobby. The woman passed under the gas lamp and Gertie frowned. It was Mabel and she seemed in an awful hurry.

The other figure turned and started toward her. Her nerves jumped when she saw Sid Barrett grinning at her. No wonder Mabel had run off like that. He'd probably been pestering her the way he hassled all the women.

Bracing herself, she approached him with a firm step, ready to brush him aside if he barred her way.

"Hello, me old darling," he called out, while she was still a few steps away.

"I'm not your bleeding darling." She glared at him, but he seemed unfazed by her animosity toward him.

"I hear they've got a Christmas celebration going on at the George and Dragon tonight. If you'll go with me I'll buy you all the gin and tonics you can drink."

"No, ta very much."

"Oh, you don't like gin?" He tilted his head to one side. "How about a nice cherry brandy, then?"

She stared at him, jolted by the suggestion. Cherry brandy would always remind her of Ian. She drank it all the time when they were together. Ian used to tease her about it, saying her nose would turn red if she kept drinking it.

Forcing her thoughts away from the memory, she scowled at Sid. "I'm not going anywhere with you, so just bloody leave me alone."

Sid simply smiled. "Come on, luv, come and have a drink with me tonight. You need cheering up. It isn't every day you lose a husband."

She gritted her teeth. "I already told you, Ian wasn't my husband."

"He was your children's father, though, so he must have meant a lot to you at one time." He leaned forward, a sly gleam in his eyes. "He must have come visiting a lot."

Gertie frowned. "I don't think that's any of your bleeding business, is it."

"I'd like to make it my business. A nice looking woman like you shouldn't have to bring up two little ones alone."

"Yeah, well, that's for me to worry about, not you. In any case, I already got a boyfriend, so you needn't worry about me being alone." Tossing her head, Gertie marched away from him. She could feel his gaze on her back all the way down the corridor.

She was relieved when she could turn the corner and leave him behind. Cheeky bugger. What was he thinking, trying to pick up someone who'd just lost her husband?

She was getting a funny feeling in her bones about that man. He was probably chasing after all the maids and making himself a nuisance. Hoping to get one of them alone, no doubt. Well, he wasn't going to get her alone anywhere with him. Not if he offered her a hundred pounds and all the blinking diamonds she could wear.

He wasn't her type. Not like Dan. Now, if only Dan was as eager for her company as that sleazy Sid Barrett, she could be really happy.

Right now, however, she had better things to think about. She had to get supper on the tables and then get the dishes washed and put away before she could meet Dan and go down the pub. Now that was something she was really going to enjoy.

*   *   *

DECKED WITH FOLLY

It had been a long day, and Cecily was looking forward to a quiet evening relaxing with her husband. She was smiling at the thought as she approached the stairs, but the smile soon faded when she saw one of her footmen standing over by the Christmas tree.

Sidney Barrett was talking to Pansy, and judging from her expression, she wasn't enjoying the conversation. Two bright spots of red glowed in her cheeks, and she gazed at him with fire in her eyes.

There were guests passing through the foyer, and wary of drawing unwanted attention, Cecily waited until she was close behind Sid before addressing him. Just as she reached him she heard him say, "Go on, you know you want to."

Pansy didn't answer him, and he put a hand on her shoulder, as Cecily spoke in her sharpest voice. "Is there a problem here?"

Sid swung around, his face wreathed in a smile. "Mrs. Baxter! I didn't see you there."

Cecily ignored him, searching the maid's face. "Pansy? Is everything all right?"

Pansy nodded, sent a quick glance at Sid, then slid past him and scuttled off across the lobby toward the kitchen stairs.

"I've been meaning to have a word with you, m'm," Sid said, taking Cecily's attention away from the fleeing maid. "I wanted to offer my condolences."

Instantly on guard, Cecily met his gaze. "I beg your pardon?"

"I heard about the dead bloke." Sid waved a hand at the wall. "In the duck pond. Must have been a nasty shock, all right. Especially for them two little ones, losing their daddy right at Christmastime."

It was inevitable that the staff would find out about it, but that didn't mean she was prepared for this moment. Cecily drew a deep breath. "We are trying to keep the incident from the guests as much as possible. I'd appreciate it if you wouldn't discuss it among yourselves, particularly wherever someone might overhear you."

"Oh, right you are, m'm. Mum's the word, as the great bard, William Shakespeare, once said. Must be hard for the new widow. Right on Christmastime and all."

Cecily frowned. "Enough has been said on the subject," she said sternly. "The matter is closed."

Sid winked. "Gotcha, m'm. Not another word."

Cecily met his grin with a stony expression. "It might also be as well if you refrained from harassing any of my maids. They have to work extremely hard and they do not have the time or the energy to fend off unwanted overtures from you."

Sid's grin wobbled, and for a moment resentment burned in his eyes. Then it was gone, and he looked contrite. "Sorry, m'm. It won't happen again."

"See that it doesn't." Satisfied that she'd got her point across, Cecily turned her back on him and headed once more for the stairs.

Seated at her dressing table a few minutes later, she toyed with a string of pearls as she wondered how she was going to tell her husband she'd invited Ian's widow to stay indefinitely at the Pennyfoot.

No doubt he would indulge in another fit of temper. Perhaps she should wait until after supper, so that he wouldn't upset his digestion.

A vision of Archie Parker popped into her head. She could just imagine him offering Baxter a powder to settle his stomach. The image made her smile, just as her husband emerged from the boudoir, his bow tie strung about his neck and dangling on his chest.

"I can't get this pesky tie to sit straight," he grumbled. Seating himself on the davenport, he fiddled with it some more before asking irritably, "Would you please tie it for me?"

"Of course." She dropped the pearls on the table and rose from her seat. "You know you always have trouble with it. Why don't you simply let me tie it for you instead of trying to do it yourself and getting all in a dither about it?"

"Because I don't like being dependent on people."

"No, it's more likely because you are stubborn." She leaned over and took the ends of the tie. "Now, be still so I can tie it properly."

He raised his chin to give her better access. "So how did Gertie take the news that she's under house arrest?"

Cecily shrugged. "You know Gertie. She took it all in stride, though she's concerned, of course."

"Well, of course she is. Being accused of murder is a serious matter. She *should* be concerned."

"She swears she didn't kill Ian. I believe her."

"I hope she's telling the truth. If only she hadn't gone around threatening the man loud enough for everyone to hear, Northcott might not have been in such a blasted hurry to arrest her."

97

"There." Cecily surveyed her handiwork with a nod of satisfaction. "Perfect, if I do say so myself."

Baxter grunted and got up from the bed to peer at himself in her mirror. "Looks all right. Thank you."

"Not at all." Cecily sat down at the dressing table once more. "Actually, you know, that's what puzzles me."

Baxter frowned. "What? That I can't tie a bow tie and you can?"

Cecily smiled. "No. It was Northcott saying someone told him that Gertie had threatened Ian with a knife. Yet Gertie insists she and Ian were alone in the kitchen when she did that. So how could anyone have known about it?"

"Well, someone must have seen or heard her."

"But who? Gertie was quite sure they were alone. Until Clive came along, that is."

"Clive?" Baxter gave her a sharp look. "Where does he fit into all this?"

"He came to the back door when Gertie was arguing with Ian. Apparently he ran Ian off the premises."

"Well, good for him." Baxter paused, an odd look on his face. "You don't think Clive could have killed him?"

Cecily swallowed, afraid to admit the thought had crossed her mind. "No, of course not. Clive wouldn't step on a spider, much less kill a man."

"I don't know. He's quite protective of Gertie and the twins."

"Whoever hit Ian took the candlestick from the hallstand. Clive was in the kitchen. I think Gertie would have seen a candlestick in his hand, and I hardly think he dragged Ian into the hotel to get the candlestick to hit him, do you?"

Baxter's frown cleared. "Does seem a bit far-fetched. Then again, who else would want to kill Rossiter? He hasn't lived here in years. He doesn't know anyone here."

"He knows just about everyone who works here. Or . . ." She paused, staring at her reflection in the mirror.

"Or what?"

Cecily looked up, meeting her husband's concerned gaze. "Perhaps he fell into bad company when he moved down here. His wife did say she didn't like the company he kept."

Baxter stared at her. "His *wife?* Where did you see his wife?"

Cecily took a deep breath, then spoke in a rush to get the words out. "Right here in the hotel. She came looking for Ian. I had to tell her he'd died. She was so upset, she had nowhere to go and I felt so sorry for her, I offered her a room here until she can get settled somewhere else." Running out of breath, she braced herself, waiting for her husband's wrath to explode once more.

To her surprise, after a moment's tense silence, Baxter said quietly, "That might have been a mistake."

"Yes," Cecily said slowly, "I realize that now. I just hope she doesn't cause Gertie any trouble."

"She has no cause to be angry with Gertie. After all, Gertie had no idea Ian was already married to someone else when she married him."

"Maybe not, but I do think that Gloria blames her all the same."

Baxter grunted. "Well, Ian's gone. The problem is, now that you've offered his widow free room and board, she is likely to take advantage of it and you might never be rid of her."

"In that case, I shall ask her politely to leave."

Baxter smiled. "That, my dear, would be quite remarkable indeed."

"Piffle." She returned his smile, but couldn't quite banish the uneasy feeling under her ribs. She didn't feel comfortable with Ian's widow in the hotel, and she wished now she hadn't been quite so accommodating with her. But she wasn't sure exactly why it bothered her. It could be because of Ian's attempted kidnaping of his daughter, though it didn't seem likely that Gloria would want to steal either of the twins away, now that Ian was no longer alive.

Whatever the reason for her apprehension, she would have to make sure to keep an eye on Gloria Johnson. With any luck, the woman would soon find other accommodations and leave them in peace. For until she did so, the memory of Ian Rossiter would hang over their heads and be a constant reminder that another murder had been committed, and that his killer was still on the loose.

CHAPTER
❀ 9 ❀

"I do love riding in this motorcar." Gertie snuggled back in the soft leather seat and drew the collar of her wool coat closer around her neck. "It makes me feel like royalty. I want to wave at everyone as we go by."

Seated next to her behind the huge steering wheel, Dan chuckled. "Go ahead and wave. I'm sure they'll all wave back."

"Nah. They'll just think I'm showing off." She ran a finger along the walnut dashboard. "It's a real pretty motorcar, though. I see lots of people looking at it as we drive down the street."

"These Austins are well built." Dan patted the steering wheel. "It can go sixteen miles an hour downhill. Maybe even faster on a long slope."

Gertie gasped. "That sounds really fast."

Dan nodded. "They are building bigger and better motors all the time. I wouldn't be at all surprised to see a motorcar going twenty-five, thirty miles an hour in a year or two."

"Blimey, that's dangerous. What happens when you cross the road and one's coming at you? Like what happened to you yesterday. You wouldn't have time to get out the bloody way, would you."

"You'd have to keep a sharp lookout for them, that's all. Just like you do horses."

Gertie thought about that. "I dunno. I think I'd rather dodge horses than motorcars. I don't know what the world's coming to, what with all this new stuff going on. I heard some blokes talking the other day about someone in America making a machine that can fly off the ground." She shook her head. "Can you imagine that?"

"The Wright brothers." Dan did something with a stick near his knees and the car jerked, sending Gertie lurching forward. "They say one day they will build a machine that will fly them all the way across the country."

Gertie found that hard to believe, but not wanting to seem ignorant, she refrained from saying so. "Well, I'd rather go out in this motorcar than in a flying machine any day. I like to feel the ground under me."

Dan grinned. "I can't say I blame you."

Remembering something, Gertie sat upright. "I thought you said you got hit by another motorcar last night."

"No, I said I swerved to avoid getting hit."

"But I thought you said you got bumped and that's how you hurt your face."

Dan sighed. "Maybe I did."

DECKED WITH FOLLY

"So where is the dent in the motorcar? Is it a bad one? I didn't see it when I got in. Will it cost a lot to mend it? How—"

"Gertie!" He sounded irritable and she snapped her mouth shut. "It was just a light scratch. I rubbed it out with some polish so you can't see it."

"Sorry."

She'd mumbled the word and he was quick to make amends. Reaching for her hand he gave it a light squeeze. "Never mind, luv. It was nothing, honest. Tell me about the carol singing at the hotel. Will you be able to go?"

"I hope so." She stole a quick glance at him and was relieved to see his jaw relaxed again. "Will you come if I can go?"

"Will it be all right with Mrs. Baxter?"

"Course it would. You haven't seen the decorations yet, have you. Miss Pengrath does a lovely job with them. Oh, I mean Mrs. Prestwick. I keep forgetting she's married now."

If she'd hoped the subject of marriage might start a conversation about their own relationship she was soon disappointed.

"If she did half as well as she did last year with the decorations," Dan said, bringing the motorcar to a halt, "it's bound to look fantastic. She really does make it look good. In fact, the windows were lit up so bright last night I thought the hotel was on fire, until I realized it was candles on a Christmas tree. Must have been dozens of them." He shut off the engine and the motor shuddered into silence.

Glancing out the window, Gertie saw that they were in the courtyard of the George and Dragon. On either side carriages were lined up one behind the other, while the horses were gathered in a pen in the field beyond.

Light flowed from the lattice windows of the pub, and the sound of laughter echoed into the night. The tinkling notes of an out of tune piano could be heard above the chatter, and someone was singing with great gusto and painfully off-key.

It all sounded so festive, and she felt a stir of excitement. Thank goodness she'd told Dan earlier about Ian. He'd been shocked, as she'd expected, but he'd got over it really fast, and now they could put it behind them, at least for tonight.

She waited for Dan to open the door for her, then stepped out onto the pavement. This was the moment she loved, stepping down from the beautiful motorcar with Dan holding her hand like a prince escorting a princess.

That's how he always made her feel. Like a princess. No one had ever made her feel that way before. No one had ever treated her the way Dan treated her. She could be really, really happy, if only he would say something about their future together. Even if she had to wait a year or two to get married. It was the not knowing that bothered her.

"Don't look so worried," Dan said, as he tucked her hand into his elbow. "The private lounge will be just as much fun as the public bar. From what I hear they have a nice supper laid out and there'll be singing and dancing."

Gertie began to feel nervous. What if someone saw her and told madam? She'd be in hot water all right. "I can't sing or dance."

"Then we'll watch." He laughed, and pulled her to the door. "I'll teach you to dance, Gertie McBride, and if you come out of here tonight without saying you had the best night out ever, I'll walk all the way to the motorcar on my hands."

"Now that's something I've got to see." Putting her qualms behind her, Gertie stepped through the door into the warm, smoky chaos of the Christmas party.

After having enjoyed supper in the dining room, Cecily sat opposite her husband in front of a crackling fire in their suite and did her best to concentrate on the conversation.

She found it hard to relax, however, unable to prevent the questions haunting her, mainly how someone had known about Gertie threatening Ian with a knife. She felt sure it had to be a key to the puzzle, and the only way she was going to solve it was to ask everyone who might have overheard the quarrel. Starting with Mrs. Chubb. She would tackle her first thing in the morning, she decided.

"May I ask what is troubling you to the extent you are completely ignoring me?"

Baxter's voice cut into her thoughts, jarring her to attention. "Oh, I'm sorry, darling. I was thinking about the Christmas pantomime tomorrow night. Phoebe promised to be here early tomorrow to go over the final arrangements." Feeling guilty for having been less than truthful, she leaned forward and patted his hand. "I promise you will have my undivided attention for the rest of the evening."

"I certainly hope so." He caught her fingers in his and raised them to his mouth. "I'm aware that we have been married long enough for you to grow weary of my company, but I sincerely hope we have not reached the point of shutting each other out completely."

"Nor shall we ever, my love." She sent him her warmest smile. "And neither am I, nor shall I ever be, weary of your company. I simply have a lot on my mind, that's all."

"Humph. Well, I hope at least you're not stewing over the unfortunate demise of Mr. Rossiter." He let go of her hand and reached for his brandy glass.

Knowing how upset he'd be if he knew that's exactly what had been occupying her mind, Cecily made a determined effort to banish all thoughts of the murder from her mind. Tonight belonged to her husband. Tomorrow would be soon enough to continue her investigation.

It was almost midnight when Dan pulled up outside the Pennyfoot. Already half asleep, Gertie returned his goodnight kiss. "You were right," she said, snuggling into his shoulder, "it was the best night ever." Or it would have been, she added inwardly, if he'd said something, anything, that would let her know he really, truly loved her. Then she could look forward to the day he asked her to marry him.

"Well, I'm happy to hear that." Dan gave her shoulders a squeeze. "I wasn't looking forward to walking on my hands on this wet road."

She laughed. "I wouldn't have let you do that. Besides, every time I go out with you is the best time I've ever spent in my life."

"Me, too." He dropped a kiss on her forehead. "Now you'd

better run along. It's getting late and I know you have to be up early in the morning."

Feeling a stab of disappointment, she pulled away from him. "Yeah, you're right. I wouldn't want to be worn out and dragging around the kitchen all day."

He must have heard something in her voice, as he caught her arm just as she was slipping away from him. "Gertie? Is something wrong? You're not worrying about this Ian business are you? The constable can't arrest you without evidence, and since there isn't any, you'll be all right. Mrs. Baxter will see to that."

"I know. It's not that." She hesitated, afraid to say too much in case she frightened him off. "I was just wondering. You do like me, don't you?"

For a long moment he just sat there looking at her, until she got really nervous that she'd gone too far. "Of course I like you," he said at last. "You're the reason I came back from London. I thought you knew that."

"Yes, of course I know that." She smiled. "I just like to hear you say it, that's all."

"I like you, Gertie McBride." He leaned forward and kissed her nose. "Sleep well. I'll see you soon."

She nodded. "You sleep well, too." She slammed the door shut and watched him drive off, already missing him.

I like you, Gertie McBride he'd said. Like, not love. He'd never said he loved her. Not once. So many times she'd been tempted to say it, but had always changed her mind at the last minute, afraid he'd feel trapped or something and she'd never see him again.

It was hard, loving him like she did, without ever knowing how he really felt about her. It was all very well for him to say he'd left London to be with her, but that could simply mean he liked living on the coast better than the city and enjoyed her company.

If only she knew for sure, one way or the other. How she hated all these guessing games. One of these days she'd just come right out and say it, and then it would be up to him. Only she knew full well that she'd be a lot more miserable without him than she was now, even with the not knowing.

"Men," she muttered, as she closed the yard gate behind her. "Bleeding more trouble than they're worth, they are." Shivering in the cold, she drew her thin shawl closer to her neck as she hurried across the yard to the kitchen door. All she hoped now was that no one would see her sneaking back to her room.

It was warm inside the kitchen, with coals still glowing in the stove. She held her hands out to the heat, and breathed in the delicious spicy aroma of mince pies and fruit cake. Mrs. Chubb had been busy.

The smell made her hungry, and she turned her back on the stove, knowing she should get to her room so that Daisy could get some sleep. Reluctantly she left the kitchen and made her way down the darkened hallway to her room.

Quietly opening the door, she peeked in. The twins were asleep in their beds, and Daisy was on her back on Gertie's bed, snoring like a drunk docker.

Gertie crept across the floor, wincing as the floorboards creaked under her feet. She shook Daisy's arm, and the snoring cut off with a snort.

DECKED WITH FOLLY

The nanny stirred and slowly opened her eyes. Blinking, she demanded, "What time is it?"

"Shhshh!" Gertie put her finger to her lips. "You'll wake the twins."

"Sorry." Daisy swung her feet to the floor. "I'll get off to my room."

"Thank you, Daisy. See you in the morning. And remember, mum's the word."

Daisy nodded, blew a kiss to the sleeping twins, then disappeared into the darkness.

Gertie closed the door and sank onto the edge of the bed. She was too hungry to go to sleep. Having been so excited at the thought of going out with Dan, she'd hardly eaten any supper, and the pickled egg she'd eaten down the pub didn't exactly fill her up.

The thought of all those mince pies cooling in the pantry made her stomach growl. If she was going to get any sleep at all, she'd have to eat something. Surely Mrs. Chubb wouldn't miss one or two mince pies.

After making sure the twins were still sleeping peacefully, she picked up the oil lamp and crept to the door. She'd only be gone a minute or two. Just long enough to grab something to eat and a glass of milk. But just in case, she left the door open a little bit. If the twins cried out she'd hear them down the hallway. Hurrying toward the kitchen, she licked her lips in anticipation of the treat in store.

The coals had died down in the few minutes she'd been gone, with only a faint glow left to warm the room. Carrying the lamp over to the pantry, she looked inside. There on the shelf stood platters of mince pies and five large fruitcakes waiting to be decorated with royal icing.

The smell made Gertie feel faint. She would have loved a hefty chunk of fruitcake, but she could just imagine Chubby's face if she walked into the pantry the next morning and saw a slice cut out of her precious cake.

Gertie grinned at the thought. Mince pies now, well, that was a different matter. She balanced the lamp on the shelf, then scooped up three of the miniature pies. After slipping two of them into her pocket, she took a bite out of the third.

With a sigh of pure pleasure she chewed it down, then shoved the rest of the pie in her mouth. It tasted even better than it smelled. Swallowing the last of it, she reached for the jug of milk.

She thought about getting a cup, then shrugged and tipped the jug so she could drink a few mouthfuls from it, before replacing it on the shelf. With a quick swipe of her mouth with her sleeve, she grabbed the lamp and hurried out of the pantry, being careful to close the door behind her.

A moment or two later she was back in her room and closing the door. As she was putting the lamp back on the dresser, James spoke from his bed. "Where have you been?"

Gertie spun around, to see both twins sitting up in bed staring at her. "I went out tonight. Remember? I told you I was going to see Uncle Dan."

"Where did Daisy go?"

He sounded accusing, and Gertie felt guilty. They must have woken up and realized they were alone. "I went to get you these," she said quickly. She pulled the mince pies from her pocket and took them over to the beds. "Here, you can eat it now if you like."

James took his and immediately jammed it in his mouth.

Lillian looked at hers as if it would bite her. "What is it?"

"It's a mince pie." Gertie nodded at James. "Look, he likes it. You've eaten them before. Last Christmas you ate a lot of them, remember?"

Lillian gingerly took the mince pie in her fingers. "Where did the elf go?"

Gertie frowned. "The elf?"

"She's been dreaming," James said, his mouth still full of mince pie. "She's always dreaming, aren't you Lilly."

Lillian took a small bite of the pie. "I don't like it." She held it out to Gertie.

"I'll have it." James grabbed it before Gertie could take it.

"I bet the elf would have liked it," Lillian said.

"Give that to me." Gertie took the mince pie away from James. "One is quite enough. Now the two of you, go to sleep. You know Father Christmas is watching you, and if you don't do what you're told, he won't leave you no presents."

"He sent the elf to watch us, too," Lillian said, snuggling down under the blankets.

"I told you she's always dreaming." James plopped down, too. "Go back to sleep, Lilly."

For answer Lillian murmured a sleepy "G'night."

Gertie smiled. "Goodnight you two precious things." She tucked them up then went back to her own bed. The bedclothes were still rumpled from Daisy's doze, and she straightened them, then glanced over at the twins. They both appeared to be sleeping. Quickly she popped the rescued mince pie in her mouth, and went over to the dresser.

After pulling out all the pins from her hair she dropped them in the little dish she kept on her dresser. As she did so, she noticed a piece of white cotton poking out from one of her drawers.

Easing the drawer open, she saw all her unmentionables rumpled up and thrown about. That Lillian, she thought darkly. She was always getting into her clothes and trying them on. She'd asked Daisy to see that the twins didn't touch anything while she was gone, but once that girl got her nose in a book she wouldn't notice if Father Christmas hisself came down the chimney.

Glancing over at the bedside table, she saw that the clock and the photograph of her, Dan, and the twins had been moved as well. The twins must have had quite a game together while she was gone.

On impulse she crossed the room and opened the wardrobe. Sure enough, her clothes were shoved back to one side and the lid was off her good shoe box. She'd have a word with those little blighters in the morning and set them straight once and for all. No doubt Lillian would blame it all on a bloody elf.

Quickly she undressed and climbed into bed. Now she could close her eyes and dream about Dan asking her to marry him, which was a whole lot more interesting than Lillian's elves.

CHAPTER
❈ 10 ❈

Cecily awoke the next morning with a feeling of urgency. Christmas Eve was almost upon them, and once she got caught up in the festivities, there would be no time to pursue her search for Ian's killer.

The sound of melodic voices drifted down the hallway as she hurried to her office. The carolers were rehearsing for the Christmas Eve carol singing around the Christmas tree.

Cecily couldn't help the shudder that always ran through her at the thought of candles on the tree. At one time they had been lit as part of the ceremonies, but ever since the day she'd almost lost her life when the tree had burned down, she had forbidden anyone to light them.

At first, she'd wanted to have the trees decorated without candles, but they were so much a part of the tradition, the tree just didn't look the same without them. In the end she'd asked Madeline to include them in her decorations, just as long as they were never lit again.

Still lost in the unsettling memories, she started violently when a man stepped in front of her in the shadowed hallway.

"Good morning, Mrs. B." Archie Parker ran a hand across the bald patch on his head. "I was hoping to bump into you. I wanted to ask you about the unfortunate death of that young man. Must be upsetting for you."

Cecily's spirits plummeted. Perhaps she'd been naive to think they could keep it a secret from the guests for long, but the last person she wanted to hear of it from was the man standing in front of her. She had no doubt he'd be the kind of person who would delight in spreading the news.

"Most upsetting indeed," she said, giving him a mean-ingful look. "Which is why I would hope that our guests do not hear of it. News like that would most certainly put a cloud over the celebrations of Christmas."

"Oh, indeed." Archie laid a finger against his nose. "Rest assured, Mrs. B. I wouldn't mention a word of it to anyone else. Oh, no. Wouldn't want to spoil it for everyone, now would I. Murder is such a nasty subject at the best of times."

Cecily regarded him, disturbed once more by the little man's audacity. "May I ask why you would think the man was murdered?"

Archie's eyes gleamed in the reflection of the lamplight. "Just a slip of the tongue, Mrs. B. What I meant was, sud-den death is never a popular topic of conversation, no matter how it happened."

"Quite. In any case, at this point we are not in possession of all the facts. Therefore it would be unwise to make assumptions." Cecily fixed him with a stern glare. "I certainly hope you won't repeat your conjectures to any of the other guests."

Archie seemed unfazed by her displeasure. Nodding emphatically, he assured her. "Mum's the word, Mrs. B. You can rely on me to keep my mouth shut."

Cecily seriously doubted that, but she couldn't think of anything else to say that would convince him to keep quiet.

"Must be hard on his wife," Archie said, his nose twitching. "Rotten time to lose a husband, it being Christmas and all."

Taken aback, Cecily tried to gather her thoughts. It seemed everyone had sympathy for the grieving widow. It amazed her how fast the news could travel on the grapevine.

This man seemed to know far more than he was entitled to, though it wasn't clear if he was referring to Gertie or Gloria when he'd mentioned a wife, and she could hardly ask him without saying too much herself.

Archie nodded, taking her silence for agreement. "Yes, indeed. Can't be easy, what with his two little ones running around to remind her of her loss. I feel sorry for her, that I do." He paused, looking up at Cecily with a sly expression on his mottled face. "I'd like to offer my help, Mrs. B. I'm . . . ah . . . rather good at ferreting out clues and such, and I'd be happy to make a few discreet enquiries on—"

"No!" Aware she'd spoken more sharply than she'd intended, Cecily summoned a smile. "That's very kind of you, Mr. Parker, but—"

"Archie, please."

Cecily drew a deep breath. "Thank you, Mr. Parker. But there's really nothing to investigate. As far as we know, Mr.

115

Rossiter's drowning was an accident. The constable will be taking care of any necessary details when he returns, and until then, I suggest we all put the unfortunate matter out of our minds and concentrate on enjoying the Christmas season. Now, if you will excuse me, I have urgent matters to attend to and I'm running late."

Brushing past him, she reached out for the door handle of her office.

"Very well," Archie said quietly behind her. "I take it the matter's closed then."

She looked back at him. "Most definitely."

Without another word, he turned and ambled away.

Staring after him, Cecily waited until he had disappeared around the corner before opening her door. There was something unsavory about that man. He'd be the last person she'd go to for a medicinal remedy, she was quite sure of that.

She had the distinct impression that his cures might well do more harm than good, and it was not a comfortable feeling to have what Madeline referred to as a charlatan mingling with her guests. All she could hope was that he didn't attempt to offer his wares to any of them, or she might have a case of poisoning on her hands. On top of everything else, that would be a disaster indeed.

"All right, you two." Gertie folded her arms and glared at the twins, who sat on the bed with stubborn looks on their faces. "I want to know what you got up to while I was gone last night. Lillian, did you play dress up last night with my clothes again?"

Lillian's eyes grew wide. "No, mama. You told me not to touch your clothes."

"She didn't," James put in earnestly. "She really didn't, mama. I was watching her the whole time."

Gertie frowned. She usually knew when the twins were lying. For one thing, they could never look her in the eye if they were telling fibs, but both of them sat there staring at her with all the innocence of newborn lambs.

Daisy was due any minute, and Gertie decided to give her offspring the benefit of the doubt until she could question the nanny. "Well, all right, then. You know what will happen if I catch you touching my things. One word from me and Father Christmas will fly his reindeer right over this roof without stopping."

Lillian's face filled with wonder. "How do all the reindeer fit on the roof?"

Gertie coughed. "They land in the roof rose garden, don't they." She wished Daisy would hurry up and get there. She never felt comfortable making up stories to her kids about Father Christmas. In her opinion it came perilously close to lying, and if there was one thing Gertie couldn't abide, it was a liar.

"How does Father Christmas get all those toys for all the kids on his sleigh?" James demanded. "It would have to be a jolly big sleigh. It couldn't fit in the roof garden with all the reindeer, could it?"

Gertie fidgeted with her hairpins, pretending to pin her hair under her cap. "I don't know. You'll have to ask Father Christmas."

"How can we ask Father Christmas when he won't come until after we're asleep?"

"Write a letter and send it to him."

James's doubtful expression changed to one of delight. "We can send him a letter?"

"Yes, you can." Gertie smiled at them both. "Both of you. It might help to keep you out of mischief. Write them and I'll post them for you."

James looked suspicious. "Do you know his address?"

"Course I do, silly. Everyone knows Father Christmas lives at the North Pole."

"P'raps the elf can take them to him," Lillian said.

James gave her a hefty nudge. "You've been dreaming again, silly Lilly."

Lillian pouted. "Don't call me that."

James jumped off the bed and started marching around the room chanting, "Silly Lilly, silly Lilly."

Gertie reached out and cuffed his ear. "Stop that. Go and write your letter."

James rubbed his ear. "We don't have any paper."

"I'll get you some."

The welcome tap on the door came at last and Gertie hurried to open it. Daisy seemed half asleep as she wandered into the room. She mumbled something Gertie couldn't hear and flopped down on the bed.

"What's the matter with you? Not ill are you?" Gertie peered at her nanny in dismay. That's all she needed was for her twins to be ill over Christmas.

Daisy shook her head. "Just tired. I didn't get to sleep until late."

Guilt washed over Gertie. "Sorry, that was my fault. I'll be here tonight so you can go to bed early."

Daisy nodded, and yawned.

"By the way, before I go, there's something I need to ask you." Gertie glanced at the twins, but they were already arguing over who was going to write what to Father Christmas and weren't paying attention to anyone else.

Daisy looked up with heavy-lidded eyes. "What is it?"

"Did Lillian get into my wardrobe last night?"

Daisy stared at the wardrobe as if she expected it to answer for her.

"Get into it?"

Gertie sighed. "Was she dressing up in my clothes?"

"Oh! No, she wasn't. She never went anywhere near the wardrobe."

"What about my dresser?"

Daisy shook her head. "I didn't see her touch any of your things. She was playing with James and then I read them a story and then they went to bed."

Gertie was beginning to get a nasty feeling in the pit of her stomach. "You were here the whole time I was gone?"

Daisy tossed her head. "Of course I was. That's what you pay me for, isn't it. I wouldn't leave them alone, anyway. You know that."

Yes, she did know that. That's what worried her. If Lillian hadn't been in her wardrobe shoving her clothes around, then who had? And why?

While she waited at her desk for Mrs. Chubb to answer her summons, Cecily mulled over the information Gertie had given her the day before. Someone must have overheard the housemaid threatening Ian, and reported it to the constable.

Who would do that? Surely not one of the staff? Gertie was blunt and spoke her mind, but everyone liked her as far as Cecily knew. So who would deliberately throw suspicion on her for murder?

Only one person came to mind. The real killer. Making Gertie look guilty would certainly help to keep the constable's attention away from anyone else. Cecily leaned back in her chair. If she could find out who told Sam Northcott about Gertie's argument, she just might have found the person responsible for Ian's death.

Mrs. Chubb seemed out of breath when she entered the room a few minutes later. "Sorry it took me so long, m'm," she said, as she plopped down on a chair. "I had to get me scones out of the oven before I could come up."

"I'm sorry, Altheda." Cecily leaned forward, her hands folded on her desk. "I know this is a busy time for you and I wouldn't have brought you up here if it wasn't vitally important."

Mrs. Chubb looked unhappy. "Is this about Ian dying?"

"Yes, I'm afraid it is."

Mrs. Chubb nodded. "I thought so. Gertie's really worried about it. She says she's going to be arrested for murdering Ian." A shudder went through her body. "She doesn't really mean that, does she, m'm?"

"Not if I can help it." Cecily paused, measuring her words. "Mrs. Chubb, did you know Gertie had an argument with Ian the night he died?"

"Yes, m'm. I did." The housekeeper's forehead was creased

with worry. "Gertie told me about it yesterday morning. That was before we heard that Ian had died."

Cecily nodded. "You didn't know about the argument until Gertie told you, then?"

"No, m'm. I didn't. I was in the laundry room counting the sheets and pillowcases when all that was going on. By the time I got back to the kitchen, Ian was gone and Gertie was shaking like a lost lamb. I asked her what the matter was and she told me Ian was drunk and tried to come in, and then Clive came along and chased him off."

Cecily met the housekeeper's gaze. "Did she tell you she threatened him with a carving knife?"

"What!" Mrs. Chubb shot up on the chair. "No, I don't believe it. Gertie wouldn't do that."

"I'm afraid she did. She told me so herself."

Mrs. Chubb shook her head. "Oh, my, what trouble has that girl got herself into this time."

"So you didn't tell the constable about the argument?"

The housekeeper's face flushed a deep red. "Me? I wouldn't tell that pompous fool what I had for breakfast." She paused, a look of defiance in her eyes. "What's more, even if Gertie had told me she killed Ian Rossiter, I would never have uttered a word of it to anyone. Not even to you, m'm, begging your pardon."

Cecily smiled. "I would expect nothing less from you, Altheda."

"Yes, m'm." The housekeeper leaned forward. "Not that she did, of course. Gertie wouldn't do anything that dreadful. She just doesn't have it in her."

"I certainly hope not."

Mrs. Chubb leaned back, a thoughtful look on her face. "I wonder if she told Dan about the knife last night."

"Dan was here last night?"

The housekeeper nodded. "He got here just as Gertie was starting to tell me about Ian. Must have been around seven or so. She ended up telling us both what happened."

Cecily frowned, wondering why Gertie hadn't mentioned seeing Dan. "I imagine he wasn't happy to hear the news."

"No, m'm, he certainly was not. In fact, he got really angry. Said as how Ian needed to be taught a lesson. He—" She broke off with a gasp of horror.

For a long moment the two women stared at each other, then Cecily shook her head. "No, I can't believe Dan would do something like that." She'd tried to sound convincing, but the truth was, she didn't know what to think.

Dan Perkins seemed to be a nice enough man, but none of them really knew much about him, save for the fact that he had money and owned more than one butcher's shop in London, and that he seemed to care a great deal about Gertie.

It didn't help to see Mrs. Chubb's worried frown. "I do hope he didn't go and do something silly. Gertie would never get over it if she knew he'd . . ." Her voice trailed off, as if she couldn't bear to put her thoughts into words.

"I'm quite sure we are letting our imaginations run away with us," Cecily said firmly. The last thing she wanted was for the housekeeper to start spreading rumors that were entirely unfounded. "After all, you saw Dan leave, didn't you? How did he seem then?"

To her dismay, Mrs. Chubb shook her head. "No, I never

did see him leave. I left the two of them alone together in the kitchen while I went to check on Mabel." She shook her head. "I tell you, that girl was never cut out to be a housemaid. You should see the mess she made of the serviettes. Little Lillian could have done a better job than that."

The last thing Cecily needed just then was to get into a conversation about Mabel's inadequacies. "You said you left Gertie and Dan alone in the kitchen?"

"Oh, right. Anyway, I went back about half past seven to send Gertie down to the wine cellar, and Dan had already left by then."

"Did Gertie seem upset?"

Mrs. Chubb took a moment to think about it. "No, I don't think she was. I think she rather liked it when Dan got upset over her and Ian. She was in a much better state of mind when she left to get the wine."

Cecily relaxed her shoulders. "Well, then, I think we needn't worry about Dan. If he'd gone storming out after Ian I'm sure Gertie would have been noticeably worried."

Mrs. Chubb nodded. "I reckon you're right, m'm."

"Good, then that's settled." Cecily rose to her feet. "I won't keep you any longer, Altheda. I know you are busy. And I'd rather you kept our little talk to yourself, at least for the time being."

"Oh, of course, m'm. Not a word." Mrs. Chubb got up and hurried over to the door. Reaching it, she paused and looked back over her shoulder. "She's going to be all right, m'm, isn't she? Gertie, I mean. She's not going to be arrested?"

"I will certainly do everything I can to prevent it."

Mrs. Chubb nodded, though she looked far from convinced. "So will I, m'm. Just let me know what I can do."

"I'll keep that in mind, Altheda. Thank you."

"It's turning out to be a rotten week all round." Mrs. Chubb pulled the door open. "I lost my ring down the sink yesterday. My mother gave that ring to me. I've had it since I was a little girl."

"Oh, Altheda, I'm so sorry. Perhaps Clive can get it back for you."

The housekeeper's face lit up with hope. "You think so? I didn't think to ask him."

"Well, I think he can take the drainpipe apart or something. I don't know if he will find your ring, but it's certainly worth a try. Why don't you ask him."

"I will, m'm. Thanks ever so!"

Cecily watched the door close behind her housekeeper and let out her breath on a sigh. Gertie, Clive, and Dan. All of them had a reason to be angry enough at Ian to strike out at him. Yet she couldn't bring herself to think that any one of them might have been responsible for his death.

Then there was that nasty little man, Archie Parker. How did he know so much about Ian's personal life? Could he have known the dead man? If so, was it more than a coincidence that he was staying at the Pennyfoot at the same time Ian was in Badgers End?

One thing seemed certain. Whether or not the blow to Ian's head was meant to kill or just to punish, a man had died, and someone would have to pay for it. Cecily could only hope and pray that an innocent person would not have to suffer the consequences.

CHAPTER

❁ 11 ❁

Later that morning Dr. Kevin Prestwick rang Cecily with the distressing news that the autopsy had shown no water in Ian's lungs. "It would appear," Kevin said, "that the blow to the head was the cause of death. I'm afraid Northcott was right. It appears that Ian Rossiter was murdered."

"Oh, dear." Cecily tightened her grip on the receiver. "I'm afraid Gertie is in a lot of trouble unless we can find out who did this."

"And you're quite convinced your housemaid isn't responsible?"

Cecily wished she could answer that, but at this point, she wasn't sure of anything. "All I can say is that I find it hard to believe Gertie could do such a thing."

"Who knows what we are capable of when acting out of anger and fear."

"Well, I certainly think that Sam Northcott needs a lot more evidence before he can accuse Gertie of murder. She wasn't the only one angry with Ian."

"Seems to me you have a large pot of trouble coming to the boil."

"I'm afraid you're right. I'll just have to do my best to find out what really happened that night."

"You will be careful?"

She smiled at the concern in his voice. "I'm always careful, Kevin. Just ask my husband." She thanked him, then replaced the receiver on its hook.

Leaning her elbows on the desk, she rested her chin on her folded hands. Something Northcott had said had come back to her. *She was the last one to see the victim alive last night.* But according to both Gertie and Mrs. Chubb, Ian had left before Dan got there around seven o'clock. There could have been many people who had seen Ian after that.

She shook her head. None of it made sense. Her best move was to try and find out who told Sam Northcott about Gertie threatening Ian with a knife.

It took her fifteen minutes to track down Michel. She found him in the saloon bar, sipping a cup of coffee that no doubt had a measure of brandy in it.

She motioned him away from the counter, where he was exchanging jokes with the barman, and led him out into the hallway, where they were unlikely to be overheard.

"I understand that Gertie had an argument with Ian in

the kitchen the night he died," she said, keeping her voice low. "I was wondering if you happened to overhear them."

Michel's face looked pale in the dim light from the window at the end of the corridor. It was a gray day outside, and since the rain had washed the snow away, there was no bright reflection to light the dark hallways.

Cecily made a mental note to have the gas lamps lit while she waited for Michel's answer.

"No, madame, I did not see or hear them at all." Michel shook his head for emphasis. "I leave immediately after cooking the supper. I had the plum puddings in the oven and they would not be cooked until nine o'clock that night, *oui*? I do not want to wait around all that time, so I go home early and come back later." He pinched his fingers together, touched them to his lips then spread them open. "Ze puddings, ah! They smell divine, *oui*?"

"They do, indeed, Michel. Thank you."

She was about to turn away when he added, "I did see Clive Russell, however. I did not expect anyone out in the yard so late. He made me jump in my skin. He came up behind me as I went in the back door. Sacre bleu! That man is a giant."

Cecily frowned. "What time was that?"

Michel shrugged. "Nine o'clock, perhaps. Maybe a little later. I had come back to take out the puddings."

"Well, thank you, Michel. You can go back to finish your coffee now."

"Yes, madame." Michel gave her a little bow, then disappeared back into the bar.

Walking back to her office, Cecily wrinkled her brow.

Clive always left about six o'clock, unless she specifically asked him to stay longer to work on something. She hadn't had to ask him to stay for at least a month. So what was he doing in the kitchen yard at nine o'clock that night?

Deep in thought, she didn't see the woman standing by her door until a shrill voice shattered her concentration.

"Cecily, dear! I was just coming to see you! I peeked in the ballroom and I noticed the backdrop isn't in place on the stage." The petite woman flapped a hand in front of her flushed face. "I do hope and pray it will be ready for the performance tonight."

"Hello, Phoebe." Cecily smiled at the newcomer, more to put her at ease than because she felt like smiling. Phoebe could be exhausting at the best of times, and if she'd brought the colonel along, things could get even more difficult.

Colonel Frederick Fortescue had fought in the Boer War, and as a result of his experiences had returned home with an addled brain that fluctuated between endless memories of his war days and, at times, a belief that he was still on the front line.

Dealing with the colonel kept one on one's toes, in more ways than one. Phoebe's way of dealing with him was to ignore his problem and convince herself he was completely normal.

Right now, however, the lady seemed extremely upset by the lack of a perfect setting for her pantomime. "Really, Cecily, I should have thought everything would have been ready. I have quite enough to worry about getting my girls organized and in place. I really can't be fretting about the stage scenery as well."

DECKED WITH FOLLY

"Don't worry, Phoebe." Cecily opened the door of her office and ushered her visitor inside. "The backdrop is getting a little touch-up of paint, that's all. It was looking a bit drab, and I knew you wouldn't be happy to see it in that state so I had Clive freshen it up for you."

"Oh." Phoebe's wide-brimmed hat, loaded with pink ostrich feathers, blue ribbons, and purple grapes, wobbled precariously on her head as she plopped down on a chair. "Well, I certainly hope he has it done before curtain this evening."

"He has promised to have everything set up by this afternoon."

"Well, good." Phoebe fanned her face again. "I don't know why I'm so warm. It's quite chilly outside, though I'm happy to say the snow has all gone. All that slush does dreadful things to the hems of my skirts."

Cecily sat down at her desk. "Is there anything we can do for the pantomime, apart from getting the scenery in place, I mean?"

Phoebe's frown relaxed. "Thank you, dear, but I have everything under control." She leaned forward. "What is this rumor going around about a man being found dead in your duck pond? I do hope that isn't true."

"Where did you hear that?"

Cecily had spoken more sharply than she'd intended. Phoebe's eyebrows raised. "Cecily! Are you saying it *is* true? My dear! Who is he? One of your guests?"

Struggling to find an answer that would satisfy her, Cecily shook her head. Just as the pause had become uncomfortably long, a sharp rap on the door snatched Phoebe's attention away.

Kate Kingsbury

"Oh, that's probably Frederick. I left him to see to the carriage. I made him promise he would pop in to see you before going down to the bar. Come in, darling!"

The door opened and the colonel's bewhiskered face peered in. "Oh, there you are, old bean. I was wondering where you'd gone."

Phoebe clicked her tongue in annoyance. "I told you I'd be in Cecily's office. Do come in, Frederick. It's drafty with that door open."

The colonel shuffled into the room and leaned on the door to close it. "What ho, there, Mrs. Baxter. All ready for Christmas, I see! What? What?"

"Yes, indeed, Colonel." Cecily waved her hand at the vacant chair. "Have a seat."

"Don't mind if I do, old girl. The old legs are not what they used to be."

"Frederick!" Phoebe looked scandalized. "Gentlemen do not refer to their . . . er . . . personal body parts in the presence of a lady."

The colonel seemed confused, as well he might. "Personal body parts?"

Cecily hastened to intervene. "It's quite all right, Colonel. Do sit down."

"Oh, right." Parting the tails of his coat, Colonel Fortescue sat down heavily on the chair.

"Anyway," Phoebe said, "as we were saying, Cecily. We have been rehearsing for two weeks in the church hall and I think you are going to be pleased with the pantomime this year. We are doing Cinderella. I think I told you about that."

DECKED WITH FOLLY

Thankful that Phoebe had lost the thread of their earlier conversation, Cecily smiled. "Cinderella. How nice. One of my favorites."

"Is that the one about the young lady who couldn't wake up?" the colonel asked.

Phoebe gave him a scathing look. "Of course not. That was Sleeping Beauty."

"Ah, I knew it had a beauty in there somewhere."

Phoebe bristled. "Really Frederick, if you intend to go on being such a bore, why don't you just toddle off down to the bar. I'm sure you'll find someone to listen to your nonsense."

"Good idea, old bean." The colonel heaved himself out of the chair again. "Just hope there's a bit more peace and quiet in there than in the George the other night. All that blasted racket gave me a headache."

Phoebe rolled her eyes at Cecily. "He came home and complained for over an hour about some kind of brawl in the courtyard. Serves him right, I told him, for rubbing elbows with the riffraff."

"They were going at it hammer and tongs, old girl. Yelling and hitting and kicking . . ." The colonel shook his head. "Reminds me of the time I was in India watching a cricket match. The bowler hit the batter on the hip with the ball and the batter swore he did it on purpose. Went tearing up to the bowler waving his bat—"

"Frederick," Phoebe said sternly. "Please, just go to the bar. I'm sure you'll find someone there who'll listen to your stories."

"—and swung it at the poor chap," the colonel blithely

continued. "Missed the bugger, tripped over the bat and fell on it. Took out his two front teeth, just like that."

Cecily winced, while Phoebe's cheeks grew red. "Frederick! The bar!"

"All right, all right, I'm going." The colonel shuffled to the door. "Never could talk right after that, but he had a hell of a whistle."

Phoebe looked as if she was about to have a stroke.

"Enjoy your sherry, Colonel," Cecily said, hoping the man would get out of her office before Phoebe actually came to blows herself.

"Will do, old girl." He pulled the door open then looked back at her. "Oh, by the way, I recognized one of the blighters in the courtyard. It was that young chap who used to own the butcher's shop in the High Street. Never thought he was the type to resort to fisticuffs. Then again, he only kept the shop for a few months. Just goes to show, he's not exactly reliable, what? What?"

He was almost out the door before Cecily stopped him. "Colonel, are you quite sure it was the previous owner of Abbitson's, the butcher's shop?"

"Oh, quite, quite." He paused, his head poked in the doorway. "Big strapping lad. Got the best of the other chap, I can tell you." He frowned. "Funny thing, but I thought I recognized the other chap, too. Can't place him, though. Ah well. Toodleloo, then, Mrs. Baxter." He waved his hand at her and closed the door.

Cecily looked at Phoebe, who was mopping her forehead with a lace handkerchief. "When did the colonel say he saw those two men fighting?"

"The night before last." Phoebe lowered the handkerchief. "Why do you ask?"

"Oh, I don't know." Cecily forced a smile. "Idle curiosity, that's all. You were telling me about your rehearsals?"

"Ah, yes. Well . . ."

Cecily let her prattle on without really listening to her. Her mind was on the colonel's words as he'd gone out the door. It seemed as though Dan had been fighting the night Ian died. Somehow she had no doubt that the man with whom he'd exchanged blows was none other than Ian himself.

That must have been after Gertie had told Dan about Ian confronting her in the kitchen. Something else that Gertie had neglected to tell her. If that were so, that meant that Dan, along with whoever else was in the George that night, had contact with Ian after he'd left Gertie. So how could Sam Northcott possibly think that Gertie had been the last person to see Ian alive?

Cecily glanced at the clock. Gertie would be busy now, getting things ready for the midday meal, but as soon as that was over, she intended to have another talk with that young lady, and find out what else she was keeping to herself.

"Anyway," Phoebe was saying, "I do think the acrobats will provide an admirable conclusion to the pantomime, don't you think?"

Cecily made an effort to concentrate. "Acrobats?"

"Yes, dear." Phoebe leaned forward, her gaze probing Cecily's face. "You seem somewhat detached this morning. Is anything wrong?"

Before Cecily could answer, the door burst open without so much as a warning tap. Startled, she stared at the colonel as he marched into the room and thumped a triumphant fist on her desk. "That Rossiter chap! I knew I recognized him from somewhere. He used to work for you, what? What?"

Phoebe looked intrigued. "Ian Rossiter? I wondered what had happened to him. Has he come back to work here?"

"He'd have a hard time doing that, old bean." The colonel turned to her, his whiskers quivering with relish. "The poor blighter bought it, didn't he. Someone bashed him over the noggin and killed him stone dead."

Phoebe uttered a little shriek and slapped her gloved hand over her mouth. Above it her eyes were wide with shock.

Cursing herself for not telling her friend the truth earlier, Cecily got up from her chair and hurried around to her. "I'm sorry, Phoebe. I'd hoped you wouldn't have to know. I know you always had a soft spot for Ian."

"Who killed him?" Phoebe whispered behind her hand.

"We don't know." Cecily looked at the colonel. "I'd appreciate it if you didn't spread the news around the hotel. I would like to know who told you."

The colonel looked sheepish. "Sorry, old girl. Shouldn't have blurted it out like that. I just now overheard a chap talking about it. Short little bald-headed chappie with a rather twitchy mustache."

Cecily knew immediately to whom he referred. Archie Parker. "Did you happen to notice to whom he was speaking?"

"Oh, yes, indeed, old girl. Young woman, she was, red hair, green eyes, and a face full of freckles. Spoke in a soft voice, as if she were running out of breath."

He'd described Gloria Johnson perfectly. Cecily frowned.

DECKED WITH FOLLY

Had Archie Parker somehow discovered that Gloria was Ian's widow? If so, then no doubt he was eagerly satisfying his curiosity with all the gory details. Not that Gloria could tell him much.

Still, it unsettled her to know that Ian's death was now a topic of conversation among the guests. Especially since she had made Archie Parker promise not to mention it. Obviously the man was not to be trusted.

In fact, right at that moment, she had difficulty knowing just whom she could trust. It was not a comfortable feeling.

"So did you have a good time last night down the pub?" Pansy picked up a fork from one of the dining room tables, examined it with a critical eye, then took a corner of her apron and briskly rubbed at the prongs.

Gertie finished dusting the back of a chair and looked up at her. "It was smashing. We had hot cider and rum, and sausage rolls and cheese and pickled onions, and trifle in brandy glasses." She grinned. "We sang lots of songs and Christmas carols and Dan even taught me to dance. A little bit, anyway. It was a lovely evening."

Pansy clasped her hands together and rolled her eyes at the ceiling. "Dancing. Oh, that sounds lovely. I've never been dancing."

"Do you know how?"

"Well, no, but I bet Samuel does. He could teach me how to do it."

"Well, I can teach you a step or two." Gertie dropped her duster on the table. "Come here, and I'll show you."

Pansy hurried over to her. "Is it hard?"

"Nah, not if you concentrate. Look, I'll show you how to do the two-step." She started humming, sliding her foot to one side and then bringing the other one back to meet it. After gliding between the tables for a few steps, she nudged her chin at Pansy. "Now you do it."

Pansy hummed and sidestepped around the floor. "I like it! It's easy!"

"See? I told you."

Together the two of them hummed and glided around, until Pansy burst out laughing. "I bet we look silly dancing without a partner."

Gertie opened her mouth to answer her but just then a loud clapping of hands interrupted her. Both she and Pansy swung around just as Sid Barrett sauntered into the room.

"Very nice," he said, in his smarmy voice. "I wouldn't mind being your partner." He held out his hands to Gertie. "How about it?"

Gertie sniffed and tossed her head. "I wouldn't dance with you if my blinking life depended on it."

Sid dropped his hands. "It wouldn't hurt you to be polite for a change, now would it."

"I'm polite to them what are respectful."

For an instant he looked annoyed, then his face relaxed in a smile again. "Well, me darlin', I have the greatest respect for you. How about joining me in the bar for a drink to-night? Not seeing the boyfriend, are you?"

"What if I am?"

He shook his head. "I'm surprised you feel like going out, seeing as how your husband was murdered."

DECKED WITH FOLLY

"I told you he wasn't my husband. And how'd you know he was murdered, anyhow?"

Sid smiled. "You'd be surprised what I know."

Gertie was getting a nasty feeling in her stomach. "Well, I don't have time to talk to you no more. I've got work to do." She made to move forward, but Sid blocked her way, placing a hand on either side of the door.

"Well, then, you and I will have to have a cozy little chat when you do have more time."

For several long moments Gertie stared into Sid's eyes. She didn't like the way he looked at her. Neither did she like the feeling of being trapped, even though she knew a knee in the right place would move him fast enough. "Get the bloody hell out of our way," she muttered, "or you'll be walking funny for a week."

For a second or two mischief gleamed in his eyes. Then he laughed, dropped his hands, and stood back. "All right. Until later then, luv."

She itched to slap his face, but there were some things madam would never allow. Shoving her way past him, Gertie stomped toward the door with Pansy scrambling along close behind her.

She was still frowning when she reached the kitchen. She hadn't spoken one word all the way downstairs, but the minute they entered the kitchen words burst out of her mouth.

"That bloody Sid Barrett." Gertie dug her fists into her hips. "He blocked the door of the dining room and wouldn't let me pass."

"Oh, dear." Mrs. Chubb wiped her hands on her apron. "I shall have to have a word with that young man. I can't have him aggravating the staff like that. I'm sure he means no harm, though. He just likes to play pranks. No doubt he thinks it's funny."

Gertie snorted. "I don't think it's very funny when he keeps asking me to go out with him and won't take no for an answer." She shuddered. "I'd rather eat worms than go out with the likes of him."

Standing at the stove, Michel rapped a wooden spoon against a steaming pot of stew. "Worms are all ze guests will have to eat if someone does not start preparing the vegetables, *oui?*"

"All right. Keep your bleeding hair on." Gertie started for the sink. "I just hope that bugger stays out of my way or I might be tempted to sock him one. He gives me the creeps, he does."

"If he's really being a nuisance," Mrs. Chubb said, "perhaps you should have a word with madam about it."

"I will." Gertie grabbed a carrot from the bowl on the counter and picked up the peeling knife. "Just as soon as dinner is over with." And she wasn't going to mince words, neither. No one treated Gertie McBride like that and got away with it. Nobody.

CHAPTER
✿ 12 ✿

After enjoying a tasty meal with her husband, Cecily left him to enjoy a quiet afternoon in their suite while she returned to her office.

When she reached the foyer, however, she was once more waylaid by Archie Parker, who gave every indication of having lain in wait for her. He practically pounced on her as she reached the last step, obviously determined to speak with her no matter how much she might attempt to avoid him.

"There you are, Mrs. B!" He beamed at her, nose twitching furiously. "I've been wanting to have a private word with you, if you can spare the time."

She was tempted to tell him she didn't have a moment to spare, but knowing that would simply delay the inevitable, she nodded. Glancing around the foyer, she saw a group of guests chatting together by the reception desk, and a couple deep in conversation wandering to the front doors.

Wondering just how "private" Archie's intended discussion could be, she said with some reluctance, "Perhaps we should go along to my office. It will be more quiet there."

"Excellent!" Archie rubbed his hands together. "And warmer, I trust."

Since the constant opening and closing of the front doors allowed all warmth to escape from the foyer, Cecily could at least agree on that point.

She led the way, with Archie scuffling along close behind her, and made a mental note to send for Gertie as soon as she got rid of Mr. Parker. Which, she hoped fervently, would be in short order.

Settling herself behind her desk in her office, she offered him a chair. "I trust you enjoyed the midday meal?"

"Excellent! Excellent meal." Nodding and twitching, Archie waved a hand in the air. "Every meal here is excellent. You are fortunate to have such a masterful chef."

"I am indeed." She straightened the papers on her desk then sat back in her chair. "Now then, what is it you wish to discuss with me?"

Archie's eyes gleamed as he sat forward. "I happened to overhear it mentioned that the young man found in the duck pond was, indeed, the victim of murder."

Since by now the news was apparently all over the Pennyfoot, Cecily saw no reason to hedge any further. "Unfortunately, yes. It appears that way."

"And . . . do you have any idea who might have perpetrated the crime?"

She looked him straight in the eye. "I'm afraid I don't. None at all."

"Ah!" He sat back, hands folded across his chest. "I suppose anyone could have done it. A prowler, perhaps. After all, anyone could have walked in off the street into the foyer. It would have taken only a moment to snatch the candlestick off the hallstand to carry out the dirty deed." He nodded, as if pleased with his own cleverness.

Cecily stared at him for a long moment before answering. "Yes, I suppose someone could have done that."

"Did he have many enemies? The deceased, I mean." Archie's gaze probed her face. "Someone who had good reason to want him dead, perhaps?"

"Mr. Parker." Cecily controlled her annoyance with difficulty. "I'm not at liberty to discuss the matter, and even if I were, I know nothing that could possibly help determine who was responsible for what happened. Furthermore, I dislike discussing it, so I'd appreciate it if you would not bring up the subject again."

Archie nodded, though he seemed quite unaffected by her reprimand. "I imagine all this turmoil would be upsetting, yes. I simply wanted to offer my help. After all, you must want to discover the identity of the perpetrator. It can't be a comfortable feeling knowing there is a killer loose on the premises."

"There is no indication that the killer is still on the premises." Cecily met his gaze, determined not to be unnerved by the man's persistence. "As you yourself pointed out, it could have been a prowler, a complete stranger having wandered in off the street and possibly long gone from the town now."

Archie nodded. "Quite, quite."

Cecily slowly let out her breath. "Was there something else you wanted to tell me?"

Archie twitched his nose and frowned. "What? Oh, right, Mrs. B. Actually I came to ask you if I could have a bed warmer at night. The fireplace helps to keep the room warm but my bed is always cold. I can't sleep when my feet are cold. That's the curse of sleeping alone, what?"

Confused by the abrupt change of subject, Cecily struggled to make sense of the words. "A bed warmer?"

Archie nodded with enthusiasm. "Yes. You know, one of those pans you fill with hot coals from the fire and rub it all over the bed."

"I know what a bed warmer is, Mr. Parker." She squared her shoulders. "I'll see that your request is taken care of this evening."

"Good, good." Archie rubbed his hands together. "Perhaps that maid, McBride, could come up at bedtime and see to it for me?"

Cecily narrowed her eyes. "I'll send one of the footmen," she said shortly.

Once more Archie seemed unfazed by her disapproval. "Well, all right. As you wish." He got up from his chair. "I hope you soon find out who clubbed Mr. Rossiter to death. Nasty business that. I suppose you'll be calling in the inspector?"

Cecily rose, leaning her hands on the desk. "I can assure you, Mr. Parker, that everything is being done to apprehend the criminal."

"Ah, yes. Right. Right. Thank you, Mrs. B." Nodding and backing away, he came up hard against the door. "Oops! Didn't see that there." He grabbed the handle, opened the door, nodded at her once more, then disappeared.

Cecily stood where she was for a long moment, staring at the closed door. Then she shook her head, sat down, and pulled the bell rope. While she waited for one of the maids, she opened the ledger and began writing down the bills that had been paid that morning.

After having to erase a figure twice, she gave up and closed the ledger again. There was too much occupying her mind. Too many questions. It was time she started getting some of the answers.

She was hoping that Gertie would respond to her summons, but it was Mabel who stood hesitating in the doorway.

"Will you please ask Clive to come to my office right away, and tell Gertie I would like a word with her just as soon as she is free."

Mabel ducked a curtsey. "Yes, m'm." She turned to go, then paused as Cecily asked, "How are you settling in here, Mabel? Are Gertie and Mrs. Chubb taking care of you? I know this is a busy time, but I hope they are finding time to show you what you need to know."

Mabel avoided her gaze, staring at the carpet instead. She was a rather plump young lady, with pale cheeks and gray eyes that for the most part seemed devoid of expression. Her fair hair was scraped back from her face, and her short stature made her look like a young schoolchild.

There was an air of deep sadness about her that for some reason made Cecily feel protective. Mabel had told her that her mother had died when she was a baby and she'd been brought up in London by her grandmother. Judging from her demeanor when she'd divulged this piece of information, Cecily gathered that the relationship was not a happy one.

Since Mabel seemed disinclined to answer, Cecily tried again. "Is anything wrong, Mabel? Is there something we can do for you?"

Mabel shook her head and muttered, "No thank you, m'm. Mrs. McBride is being really helpful and so is Mrs. Chubb."

"Well, that's good to hear." Cecily smiled back. "Run along then, and don't forget to tell Gertie I need a word with her."

"Yes, m'm. I mean no, m'm. I won't forget." Looking as if she were desperate to escape, Mabel slipped from the room.

Cecily frowned, disturbed by the young woman's obvious melancholy. She would have to talk to Mrs. Chubb about her, and see if there was something they could do to cheer up the new maid. She didn't like to think that a member of her staff was unhappy with her job.

A few minutes later a thump on the door warned Cecily that Clive was about to enter. The big man seemed to fill the doorway as he stood waiting for her to speak.

"Come in, Clive, and close the door behind you." She smiled, but her words must have struck a warning note, as he seemed wary when he sat down opposite her.

She wasted no time in coming to the point. "Michel tells me he bumped into you the night before last. I understand it was quite late."

"Yes, m'm." Clive looked down at the cap he held in his hands. "I was late leaving."

"Very late. After nine o'clock, Michel said."

"Yes, m'm."

"Would you mind telling me what you were doing in the yard at that hour?"

"I was on my way home, m'm."

Cecily frowned. "But your day ended at six. I don't remember asking you to stay after that."

"No, m'm. You didn't. I . . . had a job to do and it took a lot longer than I thought it would."

"I see." She rested her hands in her lap. "What kind of job?"

He glanced up at her, then back down at his feet. "I . . . ah . . . was down in the wine cellar working on the water pipes."

Worried now, she leaned forward. "Do we have a problem with the pipes?"

"Not anymore, m'm."

She pressed her lips together. He gave her the distinct impression that he was avoiding the truth. She had to ask herself why, and she didn't like any of the answers that presented themselves. "Gertie tells me you came to her aid that night, when Ian was pestering her."

"Yes, m'm."

"What happened exactly?"

Clive took his time thinking about that. After a long pause, he said slowly, "I was walking past the door and he was in the kitchen and I heard her yelling at him. I opened the door and she had a knife in his face. She was quite angry, and I was worried she might use the knife on him, so I hustled him out of there and out of the gate."

"Just like that?"

Clive shuffled his feet. "He took a bit of persuading, m'm."

"I imagine he did."

"He came back later, though."

Cecily straightened her back. "Ian came back after you threw him out?"

"Yes, m'm." Clive hunched his shoulders and twisted his cap in his hands. After a significant pause, he blurted out "Gertie told me later that night that he'd come back. He wanted to see the twins, she said."

"Did you escort him off the premises again?"

Again the odd pause before he muttered, "No, m'm. He wasn't there when she told me that so he must have gone home."

"I see." Cecily leaned back in her chair. It seemed that Gertie had left out quite a lot of what had happened that evening. "Did Gertie happen to mention what time Ian left the second time?"

Clive thought about it. "Must have been about nine o'clock, or thereabouts."

Nine o'clock. So Sam Northcott could have been right. Gertie might well have been the last person to see Ian alive. But then, how did the constable know that? Who was giving him all this information?

She gave Clive a stern look. "Have you been talking to P.C. Northcott about this?"

The maintenance man looked offended. "I have not, m'm. I haven't spoken to the constable in quite some time."

Remembering Northcott's cryptic comment the day before, Cecily was tempted to ask Clive about his former association with the constable. Before she could do so, however, he supplied the answer.

"I haven't spoken to him since he tried to arrest me for trespassing."

"Trespassing?"

"Yes, m'm." Clive shifted his feet. "It happened before I came to work here. I was doing odd jobs around town and I'd been hired to repair the roof of one of the cottages down by the harbor. The owners were visiting relatives while I worked on it and the constable came by to call on them. He saw me in the backyard and arrested me for trespassing." He pursed his lips. "It took quite a while to sort everything out. He never did apologize for arresting me and hauling me off to the station. I haven't spoken to him since. Except for when I bumped into him yesterday, that is."

Cecily really hadn't believed Clive to be the informant, but had felt compelled to ask. Someone had been very forthcoming with the constable, however, and she was becoming convinced that finding that person would lead her to the killer. "Thank you, Clive. That will be all."

"Yes, m'm." He stood, hesitating in front of her desk until she looked up at him. "Gertie didn't kill Mr. Rossiter, m'm. I'd stake my life on it."

With a heavy sigh, she nodded. "I hope you're right, Clive. Right now, I don't know what to think."

"We'll soon find out who did it, m'm. I can promise you that."

She looked at him in alarm, worried that he'd start investigating on his own. She knew from experience how much trouble that could cause. "We should leave that to the police. Apart from the fact that it's dangerous to meddle with murder, the constabulary won't thank us for interfering in their business. Let them handle it, Clive."

His expression portrayed clearly what he thought of the constabulary, and considering his false arrest, she could hardly blame him. She was relieved, however, when he gave her a brief nod. "I'll get back to my work then, m'm."

She watched him leave, feeling a deep sense of sympathy. Clive was an educated man, once a respected teacher in a London school. Unfortunately he'd taken to drinking and it had eventually cost him his career and his marriage. He'd taken steps to control his addiction, but he would never again be trusted to teach children.

Maintenance work was the only occupation he could find, and when she'd interviewed him, Cecily had sensed how very much he missed his vocation. She had appreciated the fact that he'd been honest about his past and had never regretted giving him the job. Though she often wondered how he could be happy doing menial work when he was capable of so much more.

Sighing, she opened her ledger again. She was no closer to finding out who killed Ian, or who had given the constable so much information. Time was ticking away, and unless she found out something soon, Sam Northcott would be back ready to arrest Gertie and take her into custody.

There was one question hovering around in her mind to which she would like an answer. She would very much like to know how Archie Parker knew that the murder weapon was taken from the hallstand in the foyer.

All in all, there was a great deal of information being passed around the Pennyfoot, and she would give anything to know who was doing the talking.

*   *   *

DECKED WITH FOLLY

Gertie finished polishing the last wineglass and stuck it on the shelf in the cabinet. Mabel had given her the message earlier that madam wanted to see her, and Gertie was anxious to get it over with. Any time someone wanted to talk to her she got nervous now. She couldn't forget that the constable thought she'd killed Ian, and she was really hoping madam was going to tell her that the killer had been found and arrested and that she had nothing more to worry about. But it was almost three o'clock, and she wanted to spend a little time with the twins before getting the ballroom ready for the pantomime that evening. The way things were going, it looked as if she'd get no more than five minutes with them.

Pansy had already disappeared, probably gone looking for Samuel. Mrs. Chubb was in her room and Michel was out somewhere for a walk. This was the quietest time of day for the staff, and Gertie always tried to make the most of it.

Hurrying along the corridor to her room, she thought about how she'd get the twins to make paper chains so they could hang them on the walls. It would keep their minds off Father Christmas and how soon he was coming.

She could hear their voices as she reached the room, arguing again. Pulling a face, she opened the door and looked in.

Daisy sat on the bed, reading as usual. The twins were playing tug-of-war with a toy boat, Lillian insisting it was her turn to play with it and James loudly arguing that it was his boat.

Gertie rolled her eyes. "James! Let Lilly play with that for a while. I have to go and talk to madam but I'll be back in a little while and we'll make paper chains, all right?"

The twins went on wrestling with the boat.

Daisy looked up. "Will you be long? I wanted to go into town to get some knitting wool."

Gertie blinked as James raised his voice even higher. "I'll only be a minute or two," she said, raising her own voice above her child's. "Try and keep those two quiet until I get back." She shut the door on the noise and fled back down the corridor to the stairs.

She reached the main hallway and was halfway across the foyer when someone called her name. Turning, her stomach dropped when she saw Ian's wife, Gloria Johnson, walking toward her. The last thing she needed was a fight with her. Clenching her fists, she waited for the other woman to reach her.

Gloria stopped a few feet from her, her face full of hostility. "I wanted to talk to you," she said, her voice low and angry.

"What about?"

"About my husband, of course."

Gertie glanced around the empty foyer. Everyone was taking a little time off or a nap in their rooms. Though it wouldn't be long before someone would come in and disturb them. "What about Ian?"

"I want to know why he came to see you the night he was killed."

"He didn't come to see me. He came to see the twins."

"That's what he said."

Gertie sighed. "That's what he meant. There was no love lost between me and Ian. We hated each other."

"That's not what I heard."

"Well, then you heard wrong." Gertie made a move to leave, but Gloria's next words stopped her.

"Do you know who killed him?"

Taking a deep breath, Gertie turned around. "I haven't got the faintest idea who killed your husband. The last time I saw Ian Rossiter he was alive and kicking. You can bloody believe that or not, I don't care."

"I think your boyfriend killed him."

Gertie blinked. "What? Who? Are you talking about Dan Perkins?"

"If that's his name." Gloria kept looking over her shoulder as if she were afraid of being overheard. "All I know is that he was punching the daylights out of my husband down at the pub the night he died."

Gertie felt her jaw drop. "My Dan was fighting with Ian? What for?"

The front door opened suddenly, making Gloria jump. She sent a scared glance at the door then seemed to relax as an elderly couple strolled in. Moving closer to Gertie, she lowered her voice even more. "I don't know what it was about, but yes, he was fighting with Robert. Where do you think my husband got that black eye? If you don't believe me, ask them down at the pub. They'll tell you. Lots of people must have seen them going at it."

Gertie stared at her for a long moment, then said quietly, "I never pay any attention to gossipmongers. I have to go now." This time she didn't wait for Gloria to answer. Turning her back on her, she strode purposefully toward the hallway and didn't stop until she reached madam's office.

CHAPTER
❁ 13 ❁

Seated at her desk, Cecily raised her head at the sound of Gertie's knock. "Come in!"

Gertie appeared in the doorway, her cap askew as usual and strands of hair falling across her forehead. She barged into the room and shut the door with a resounding thud. "You wanted to see me, m'm?"

Noting the two bright spots of red on Gertie's cheeks, Cecily waved at a chair. "Sit down, Gertie."

The housemaid sat, her chest heaving as if she was having difficulty breathing.

Cecily waited a moment to give her time to calm down, then enquired gently, "You seem to be upset about something. Do you want to tell me what happened?"

Gertie pressed her lips together, then let out her breath in an explosive sound of exasperation. "Gloria. I just bumped into her in the foyer."

"I see. I assume the exchange was less than cordial."

"She wanted to know if I knew who killed Ian. She told me she thought it was Dan Perkins."

"Oh, dear." Cecily closed her ledger and set it aside. "I hope you set her straight."

"You bet I bleeding did . . . sorry, m'm."

"Quite all right, Gertie."

"Yes, well, that weren't the worst of it."

Eyeing her warily, Cecily waited for her to continue.

"She said Dan was fighting with Ian down the pub that night," Gertie burst out at last.

"Oh, I see." Cecily paused, wondering how much to tell her. "Actually, I had heard that from someone else."

"Who?" Gertie leaned forward, eyes blazing. "Well, they was wrong. My Dan wouldn't—" She broke off, her eyes growing wide. "Oh, bugger."

Cecily waited.

Gertie fidgeted around for several seconds, before saying carefully, "If I tell you something, m'm, can you promise not to tell the constable?"

"I wish I could." Cecily sighed, "I'm sorry, Gertie. We are dealing with a murder here. After all, someone brutally hit Ian over the head and killed him. I can't promise to keep important information from the police. I think you'd better tell me what you know, or you could end up in a great deal of trouble."

"If I'm not already." Gertie stared gloomily at her knees. "It's just that, well, I was out with Dan last night and he had this graze on the side of his face. He said he had an accident in the car, but I couldn't see no mark on the car but he said he'd rubbed it out, but then Gloria said he was fighting and . . ." She paused for breath.

"You think he might have got the graze from the fight," Cecily finished for her.

Gertie nodded, her face a sea of misery. "That doesn't mean he killed him, though, does it. I saw Ian later that night and he had a black eye. Gloria said Dan gave it to him. But then if I saw him after the fight was over it could have been anyone what killed him. It doesn't have to be Dan."

"No, it doesn't."

"I just can't help wondering why he didn't tell me about the fight."

"Most likely he didn't want to upset you."

Gertie was silent for a moment, then muttered, "Yeah, that was probably it."

Cecily folded her hands on the desk. "How did Gloria know that Dan and Ian had been fighting?"

Gertie looked startled. "What?"

"Or that Ian had a black eye? Gloria told me that when Ian left her at the cottage to go to the George and Dragon, she went to bed. She said that was the last time she saw him. So I'm wondering how she knew he'd been fighting with Dan and received a black eye."

"I don't know." Gertie pondered the question. "She must have been lying about going to bed. Perhaps she went down the pub to look for him and someone down there told her."

"That's possible. But then why would she lie about it?" Cecily glanced at the clock. "While we're on the subject, is there a reason why you didn't tell me earlier that Ian came back again later that evening?"

Gertie looked surprised. "I didn't?" She thought about it. "Oh, well, I was going to, but Gloria walked in while we was talking and I never got a chance to tell you the rest."

She was right, Cecily realized. Gloria had interrupted their conversation. "Well, why don't you tell me the rest of the story now."

Gertie heaved a sigh. "All right. I might as well. Nothing is a bloody secret around here, anyway. Sorry, m'm."

Cecily smiled. "Go on." She settled back, eager to hear Gertie's side of the story. Perhaps now she'd get some of the answers that kept eluding her and they'd help clear up some of her suspicions.

"Well, it was like this," Gertie said. "As I told you before, Ian came to the back door demanding to see the twins. I told him he couldn't see them. He got nasty and that's when I picked up the knife. I was hoping to scare him off. Then Clive turned up and took him away." Gertie shuddered. "I don't know what I would have done if he hadn't got there right then."

"Then it's just as well that he did. So what happened after that?"

"Well, like I said, Dan came over and we talked a bit. I told him what happened and he was pretty cross." Gertie shook her head. "He must have gone down the pub after that and had it out with Ian."

"Well, then—" Cecily broke off as something popped into her mind. Her conversation with Mrs. Chubb. *I went back about half past seven to send Gertie down to the wine cellar.*

Gertie looked worried. "Yes, m'm?"

"I was just thinking about something." Cecily paused, then said abruptly, "I understand Mrs. Chubb sent you down to the wine cellar that night."

Gertie's frown deepened. "Yes, m'm. She wanted me to bring up a case of wine."

"Did you happen to see Clive down there while you were there?"

Gertie looked surprised. "No, m'm. I didn't." She fidgeted her feet, staring down at them as if she'd never seen them before.

So Clive had lied about where he was that evening. Cecily was getting a very bad feeling about the maintenance man. So far she had resisted the possibility of him being involved, but there were just too many lies and evasions about that night for her to rule him out.

Much as she hated to admit it, the circumstances seemed to point rather strongly in his direction.

"Did I say something wrong?"

Gertie sounded worried, and Cecily forced her mind back to the subject at hand. "It's nothing important. Now, where were we? You said that Ian came back here later that night, after you went to the wine cellar?"

"Yes. It was just before nine o'clock. I went out to fill the coal scuttle 'cos I knew Michel was coming back to take his puddings out the oven at nine and he'd raise merry hell if he saw the scuttle was empty."

"Yes, Michel told me he came back here to take out the puddings."

Gertie raised a hand to sweep the stray hair from her eyes.

"Yes, well, I was opening the coal shed door when Ian came up behind me. I could smell his breath from where I stood. I knew he'd had a bellyful of beer. I could see the black eye and I thought he'd been in a fight, and I could tell he was really angry and upset."

"Did he hurt you?"

"He grabbed my arm." Gertie rubbed a spot above her elbow. "I got a bruise there now."

"So what happened next?"

"Well, he was snarling at me, threatening me with all kinds of terrible things if I didn't let him see the twins. I could see he was in a rage and he scared me. I tried to tell him they was asleep and he'd frighten them if he woke them up, but he wouldn't listen."

Gertie shuddered, and Cecily waited while she struggled to compose herself. "Anyway," she went on, "I got angry, too, and I shoved him. Hard. Being drunk and all he staggered a bit and tripped over the step. He fell backwards into the coal shed and I locked him in. I thought I'd leave him there until he cooled down a bit."

Cecily raised her eyebrows. "You locked Ian in the coal shed?"

"Yes, m'm." Gertie looked anxious. "Only for a few minutes. I went back to the kitchen and I was going to ask Michel to let him out when he got here, but then Clive came to the door. He'd heard the shouting from across the yard and wanted to know if I was all right."

Cecily took a moment to digest Gertie's tumbling words. Clive had not mentioned one word of this to her. She had to wonder why.

157

"So I asked him to let Ian out," Gertie went on, with just a slight tremor in her voice. "I gave him the key, but when he came back he said Ian had climbed out the window and was gone." She looked up, her eyes glistening with tears. "He always comes to my rescue, Clive does. He's a good man."

Cecily felt a cold chill run down her back as she met Gertie's gaze. She knew what she was thinking. What they were both thinking. It wouldn't have taken too much time for Clive to go into the foyer and take the candlestick. Perhaps thinking to protect himself.

He could have opened the shed door, and when Ian charged at him, hit him over the head. Then dragged him to the pond and left him there before bringing back the key.

Cecily cleared her throat. "How much time do you think passed after giving Clive the key, until he brought it back?"

Gertie dropped her gaze. "I don't know. I took the clean serviettes up to the dining room after I gave Clive the key. I wanted to save time in the morning. By the time I got back to the kitchen, Clive had put the key on the table and left."

She frowned. "I was gone quite a while. I went by the library and saw a strange flickering light under the door." She flicked a nervous glance at Cecily. "It was Mabel. She'd lit every candle on the Christmas tree."

Cecily felt the shiver all over her body. "Oh, good heavens."

"I know. She wanted to see how it looked. I helped her blow them all out, and then . . . I . . . went . . ."

Cecily looked at her in surprise as her words gradually trailed off. Her face seemed to be set in stone and there was such horror in her eyes Cecily felt a jolt of fear herself. "Gertie?"

The housemaid swallowed, and seemed to make an effort

to focus on her face. "Dan," she whispered. "He came back here. I never saw him, but he must have come back here. He told me he saw the candles in the window. That must have been about the time Ian was—" She gulped, unable to finish.

Cecily clenched her fingers. "All right, Gertie. Let's not jump to conclusions."

Gertie's frightened eyes pleaded with her. "Why would he come back here that late? Why didn't he come to see me? Why didn't he tell me he came back? Why didn't he tell me about the fight?"

"I wish I had the answers." Cecily got up and walked around the desk. "I do know one thing. It doesn't help to try and guess what happened. We just have to have faith in the people we know and trust, and eventually the truth will come out."

Gertie shook her head. "I don't know who to trust anymore, m'm. Honest I don't."

Cecily patted her shoulder. "Try not to worry about it all now, Gertie. You have two little ones who are really excited about Christmas, and we don't want to spoil things for them with all our questions and suspicions, do we. I promise you I will look into everything and try to get some answers, but in the meantime, you go and enjoy what little time you have with the twins, and try to put all this out of your mind."

Gertie heaved a heavy sigh and shoved herself up from the chair. "I'll do me best, m'm, but it ain't going to be bloody easy."

Cecily smiled, though it was the last thing she felt like doing. "I know you'll manage just fine. You're bringing them to the pantomime tonight, aren't you?"

Kate Kingsbury

"Yes, m'm. They're really excited about it. Though the way things are going I wouldn't be surprised if Mrs. Fortescue blows up the ballroom or something."

Cecily winced. "Don't even think it."

"No, m'm. Thank you, m'm." Gertie dropped a curtsey then trudged to the door. She had almost reached it when she paused, then spun around. "Oh, I almost forgot, what with everything else going on." She paused again, looked as if she was about to say something, then apparently changed her mind. "Never mind, m'm. I'll take care of it."

Sensing that something else was troubling her house-maid, Cecily felt compelled to pursue the matter. "Take care of what, Gertie?"

"It's . . . well, I don't like to tell tales and all, but . . ."

With infinite patience, Cecily waited.

"Well, it's that Sid Barrett." The rest of her words came out in a rush. "He's making a nuisance of himself, m'm. I mean, he keeps getting in our way, chatting us up, trying to get a rise out of us. I think he's bothering the other girls, too, from what I hear."

Cecily sighed. She had suspected as much. She might have known the new footman was too good to be true. "Thank you, Gertie, for letting me know. I'll see that Sidney behaves himself in future."

"Yes, m'm. Thank you, m'm." She looked anxious. "I don't want to get him into trouble or anything. I just want him to stop bothering us."

"I'll take care of it, Gertie."

"Thank you, m'm. Then I'll get back to me work." Reaching the door, she looked back. "I just hope we get all this sorted out in the next day or two, or this could be the worst Christmas I ever spent at the Pennyfoot."

As Cecily watched the door close behind her, she was inclined to agree.

Gertie walked slowly back to the foyer, her brain buzzing with questions. She needed to see Dan in the worst way. She needed answers, reassurance from him. Yet there was no way of knowing if he would tell her the truth.

What would she do if she found out that he'd killed Ian? She'd just about die, that's what. She couldn't imagine going on without him. Yet she'd have to, for the sake of her twins.

How could she get through Christmas, pretending to be happy and excited when all the time all this turmoil was going on inside her mind?

They had to find out what really happened. Even if it wasn't what she wanted to hear. It was the not knowing that was killing her.

Deep in thought, she reached the foyer, then jerked to a halt as a short, bald-headed man stepped into her path. Recognizing Archibald Parker, she did her best to look pleasant. "Can I help you, sir?"

"Yes, yes, I hope so." Archie glanced around the foyer, as if looking for someone, but the only person visible was Philip, the clerk, half hidden behind the reception desk. "I . . . had a word with Mrs. B. about this, and I thought I'd mention it to you, as well." His nose twitched violently, and his mustache seemed to dance in unison as he gazed at her. "I would like a bed warmer in my bed tonight."

Gertie frowned, wondering if he was being fresh, or simply meant that he wanted a warming pan.

Archie looked worried. "Mrs. B. said it would be all right. Perhaps you could bring it up after the pantomime? I can't go to sleep when my bed is so cold."

Deciding to give him the benefit of the doubt, Gertie nodded. "I'll see to it, Mr. Parker. I won't be bringing it up myself as I'll have other duties to attend to, but I'll make sure that one of the footmen warms your bed for you tonight."

"Oh, thank you. Thank you." Archie beamed at her. "I shall look forward to a good night's sleep, then."

"Very well, sir." Gertie was about to pass, when he stopped her with a hand on her arm. "I'm so sorry to hear about your loss."

She paused, with a heavy thud of her heart. "I beg your pardon?"

"Your loss. I know you weren't married to the deceased, but he was the father of your children, am I right?"

Lost for words, she could only stare at him.

"Must have been a dreadful shock. I don't suppose you know who did it?"

Gertie finally found her voice. "No, sir. I don't. Even if I did, I really don't see as how it's any of your business." She twisted away from his grasp and marched off, with his wheedling voice following her.

"I didn't mean any offense! Please forgive me if I upset you!"

Stomping down the stairs she muttered to herself under her breath. Nosy bleeding busybody. How the heck was she supposed to put everything out of her mind if everyone in the world knew about the murder and kept trying to talk to her about it?

Doing her best to curb her temper, she marched down the hallway to her room. This time, all was quiet as she reached it. Daisy must have found something to keep the twins occupied.

Opening the door, the first thing she saw was her nanny lying on the bed with her book propped up in front of her. The second thing she saw was Lillian and James on the floor. A pile of building blocks lay between them, and resplendent, in the middle of them, stood a tall, ornate candlestick.

CHAPTER

❊ 14 ❊

"I'm going out for a little while," Cecily announced, as Baxter unfolded the daily newspaper. "I thought I'd do a spot of shopping."

"Oh, right." He started to fold up the newspaper again. "I'll come with you."

"I'd rather you didn't, dear." She smiled to take away the sting of her words. "Actually I was hoping to find a very special Christmas present for you."

"Oh." His expression said that she'd left it a little late, which wasn't like her at all.

"I already have your presents," she hurried to explain. "This one will be a little extra."

Curiosity crept across his face. "Well, now you'll have to give me a hint."

DECKED WITH FOLLY

"Certainly not!" She finished tying her scarf over her hat and picked up her muff. "It's supposed to be a surprise and I'm not going to spoil it, so you'll just have to wait until Christmas morning."

"Oh, very well." He opened the newspaper again. "Samuel taking you, then?"

"Yes, dear."

"You won't be late for supper, I hope. You haven't forgotten the pantomime is tonight?"

"Of course not, dear. How could I?"

"Good. I wouldn't want to be there without you."

"There's no fear of that." She bent over and planted a kiss on his cheek. "I'll be back before you know it."

He grunted an answer and she hurried to the door, thankful he hadn't asked too many questions. She really hated to lie. As it was, as long as she actually bought something for him, she could convince herself she'd told him the truth.

For, one thing she was sure of, if she told him where she was really going, he'd have made no bones about his disapproval, and she was in no mood for an argument.

Samuel was waiting for Cecily in the foyer when she arrived there, and she wasted no time in hurrying outside. She had only an hour or so to achieve her purpose, and return in time for supper.

The wind had died down, and rain spattered on the roof and windows of the carriage as they sped down the Esplanade toward the town. Wreaths of fir and holly hung from every gas lamp along the seafront. Light from the windows of the little shops spilled across the wet pavements, and peo-

165

ple stood huddled in front of the bay windows or hurried in and out the doors.

Horses, carriages, bicycles, and motorcars crammed the High Street, and it took Samuel more than twenty minutes to get from one end to the other. It was precious time wasted, and Cecily fretted as they continued on, once more leaving the hustle and bustle of the town behind.

Rattling down the country road, Cecily peered out at the dripping trees and soaked hedges. A late afternoon mist was rolling in from the ocean, shrouding from view everything beyond a few feet. As they turned the bend, however, she caught sight of a faint light gleaming through the fog. They were almost there.

The carriage slowed, rumbling into the courtyard of the George and Dragon and coming to a halt in front of the rear door. It was not yet opening time and Cecily hoped to catch Bernard McPherson, the owner of the public house, before he went into the bar to prepare for the evening.

Samuel opened the door of the carriage and peeked in. "Would you want me to knock and announce that you have come to visit, m'm?"

"Thank you, Samuel, but I'll do my own announcing." She held out her hand and Samuel assisted her to the ground. "Come with me," she ordered, "I would like you to accompany me while I talk to Mr. McPherson." Raising her skirts, she crossed over the puddles to the door.

It opened almost immediately, and the surprised face of Bernard McPherson appeared in the doorway. "'Pon my soul, it's Mrs. Baxter!" A grin spread over his gaunt face. "To what do I owe this honor?"

DECKED WITH FOLLY

"I was hoping to have a word with you." She smiled up at him. Most of the publicans she had met were robust, stout fellows with enormous girth and sagging jowls. Bernard on the other hand was quite scrawny, though nonetheless a jolly gentleman with always a kind word or a joke for his customers.

"Of course. Come in!" He opened the door wide and stood back to let them pass. "The missus is down the village visiting our daughter, but she should be back soon."

He led the way into the parlor and beckoned them to sit. "Can I get you a wee drop of brandy, Mrs. Baxter? It's a mite chilly out there."

She shook her head. "Not for me, thank you."

"The young man, then?"

Samuel glanced at her for permission, which she gave with a nod of her head.

"Good." Bernard crossed to the door. "I'll be back in a jiff."

No sooner had the door closed behind him, than Samuel leaned forward and said in a low voice, "Begging your pardon, m'm, but does Mr. Baxter know we are here?"

Cecily looked at him. "I really don't see why that should concern you, Samuel."

"No, m'm." He was quiet for a moment, then added a little desperately, "It's just that if he doesn't know, and if he should happen to find out somehow, he's going to get really cross with me for bringing you down here."

Cecily raised her eyebrows. "You were simply following orders."

"Yes, m'm." Again a pause. "I take it he doesn't know then."

Cecily sighed. "Really, Samuel, you do like to borrow trouble, don't you. I'm here to ask a few questions, that is all. It's not as if I were in the public bar, knocking back a pint or two, now is it."

Her stable manager's face registered shock. "I should hope not, m'm."

"Well, then, I fail to see why you think Mr. Baxter would not approve."

"Yes, m'm." Yet another pause. "Perhaps it would have been better to tell him in that case."

Cecily gave him a stern look. "That is my business, Samuel."

"Yes, m'm."

She was relieved when Bernard chose that moment to return with a tray bearing a bottle of brandy and three glasses. "Just in case you change your mind, Mrs. Baxter," he said cheerfully as he set the tray down on a small table.

Glancing at the golden liquid gleaming in the bottle, Cecily imagined it sliding down her throat and warming her tummy. "Well, perhaps a tiny drop, then."

"Ah! I thought you might. Nothing like a wee drop of the good stuff to warm the cockles, right?" Smiling, Bernard poured a generous amount in the three glasses and handed one to her. Motioning Samuel to take his, the publican picked up his own glass and sat down. "Now then, Mrs. Baxter, what can I do for you?"

Cecily took a cautious sip of the brandy, then winced as it stung her throat. "I wanted to ask you a few questions about the fight in your pub the other night," she said, her voice sounding a little hoarse.

"Ah." Bernard nodded. "I thought this was more than just a friendly visit." He narrowed his gaze. "Does this have anything to do with the chap who recently died on the grounds of the Pennyfoot?"

Cecily exchanged a worried glance with Samuel. Apparently the news had now spread all over town. Avoiding his question, she said carefully, "Did you actually see the fight?"

Bernard shook his head. "No, m'm, I didn't. I was behind the bar. I heard the commotion, though, and some of my customers told me that a couple of blokes were bashing each other outside in the yard."

"So you don't know how it ended up?"

"I didn't see either of the chaps that were fighting come in the pub after that, so I reckon one got the better of the other and they both took off."

Cecily took another sip of brandy. This one went down more smoothly, and gave her a pleasant, warm sensation as it slid down to her stomach.

"There was a woman came in looking for one of them. By that time they'd left, though." Bernard downed his brandy in one gulp and smacked his lips. "Good drop of stuff, that."

"Did you speak to her?"

"Aye, I did. She came up to the bar. I was a bit surprised, since it was the public bar and this woman was a lady. Not the kind you usually see in the public bar. Things got a bit quiet when she walked in, I can tell you."

"Did she talk to anyone else while she was here?"

Bernard looked surprised. "No, she didn't. She asked if I'd seen her husband. When she described him one of the customers mentioned he'd seen a bloke like that fighting out in the courtyard. She just turned around and left without another word."

Cecily put down her glass before she was tempted to take another sip. "And you are quite sure she spoke to no one else outside?"

"As sure as I can be. I heard a horse taking off right after she went out the door, and I saw her go past the window. She didn't have time to talk to anyone else." He gave her a look full of speculation. "Does that help at all?"

"Perhaps. Thank you, Mr. McPherson." Cecily tilted her head at Samuel. "I appreciate your time. I'm afraid we must leave now. I have some shopping to do before the shops close, and the traffic in the High Street is dreadful."

Bernard jumped to his feet. "You can't stay to see the missus? She'll be disappointed to have missed you."

"Please give her my apologies. Perhaps the two of you can stop by the Pennyfoot over Christmas and sample some of Mrs. Chubb's baking. Her mince pies are legendary."

"I'm sure they are, m'm. We'd like that very much."

"Good." Cecily rose to her feet. "Come along, Samuel. We must be off."

"How are those two sons of yours?" Bernard asked, as he led them to the door.

Cecily smiled. "They are both very well, thank you."

Bernard nodded. "I often think of your Michael. Those new pumps he put in when he was the publican here are the most efficient I've ever seen."

"Michael loved this place." Cecily paused, waiting for Bernard to open the door. "I think he still misses it."

"He's happy, though, right?"

Cecily laughed. "I believe so. He's not very good at writing letters, I'm afraid."

"Ah, men usually leave that sort of thing to the women. I canna blame him too much." He opened the door and Cecily stepped out into the rain.

"Thank you for the brandy, sir," Samuel said, touching his forehead with his fingers.

"You are most welcome, laddie." Bernard smiled at Cecily. "Take care on the way back. The fog is getting thick."

He was right, Cecily realized, as she settled herself on the leather seat. The dense mist seemed to wrap itself around the horse and carriage, enfolding everything in moist arms.

Shivering, she drew her scarf tightly about her neck. "Hurry, Samuel," she called out. "We must reach town before closing time."

"Right away, m'm." Samuel cracked the whip and the horse started forward, jerking her back in her seat.

Their journey was slowed by the gray fog that swallowed up the view ahead. In a fever of impatience, Cecily leaned forward, as if by doing so she could will them to go faster, although she knew how dangerous that would be. Samuel was an experienced driver, and she respected his judgement.

At long last they reached the town, where the vehicles had thinned out considerably. Ordering Samuel to stop in front of a men's clothier store, she climbed down before he had a chance to leap to the ground and assist her.

The manager was about to close the door as she reached it, and she gave him her warmest smile. "I shan't be but a minute," she promised, and, with reluctance, he allowed her to enter.

It actually took her ten minutes to find what she wanted, a burgundy velvet waistcoat. She waited for the assistant to wrap it for her, then hurried out of the shop and back to the carriage.

More relaxed now, she had time to think about Bernard McPherson's words as they sped back along the Esplanade. Gloria had lied about the evening Ian died. Instead of waiting for him at home, as she told Cecily she had done, she must have gone to the George and Dragon to find him, but arrived after the fight and after Ian had left.

Since Bernard hadn't seen the fight, he could not have told her that Ian had a black eye. Nor, apparently, did she speak to anyone else. Which meant that Gloria must have seen her husband later that night.

Now what Cecily wanted to know was why Gloria lied about that and what it was she was trying to hide.

"Where the heck did they find this?" Gertie snatched up the candlestick and held it out to Daisy. "Where did they get it?"

Daisy dropped her book and sat up. "I dunno. I never saw it before."

Gertie swung around to face her children. Lillian looked scared, while James stared at her in defiance. "Where did you get this?" She shook it in James's face and Lillian burst into tears.

"It must have been in the room." Daisy jumped off the bed and fell to the floor on her knees. "They haven't been out since you left." Putting an arm about Lillian's shoulders, she said gently, "Tell us where you found the candlestick, there's a precious girl."

"We found it under the bed," James said, jutting out his bottom lip. "The stupid thing was just lying there. We didn't do nothing wrong, Mama!"

Realizing her hand was still shaking, Gertie clutched the candlestick to her chest. "Under the bed? Are you telling me the truth, James? Lillian! Is he telling me the truth?"

Lillian simply cried harder. Daisy looked up at her, accusation blazing in her eyes. "What is the matter with you, Gertie? It's just a silly old candlestick. It's not even real silver."

Instead of answering her, Gertie turned up the base of the candlestick. On the bottom was a brown stain, with a half dozen hairs sticking to it.

Fighting a sudden urge to be sick, Gertie put a hand over her mouth. "I have to talk to madam. Look after them until I get back."

"What's wrong? Gertie, whatever is the matter?"

Ignoring Daisy's anxious cries, Gertie fled out the door and ran headlong down the corridor. She reached the stairs before she thought to hide the candlestick under her apron. Clamping it against her hip, she raced awkwardly up the stairs and across the foyer.

Just as she reached the foot of the stairs, Sid appeared in the hallway. "'Allo," he called out. "What's yer bleeding rush? You look as if you've seen a ghost."

"Maybe I have." She paused on the bottom step. "Is madam in her office?"

"Nah, I just come from there. I don't know where she's gone."

Without bothering to answer him, Gertie leapt up the stairs, taking them two at once. By the time she reached the first landing she was fighting for breath and had to slow down.

Climbing the second flight more slowly, she tried to sort out her jumbled thoughts. The twins had found the candlestick under the bed. She had no doubt it was the murder weapon, but what in blazes was it doing under her bed? She certainly hadn't put it there.

Which meant someone else must have. The same someone who had hit Ian over the head with it? With a cold stab of fear she remembered the tumbled contents of her dresser, the clothes dragged to the side on her wardrobe.

Had there been a killer in her room? When? How?

The thought of it made her feel faint. A killer in the room with her twins. He could have killed them, too. From now on, she would make sure that the door would be locked all the time, whether anyone was in there or not.

At last she reached the top landing. Breathless and afraid, she raced down the hallway to madam's suite and rapped on the door.

Baxter's muffled voice answered her, sounding irritated. "All right, all right, hold your horses. I'm coming." The door opened, and his disgruntled face peered out. "Oh, it's you, Gertie. What is it now?"

"I'm looking for madam. Is she here?" Gertie heard the tremble in her words and swallowed.

"No, she's not. She's out on an errand. What is it?" He must have noticed her distress, and he peered more closely at her. "What's happened now? Oh, great heavens. Don't tell me someone else has been murdered?"

"Not as far as I know, sir." Gertie drew the candlestick out from under her apron and held it out to him.

For a long moment he stared at it as if he'd never seen anything like it before, then his frown cleared, to be replaced by shock. "Good Lord! Don't tell me that thing is what I think it is?"

Gertie nodded. "I think so, sir. I think it's the candlestick that killed Ian Rossiter."

CHAPTER
❦ 15 ❦

Instead of answering Gertie, Baxter opened the door wider, grabbed her arm, and dragged her inside the room. Slamming the door shut, he took a deep breath. "All right. Now tell me where you found it."

Gertie blinked hard. "It was under me bed, sir."

"Under your *bed*? What the devil was it doing there?"

"I don't know, sir. My twins found it. They were playing with it when I walked in there just now."

Baxter took the candlestick out of her hand and walked over to the dresser, where he carefully set it down. "Are you quite sure they found it under the bed?"

"Yes, sir. Daisy was with them all afternoon and they never went out of the room."

"And you've not seen it before now?"

Gertie shuddered. "No, sir."

"Then how did it get under your bed?"

"I don't know sir, but last night when I got back to me room I thought the twins had been messing around with my things. Now I think someone was in the room, and put the candlestick under my bed."

Baxter's eyebrows shot up. "Why?"

"Perhaps he was looking for a place to hide it."

"And in the entire building, all he could find was your bed?"

"Yes, sir. Or . . ." She hesitated, reluctant to put her thoughts into words.

"Or what, girl? Spit it out!"

"Or p'raps he wanted it to be found in my room, so's people would think I killed Ian."

"Oh, good Lord." Baxter ran a hand through his hair. "I suppose that could be." He thought for a moment, then said briskly, "All right. Leave this with me." He put an awkward hand on her shoulder, gave her a gentle pat, then dropped his hand again. "Try not to worry, Gertie. Mrs. Baxter and I will sort all this out."

"Yes, sir. Thank you, sir." She bent her knees, then twisted around to reach for the door handle. "I didn't kill him, sir."

"I know that, Gertie. Now run along and do try not to worry."

"Yes, sir." Feeling only slightly reassured, Gertie pulled the door open and left the room.

All the way down the stairs she thought about what could have happened to her twins with a killer in the room.

In all the years she'd worked at the Pennyfoot, she'd never felt a need to lock her door.

For one thing, she didn't have anything of value that a thief would want, but mostly, she'd always felt as if the Pennyfoot was her home, and she would never go around locking up rooms in her home. Nobody would.

Now all that security was gone. From now on she'd never feel the same about living in the Pennyfoot, and no thief could ever have taken more from her than that.

The second Cecily walked in through the door of her suite she was pounced upon by her irate husband.

"Where have you been? You're late for supper and now we shall have to gobble down our food in order to get to the dratted pantomime on time. You know how I hate to eat fast. I have a good mind to enjoy my meal and skip the pesky show altogether."

Feeling guilty, Cecily did her best to soothe his ruffled feathers. "I'm so sorry, my love. It took me longer than I had anticipated to choose just the right gift for you." She headed for the boudoir, calling out over her shoulder, "I do believe you will feel it was well worth the extra trouble I took when you see it."

After hurriedly shoving the package inside her wardrobe, she pulled off her hat and scarf and threw them on the bed. Quickly she peeled off her long gloves and threw them down, as well. She would put them all away later, she decided, as Baxter's growl reached her.

"I hope you're not stopping to change your clothes. We don't have time for that."

"No darling. I'll be out in a minute." She pulled open a drawer and snatched up a lace-trimmed shirtwaist. "I just need to tidy my hair."

He grunted a reply and she made a face at herself in the mirror. Quickly she unbuttoned her blouse, dragged it off, and slipped on the fresh one. A quick flick of the brush had to suffice, and for good measure she slid in a mother-of-pearl comb to anchor any stray strands that might escape.

A splash of toilet water on her cheeks refreshed her face, and she hurried out to join her husband, who was pacing back and forth across the carpet with his hands behind his back.

"Oh, there you are." He glared at her. "I assume we can leave for the dining room now?"

"Yes, of course, dear." She started forward, then stopped as she caught sight of the candlestick on the dresser. "What on earth is that?"

Baxter sighed. "I don't suppose it can wait until we get downstairs?"

With a muffled cry of distress, she darted forward and snatched it up. A quick peek at the base confirmed her suspicions. "Bax! For heaven's sake! Why didn't you tell me? Where did you find it?"

"I didn't find it. Gertie brought it up to me a short while ago."

Cecily listened as he repeated his conversation with the housemaid. "I told her to try not to worry," he finished. "I promised her we'd look into it."

"We will have to give this to Sam Northcott when he gets back." Cecily replaced it on the dresser with a shudder. "There's no doubt that whoever killed Ian wants the blame put on Gertie. It was most likely the same person who told Sam about Gertie's threats to Ian."

"Yes, she's come to that conclusion herself."

"Oh, dear. I shall have to speak with her."

"After supper?"

Seeing his forlorn face, she relented. "Of course, my love. We shall go down to the dining room right now, and deal with this problem later."

Her reward was a rare smile from him. Tucking her hand into his elbow he murmured, "Then let us proceed."

By the time they reached the dining room nearly all of the tables were occupied. As she threaded her way to her table by the window, Cecily exchanged greetings with guests, most of whom seemed excited about the pantomime that evening.

Considering Phoebe's reputation for disastrous presentations, Cecily found that quite heartening. She always viewed Phoebe's efforts with a certain amount of trepidation, due largely to the fact that her entourage of performers was not only inept but also stubbornly resistant to orders. They even went so far as to occasionally take a devious delight in tormenting their hapless director.

Phoebe was no match for them and was frequently reduced to a raging mass of torn nerves and shrill reprimands. Not too conducive to a successful performance. The Pennyfoot guests, however, seemed to enjoy the ensuing mayhem as much or perhaps even more than the actual presentation, much to Phoebe's utter dismay. She had sworn so many times never to direct another show that even she didn't believe her own words.

All in all, it promised to be an eventful evening, and Cecily looked forward to it as a rather masochistic way of putting her problems behind her for an hour or two.

"What are you thinking about?"

Her husband's voice interrupted her thoughts and she smiled at him. "I was just thinking about how much I'm looking forward to the pantomime tonight."

"Good Lord. Are you out of your mind? You haven't been at the gin or something, have you?"

She pulled a face at him. "Oh, come, you know you enjoy watching Phoebe make a complete fool of herself."

"A dubious pleasure at best."

"But one you wouldn't miss."

His lips twitched into a smile. "You know me too well, my dear."

She relaxed, pleased that she had coaxed him into a better mood. For the time being, all thoughts of murder and villains would be banished from her mind, while she settled back and enjoyed what had become a great British tradition—the Christmas pantomime.

Backstage in the ballroom, Phoebe was doing her best to hustle her girls into the dressing room. Several of them appeared more inclined to exchange comments with the stagehands who, instead of attending to the job, were tossing good-humored banter at the breathless dancers.

Having promised herself earlier that this time she would absolutely, definitely, not lose her temper with them, Phoebe attempted another tactic. It involved a lot of pushing and pulling, with a good deal of pinching thrown in, but one by one the young ladies were persuaded to join their companions in the cramped dressing room.

All but one. As usual, Isabelle lagged behind, lurching one shoulder up against a backdrop in a most disgusting manner. The stagehand grinning down at her wasn't helping matters at all. He gave her a lascivious wink, which reduced the ridiculous girl to silly giggling.

"Isabelle!" Phoebe pitched her voice loud enough to make them both jump. "In the dressing room. *Now!*"

"Gotta go," Isabelle said, blowing the man a kiss.

The oaf pretended to catch it and smack it against his mouth.

"Oh, for heaven's sake." Her voice thick with disgust, Phoebe grasped Isabelle's shoulder and propelled her toward the noisy dressing room. "Get in there and behave yourself for once."

Inside the room, young women were wandering around in various stages of undress. Phoebe rolled her eyes and went to work, doing up buttons and lacing ribbons, muttering all the while that this was positively the last time she would ever waste her efforts on such an ungrateful, uncooperative, unruly bunch of hooligans.

The girls, as usual, completely ignored her.

"That Sid Barrett," Isabelle said, amid giggles, "is so funny. He makes me laugh until I wet my knickers."

Howls of laughter greeted this comment, which Phoebe

immediately attempted to suppress. "The audience is coming in!" she shrieked at the top of her voice. "They will hear you cackling away like geese in here! How much respect do you expect to get from an audience when they hear you all behaving like animals! You are . . . such . . . disobedient . . ." Her voice trailed off as she realized that the girls had gone silent and she was the only one screeching.

Someone snorted, and the rest of the group dissolved once more into raucous laughter.

"Enough!" Phoebe raised her arms. "One more sound out of any of you and I will cancel this performance. Right here and now."

Apparently realizing they had gone far enough, the girls fell silent once more, and dutifully began pulling on costumes and wigs.

Trembling with suppressed fury, Phoebe fought for composure. "Dora, where are your ballet shoes?"

Dora looked down at her feet as if amazed to see they were bare. "I can't find them, Mrs. Fortescue."

"Then you will have to dance in bare feet." Phoebe stalked over to another of her dancers and began tugging at her costume. "For heaven's sake, Martha, pull this bodice up higher before you're arrested for indecent behavior."

Behind her, she heard Isabelle's low voice. "He asked me out, you know."

Dora answered in the same low tones. "Who did?"

"That Sid Barrett. He's going to take me to the George for a gin and tonic after the show."

"Oh, that one. He's nothing but a saucy rake." Dora tossed her curls so they bounced on top of her head. "He asks all the girls to go out with him. I wouldn't trust that one for the life of me."

Isabelle sounded sulky. "I didn't say as I was going, did I."

Phoebe whirled around. "I thought I said no sound."

Both girls gave her mutinous stares. "We were just—" Isabelle began, but Phoebe stopped her with a sharp raise of her hand.

"I said no sound. Or would you like someone else to play the prince?" She glanced across the room. "Martha, for instance. She knows the part."

Isabelle clamped her lips shut.

"We should have a man play the part of the prince, anyhow," Dora said.

"Yeah," someone else said. "Like Sid Barrett."

Laughter rippled around the room. "He'd make a handsome prince," Dora murmured.

"The prince is always a woman in a pantomime," Phoebe said stiffly. "You all know that very well." She paused, one hand to her ear. "Listen! That's the orchestra playing the introduction. We have five minutes to take our places. Ladies— *move!*"

To her immense satisfaction, the girls jumped into action. For a frantic moment or two they scrambled here and there tugging and pulling on their costumes, and then, at last, they were ready and dashing out the door.

Phoebe waited until the last one left, then followed at a slower pace. She felt exhausted, and the show had yet to begin. This was her last pantomime. There was no doubt in her mind.

* * *

DECKED WITH FOLLY

Out in the audience, Cecily sat in the first row, her husband on her left and Madeline on her right. Peering around her friend to where Kevin sat next to her, Cecily said quietly, "I have something of importance to discuss with you later."

Kevin nodded, and Madeline gave her a curious look. "Something's happened?"

"Yes, but I promised Baxter I wouldn't talk about it until after the show." Cecily studied the program. "I think this is the first time Phoebe has done Cinderella."

"Well, that should give her plenty of opportunities for mistakes, then." Madeline settled herself more comfortably on her chair. She wore a pale blue gown with simple lines and without any adornment. On anyone else it would have looked plain and uninteresting. On Madeline it looked elegant and sophisticated. Silver sandals peeked out from under her skirt, and she had bound her hair with silver tinsel—a decidedly Christmas touch that no one else would have dared to try.

Cecily did her best to enjoy the pantomime, in spite of the tension that kept her shoulders rigid throughout. She wasn't quite sure if it was worry about the murder or the anticipation of disaster on the stage that kept her so on edge.

For the most part, the show went quite smoothly by Phoebe's standards. Cinderella had trouble remembering her lines, and had to be prompted from the wings by the obviously irate and painfully audible director, and both Cinderella and the prince dissolved into giggles during what was supposed to be a romantic scene at the end, once more incurring the wrath of the long-suffering Phoebe.

The appearance of acrobats leaping across the stage during the finale drew surprised murmurs from the audience, however, especially since it was obvious they came as a surprise to the rest of the cast, who had to scramble to get out of their way.

As the five lithe young men balanced on each other's shoulders, Baxter leaned toward her and whispered loudly, "What the devil are they supposed to be?"

At a loss, Cecily raised her shoulders in a gesture of bewilderment. She vaguely remembered Phoebe mentioning something about acrobats, but had assumed they would be part of the show, not simply added on at the end.

"Probably had them there to take over when those worthless dancers of hers messed everything up," Baxter observed, as the curtains drew to a close amidst polite applause.

The curtains drew back again to allow the cast to take a bow, just in time to see Cinderella slap one of the acrobats across his face.

The audience rocked with laughter, and this time thunderous applause shook the rafters. Phoebe appeared on stage, red-faced and murmuring apologies, but by then her audience was scrambling to get out of their chairs and back to the dining room, where late-night snacks were being served.

"It was too much to hope that Phoebe would manage to get through an entire presentation without some kind of disaster," Madeline murmured as she accompanied Cecily to the door.

Following behind her, Baxter grunted. "That woman should be locked up. She's a menace to society."

"Well, at least they haven't hurt anyone." Cecily looked back at her husband and smiled. "That's the main concern."

"Only by a miracle." Baxter stepped in front of her and held the door open for her.

Madeline laughed. "Like the time one of her dancers in the Scottish sword dance sent a sword flying off the stage."

Baxter rolled his eyes. "Or when she lost the performing python."

"Or when the magician couldn't bring his assistant back into the magic box."

"Oh, be quiet, you two." Cecily stepped out into the hall, where small groups of people wandered toward the dining room. "You know quite well that our guests love to see Phoebe's fiascos. I think they would be quite disappointed if she managed a perfect performance."

Kevin joined them at that moment, looking anxious. "What is it you wanted to tell me? Has it got anything to do with the murder?"

Cecily sent a quick glance over her shoulder, but now they were alone in the corridor. "We have found the murder weapon," she said quietly. "It's in my suite."

Kevin's eyes opened wide. "Where was it found?"

Cecily hesitated, hating to implicate Gertie if it wasn't necessary. Before she could speak, however, Baxter answered for her.

"Gertie McBride's twins found it under her bed. She believes that someone put it there to make it appear that she killed Ian Rossiter."

Madeline drew a sharp breath, while Kevin looked worried. "If that is so, that means the killer is still here in the Pennyfoot."

"Precisely." Cecily glanced at her husband. "We have to find him before something else awful happens."

Baxter raised an eyebrow. "How, may I ask, do you intend to do that?"

"I don't know." Cecily raised her hands in a helpless gesture. "I have suspicions, but nothing tangible. It's all circumstantial." She looked at Madeline. "I don't suppose you could help?"

Madeline shot a guilty look at Kevin. "Well, I—"

"If you're suggesting," Kevin said coldly, "that my wife use her so-called psychic powers to help you solve this unfortunate murder, then I must strenuously object. We have an agreement, which I must ask her to uphold, and, which I sincerely trust she will honor."

A flash of rebellion crossed Madeline's face, then vanished. "Of course," she murmured, but her eyes sought Cecily's with a significant message. "I'm so sorry, Cecily."

"Not at all. I completely understand." Cecily smiled up at Kevin. "We shall simply have to use the tried-and-true methods of investigation."

Baxter sighed. "I sympathize, old chap. It seems as if both our wives have a problem avoiding trouble."

"Piffle." Cecily took her husband's arm to soften her words. "You are just jealous of our abilities, that is all. You men like to think of women as helpless little creatures who cannot make an intelligent decision without the guidance and wisdom of their husbands."

"If that were so, my dear Cecily, you and I would have parted company a long time ago." Patting her hand, he led her down the hallway to the dining room.

CHAPTER

✽ 16 ✽

It was the following morning before Cecily could arrange a meeting with Madeline alone. She had suggested they meet for tea and scones at Dolly's tea shop, and her friend had readily agreed.

Waiting for her to arrive, Cecily exchanged a few words with the owner of the tea shop. Dolly, a massive woman with three chins and a sharp tongue, expressed her shock and sorrow at the news that Ian Rossiter had died.

"I still remember him working for you at the Pennyfoot," she said, leaning one hand on Cecily's table to rest her back. "Bright young lad, he was. Bit of a joker but he had a good heart. I remember his wedding to Gertie, poor luv. She was so heartbroken when it turned out he was already married."

"Yes, she was." Cecily kept her voice low, aware of other

customers in the cramped restaurant. "It's all very sad the way things turned out."

"I don't suppose they know who did it." Dolly pulled a face. "Not that our brilliant constabulary could find a pickpocket in a prison yard. Still, there can't be that many people around here who would want to kill someone like Ian. He might have made his mistakes, like we all do, but he wasn't a bad person."

Cecily wasn't so sure about that. She couldn't help remembering what his wife had to say about Ian's companions. Then again, Gloria didn't seem to have much good to say about her late husband.

"Don't you think, dearie?"

Cecily looked up with a start, aware she'd completely missed what Dolly had been saying. "I do beg your pardon, Dolly. I wasn't—"

"There you are." Madeline's voice from behind her cut off Cecily's next words. "Sorry I'm late. I had to wait for Kevin to leave." She plopped down on the empty chair, her long dark hair flying all over her shoulders. Seemingly oblivious to the nervous glances sent her way from three women seated nearby, she waved a hand at Dolly. "Bring on the scones, Dolly dear. I'm utterly starving."

"They're on their way." Dolly beamed at her. "You're looking very sprightly this morning, Mrs. Prestwick."

Madeline shuddered. "I still can't get used to being called that." She gave Dolly an accusing stare. "You used to call me Madeline."

Dolly nodded, sending her chins wobbling. "That I did, but that was before you were married."

"Whatever difference does that make?"

Dolly answered by rolling her eyes, then squeezed her way through the tables in the direction of the kitchen.

Cecily shook her head. "Madeline, you are utterly incorrigible."

"I fail to see why I should be treated any differently as a married woman." Madeline flipped her hair away from her face with a careless hand. "I'm still the same person."

Cecily studied her friend. "Are you?"

Madeline gave her a rueful smile. "Well, no, I'm not. I'm not as free to do what I like when I like. I have someone else to think about now, and in several more months, there'll be a third someone else to worry about." She laid a gentle hand on her stomach.

It took Cecily a moment or two to realize what she meant.

"Madeline! Are you . . . ?"

"With child, as they say." Madeline's tinkling laugh rang out. "Don't look so stunned, Cecily. Even witches can bear babies, you know."

Shocked gasps from across the room greeted this statement, confirming that Dolly's customers had been avidly following the conversation. Not that it had been all that difficult for them, since Madeline had deliberately raised her voice in order to titillate her audience.

Cecily was far too delighted at her friend's news to scold her, however. "Madeline . . . how utterly delightful. Kevin must be over the moon."

"Kevin doesn't know yet, though no doubt he will by tonight." Madeline sent a sly glance over to the other table. "I suppose I'd better tell him before then."

"How long have you known?" Speaking in a near whisper, Cecily leaned forward. "How could Kevin not know? He's a doctor, for heaven's sake."

"Kevin doesn't know everything, even if he thinks he does." Madeline shrugged. "Besides, I only realized it myself a few days ago. I wanted to be sure before I told you."

"Well, I couldn't be happier for you." Cecily touched her friend's hand, knowing that wasn't quite the truth. It worried her that Madeline had told her before she'd broken the news to her husband. She couldn't help wondering if all was not well in the Prestwick household.

That wasn't something she felt comfortable inquiring about, however. That was Madeline's problem, and she couldn't interfere. All she could do was hope and pray that she was wrong.

"Anyway, enough of that." Madeline reached for her serviette and laid it in her lap. "What did you want to talk to me about?"

"How do you know I want to talk about anything specific? Can't two friends meet just to have a cozy chat?"

Madeline's gaze raked her face. "I know you, Cecily. You want to know if I have any revelations about Ian's death."

Cecily was prevented from answering by Dolly, who arrived at their table with a loaded tray, which she began to unload with excruciating precision. After placing each cup carefully in its saucer, she laid out a china bowl filled to the brim with cubes of sugar, into which she placed tiny silver tongs. The jug of cream followed, then the teapot dressed in a bright green knitted tea cozy.

Next, she placed in the center of the table a large platter

of scones, a bowl of clotted cream, and a jar of strawberry jam. Tucking the tray under her arm, Dolly surveyed the table. "I've just baked some Banbury cakes. They're hot out of the oven. Would you like me to bring you some?"

Cecily could already savor the aroma of the spiced raisin cakes wafting from the kitchen. "Oh, please do."

Madeline sighed. "I suppose, now that I have to eat for two, it wouldn't hurt."

Fortunately, Dolly had already moved out of earshot. Cecily frowned. "Don't you think you should tell your husband the good news before you spread it all over town?"

Madeline raised an eyebrow. "You sound a little put out with me."

"I am." Cecily leaned forward again, whispering, "Kevin should have been the first to know."

Madeline didn't answer at first, then she murmured, "I know. You're right, Cecily. I suppose I'm afraid of what he might say."

"Why? I don't understand."

"Shall I pour?" Madeline reached for the sugar bowl and picked out two lumps with the tongs, then dropped them into Cecily's cup. "Judging by our conversations on the subject, I suspect that Kevin is worried about me bringing another witch into the world." She dropped two more sugar lumps in her own cup. "I can't say I blame him."

"You must be joking." As far as Cecily could tell from her expression, however, Madeline was perfectly serious.

"He's right, you know. My child could well possess talents that are completely misunderstood by most people. Having lived with that all my life, I don't know if I want to

193

place that burden on anyone, much less my own flesh and blood."

She reached for the milk jug and poured a small amount in each cup. "Don't look so distressed, Cecily dear. This is my predicament, and I must decide how to settle it. I have no doubt it will be resolved, one way or another."

Cecily felt a pang of apprehension. "What does that mean, exactly?"

Madeline smiled. "It means I shall find a way to make everyone happy. Including you, so take that frown off your face and tell me why you summoned me here this morning." She lifted a scone from the platter and held it to her nose. "Oh, heavens, just the smell is divine. How I wish I could bake like this."

Still not reassured, Cecily took a scone and laid it on her plate. "Promise me you won't do anything drastic without talking to me first."

Madeline raised a delicate eyebrow. "Drastic? My whole life has been drastic. Why should things be any different for me now?"

"Because you are a wife and, soon to be, mother. Things have to be different."

"You worry too much. I shall take very good care of my child, no matter who she is or what happens to her in the future."

"It's a girl? Really? How do you know that?"

Madeline put her fingers to her forehead and closed her eyes. After a moment she opened them again and announced, "I don't. I'm just guessing."

Suspecting her friend was having fun with her, Cecily

gave up. "Well, do let me know what Kevin has to say. I have an idea he will be delighted."

"I hope you're right." Madeline picked up the teapot and poured the hot liquid into Cecily's cup, then filled her own. "Now, for the third time, why exactly am I here?"

Cecily sighed. "Very well." She glanced over at the occupied tables but the other customers seemed immersed in conversations of their own. Keeping her voice low, just in case, she murmured, "I saw your reaction when I told Kevin about finding the candlestick. I confess, I did wonder if you'd had . . . a moment of insight perhaps. I know he doesn't want you using your powers to help me, but frankly, I'm at a loss as to how to proceed. If I don't solve this murder before Sam Northcott returns, I'm afraid Gertie might be taken down to the station and held there on suspicion of murder."

Madeline gazed at her over the rim of her cup. "You're quite sure Gertie didn't kill Ian? After all, she has threatened to do away with him often enough."

"I'm quite sure. In fact, I have my own ideas as to who might have been responsible, but at present I don't have much evidence to substantiate my suspicions."

Madeline's eyes lit up. "So tell me, who do you think is responsible?"

"I'd rather not say at this point." Cecily hesitated, then added, "Actually, I have more than one suspect, which doesn't help matters."

"Oh, my. Poor Ian. Apparently he was not a popular fellow."

Cecily scowled. "This is not exactly a laughing matter, Madeline."

She was immediately contrite. "Of course not, Cecily. I apologize. The truth is, I don't remember my reaction yesterday. Except to wonder if Gertie really had killed Ian and had actually hidden the candlestick under the bed herself. I thought perhaps, when the twins found it, she was forced into lying about it. I suppose I was concerned about what would happen to the twins if she was convicted of murder."

Cecily shuddered. "Don't even entertain the thought. I'm as sure as I can be that Gertie didn't kill Ian. I just have to find out who did, and as quickly as possible." She studied Madeline's face. "It worries me greatly that you saw dead bodies in your vision the other day. I hope and pray that doesn't mean someone else will be killed."

Madeline shook her head. "You know most of my visions are merely symbols. We just have to work out what it meant, that's all. I'm quite sure you won't find bodies scattered all over the bowling greens, if that's what you're worried about."

Cecily gave her a wan smile. "I was rather. Silly, I suppose, but when I'm in the dark like this it's easy to imagine all sorts of horrors."

"Well, put the thought right out of your head." Madeline put down her cup and picked up what was left of her scone. "The bodies in my vision most likely represent something quite mundane, like crushed flowers, or dead spiders. You just have to work out what the connection is to your murder, that's all."

Dolly arrived at that moment with the Banbury cakes, and Cecily tried to put aside her worries for the moment to enjoy the delicious treats. The concern lingered, however, and she could not dismiss the sense of urgency. Time was of the essence, and she was fast running out of it.

Gertie hauled the carpet sweeper up the last of the stairs, puffing with exertion. Normally she took her time climbing them, but this morning she wanted to be done early. Dan had promised to stop by after the midday meal rush and there were a couple of things she really wanted to ask him.

Reaching the landing, she paused to catch her breath. She wasn't looking forward to the conversation. She thought she knew Dan well enough to tell when he was lying, but he'd lied to her about the graze on his cheek, so she had to wonder what else he had lied about.

She didn't want to even think of the answer to that one. No matter what he had or hadn't said, she couldn't imagine him ever killing anyone.

Not on purpose, anyway, a persistent voice in her head added. Stomping to the end of the hallway, she pushed the sweeper ahead of her in vicious little strokes. All right, so Dan had been fighting with Ian earlier that evening. That didn't mean he'd killed him. Yet he'd come back later to the Pennyfoot after the fight. Why? Had he known Ian had come back there? Maybe he'd followed him from the George and Dragon.

She briefly closed her eyes. The vision was strong. She could see Dan creeping across the lawn, candlestick raised above his head, ready to strike. There was Ian, standing by the pond with his back to him, unaware that he was about to die. Dan crept closer and closer, until he was right behind him. He raised his arm and—

A door opened suddenly, close by. It shattered the vision and Gertie started, jerking the sweeper toward her and stubbing her toe. "Bugger!" She stared at the young girl emerging from the guest room. "Mabel! What the bloody hell are you doing here? You're supposed to be in the dining room getting the tables ready for dinner."

Mabel dug her hands into the pockets of her apron. "M-Mrs. Chubb sent me up here. The lady wanted different pillows on the bed. She said the ones she had were too flat."

"Oh." Still distracted by the horrible vision hovering in her head, Gertie waved her arm at the stairs. "Well, you'd better get down there and work on them tables. Pansy's probably having a fit being all by herself."

"All right." Mabel slipped past her and bolted for the stairs.

Shaking her head, Gertie started rehearsing what she was going to say to Dan. All she hoped was that she'd ask the right questions and get the right answers.

Arriving back at the Pennyfoot, Cecily was filled with renewed purpose. If she was to solve this murder, she needed to put more effort into the investigation. She was well aware that her reluctance to act so far had been caused by her concern that the killer might well be someone close to her. She could not afford to dither around any longer.

After taking care of a few tasks waiting for her on her

desk, she sent for Clive. There were questions that needed to be answered.

How she hated the thought that Clive might be Ian's killer. She had always thought of him as being a quiet, private man, with a past that weighed heavily on his conscience. She just couldn't imagine him being violent toward anyone, yet he had apparently removed Ian from the premises, and if Cecily knew anything about Ian Rossiter, it was that he wouldn't have gone without a fight.

So apprehensive was she about the forthcoming exchange she jumped violently when the knock came on the door. She took a moment to compose herself before calling out, "Come in!"

Clive ambled into the room, his face a mask of tension. He obviously had a great deal on his mind, and Cecily wondered if perhaps this was the wrong time to question his recent activities.

"Sit down, Clive." She gestured at the empty chair across from her and waited for him to comply.

His forehead was wrinkled with anxiety when he looked at her, but he remained silent, waiting for her to speak to him first.

Cecily wished now she'd rehearsed what she wanted to ask him. Her heart thumped uncomfortably against her ribs, and her mouth felt dry.

Could she have misjudged her maintenance man? Was he, after all, capable of striking a man in anger, hard enough to kill him? If she questioned him would he perhaps lose control of his temper and attack her?

Wishing she had the answers to those worrisome questions, Cecily folded her hands on her desk and took a deep breath. If she was to get to the bottom of Ian's murder and determine who was responsible, then she would have to take some chances. She could only hope she hadn't underestimated the enemy.

CHAPTER
🏵 17 🏵

"I wanted to talk to you again about the night Ian was killed," Cecily began, having decided that straight to the point was the best strategy.

Clive nodded. "I thought as much."

"You told me that you spent the evening down in the wine cellar."

"Yes, I did."

She wasn't sure if that meant he was saying he did spend the evening in the wine cellar, or that he did tell her he had. She tried again. "Gertie went down there that evening to bring up some wine."

His gaze was steady on her face. "I see."

"You weren't in the wine cellar that night, were you, Clive."

201

"No, m'm. I wasn't."

She could feel her heart beginning to pound even harder. "I have to ask you where you were, Clive."

He stared at her for a long moment, then dropped his gaze. "I'd rather not tell you, m'm."

"There are a lot of things you haven't told me about that night."

"Yes, m'm."

"Gertie told me about locking Ian in the coal shed."

He looked up again, and once more his gaze was steady on her face. "Yes, m'm."

"Would you like to tell me your own version of what happened?"

He thought for a moment, then in a slow, deliberate voice, started talking. "Well, as I said before, I showed Ian the door—or to be more accurate, the gate, earlier that night. I was about to leave to go home later on when I heard voices raised in anger."

She leaned forward. "Where were you exactly when you heard these voices?"

He dropped his gaze again. "I was walking across the bowling greens, m'm."

"That late at night? In the rain?" She narrowed her gaze. "What were you doing out there?"

He sat staring at the floor for a long, tense moment, then muttered, "I'd rather not say."

Cecily clasped her hands in front of her. "Clive, I want very much to help you. I can't do that if you insist on keeping things from me."

He looked up, his eyes pleading with her. "It's a secret, m'm. A Christmas present. I want it to be a surprise."

For a moment Cecily could only stare back at him. His answer had been so utterly unexpected and mundane she would have burst out laughing if the situation hadn't been so grave.

"It's got nothing to do with Ian's death," Clive added, and placed a hand over his heart. "I swear on my honor."

At a loss for words, Cecily leaned back in her chair. Could she believe him? He'd sounded so sincere, yet she knew enough not to trust a seemingly innocent voice.

On the other hand, if he was telling the truth, and she very much wanted to believe he was, she would lose his respect by doubting him now. "Very well, Clive." She managed a faint smile. "Please go on with what you were saying. You heard someone arguing?"

Clive nodded. "I guessed it was Gertie in trouble again so I ran to the kitchen. By the time I got there, she was alone, but she told me Ian had come back and that he was drunk and she'd locked him in the coal shed."

"Yes, that's what she told me."

"Well, she gave me the key and asked me to let him out and make sure that he left. I went back to the shed, but the window was open. He must have climbed up somehow, opened the window, and got out, because he was gone when I opened the door."

"So you took the key back to the kitchen."

"Yes, m'm. Gertie wasn't there, and I waited a while but she didn't come back, so I left. I saw Michel as I was crossing the yard. I knew he was coming back to take out his plum puddings. I could smell them when I was in the kitchen."

Cecily was silent for a moment, turning over his words in her mind. He'd more or less repeated what Gertie had told her, yet his secrecy about what he was doing bothered her. A Christmas present. It was an easy enough excuse to think up, and covered a lot of ground.

There didn't seem to be anything else she could ask him that would be useful. Still troubled, she got to her feet. "Well, thank you, Clive. That will be all for now."

"Yes, m'm." He leapt to his feet, anxiety written all over his face. "I didn't kill Ian Rossiter, m'm. I swear it."

"All right, Clive." She watched him leave, still wondering how much she could trust him. He hadn't worked for her as long as most of her staff, but she had come to rely on him a great deal, to help keep the Pennyfoot running smoothly. Not only that, she had grown fond of him. She considered all of her permanent staff a surrogate family, and Clive was no exception.

She hoped, with all her heart, that he hadn't lost his temper that night and dealt Ian Rossiter a death blow.

Gertie hovered in the doorway of the dining room, disgusted to see that most of the tables were still occupied. She had been in a fever of impatience all through the midday meal, wondering if the guests were ever going to stop talking and get on with the eating.

Pansy and Mabel stood over by the dumbwaiter, whispering together about something. Gertie paid little attention to them. Her stomach was tied up in knots just thinking about the questions she needed to ask Dan, and what his answers might be.

She'd know if he wasn't telling her the truth this time. What she didn't know was what she'd do if she did catch him lying. How could she believe that her Dan, the man she loved with all her heart, had tried to make her look as if she was a murderer?

One thing she did know, if he'd been the one to kill Ian, she wasn't going to take the blame for it. Her babies needed her, and she wasn't going to prison for something she didn't do. She'd turn him in herself if she had to, no matter how much it hurt.

That would be the hard part, turning him in to the bobbies. She didn't know if she could do that, neither. Swamped in misery, she dug her hands into the pockets of her apron. It was so hard for her to believe that Dan was capable of hurting anyone.

Her Dan—the bloke who crept into the orphanage on Christmas Eve to leave presents for the children, and never let on to anyone he was the one what done it. Dan, who played with James and Lillian and gave them rides on his back.

Gertie cleared her throat. The twins would be shattered if Dan had to go to prison. They'd miss him something terrible, and so would she. Closing her eyes, she sent up a brief prayer. *Just don't let it be him.*

Someone brushed past her, and she snapped her eyes open again. The guests were leaving the dining room at last. Now she could get on with clearing the tables, and then get down to the kitchen. The sooner she got done with her chores, the sooner she could get things settled with Dan. One way or another.

It seemed to take forever to get the tables cleared. Gertie could hardly control her temper as Mabel dawdled about, and even Pansy, usually so quick and light on her feet, trudged back and forth as if she was carrying a sack of coal on her shoulders.

"What's the blinking matter with you?" Gertie demanded, when Pansy, after loading an armful of dishes into the waiter, just stood there leaning against the wall.

The young girl shrugged, and turned away. "Nothing. I'm just tired, that's all."

"Well, you'd better bleeding buck up." Gertie gave her a little push to get her going. "We've still got four more tables to clear and it's getting late."

"I don't feel like hurrying."

"What's the matter? Samuel giving you bloody trouble again?"

"He didn't come to the pantomime and he promised me he would."

Gertie sighed. "Maybe he had a job to do." She stacked dinner plates one on top of the other like a pack of cards. "Here, take these. I'll bring the rest."

Pansy looked about ready to cry. "I think he's gone off me."

"Why don't you ask him?"

"What if he tells me he doesn't want to go out with me anymore?"

"Well, at least you'll know." Gertie followed her to the

dumbwaiter, her tray loaded with glasses, plates, and cutlery. She'd know, too, once she talked to Dan. She'd know whether or not she could still dream about a life with him, or if once more she would be left out in the cold, facing a lonely and miserable future.

By the time she got down to the kitchen, she was sure she was going to be sick. She hadn't eaten anything since early that morning, yet the thought of putting food in her stomach made her heave.

She had to force herself to push the kitchen door open. The maids were busy at the sink, halfway through washing the piles of dishes on the counter. Michel had disappeared, and Mrs. Chubb had already left for her afternoon nap.

Gertie had no idea where Pansy had gone, though she suspected it was in search of Samuel. She sent up another quick prayer that her friend wouldn't have to spend Christmas with a broken heart. And that she and the twins wouldn't, either.

Of Dan there was no sign, and she felt relieved that she had a moment or two to try and calm down. She thought about sneaking into the pantry for a sip of Michel's brandy. While she was still thinking about it, however, a pounding on the back door announced Dan's arrival at last. Her stomach took a nosedive, and she hurried to open the door, ignoring the giggles and sly glances from the maids at the sink.

"Sorry I'm late, luv!" Dan dragged off his cap and stepped inside the kitchen. "I got caught up with some paperwork before I left." He bent forward to kiss her but she stepped back, leaving him poked forward like a chicken searching for food.

Looking surprised, he straightened.

Gertie nodded her head at the maids, who were still stealing glances over their shoulders. "I need to talk to you. In private."

He studied her, his face creased in concern. "What's the matter, luv? Not another . . ." He hesitated, glanced at the maids, then finished lamely, "you know what?"

She frowned, too upset to work out what he meant. "Let's go for a walk."

"What, outside? It's cold out there and it's starting to rain."

"We'll go to the wine cellar." She grabbed his sleeve. "Come on."

He followed her, silent and obviously puzzled, as she marched across the yard, heedless of the cold rain spattering across her shoulders and head.

Reaching the door, she fished for the key that she'd dropped into her pocket earlier. The door swung open, and the familiar musty smell greeted her as she stepped inside.

Feeling around in the dark, she found the oil lamp hanging on the wall. She took it down and lit it with the matches she'd brought with her, then held it up to light the way down the stairs.

She heard Dan close the door behind them, shutting them inside the damp, dark cellar. Shivering, she wished she'd stopped for her shawl on the way out.

Reaching the floor below, she hung the lamp on the wall. It swung gently back and forth, sending shadows leaping across the wall.

Dan stepped down beside her, and pulled off his coat. "Here, put this around you before you freeze to death."

DECKED WITH FOLLY

Hugging the warm wool coat around her, she fought back tears. She never cried. Well, hardly ever. This was one time when she was determined not to let the tears fall.

"Now," Dan said, leaning his shoulders against the wall behind him. "What's all this about?"

From the far end of the cellar came the echo of voices from the card rooms. At one time, when gambling had been illegal in the Pennyfoot Hotel, the rooms had been hidden below the floor in a tunnel dug by smugglers long ago.

Now that the Pennyfoot had been turned into a country club, the card games were licensed, and the rooms had been opened up. The floor above them had been removed, so they were in a sort of pit. The guests loved the atmosphere, which still bore an air of decadence without the risk of breaking the law.

Even so, Gertie could sense that sinister feeling of something forbidden closing in on her. She turned an unhappy face to look up at Dan. Had he committed murder? Was he the kind, fun-loving fellow she'd fallen in love with, or a hot-tempered coward prepared to let someone else take the blame for his sins?

Dan's eyes gleamed with the reflection of the flickering flame from the oil lamp. "What is it, Gertie? Have you had enough of me? Are you trying to say good-bye?"

Despite her best efforts, a tear escaped down her cheek. "I don't know."

He shifted away from her, as if bracing himself. "What did I do?"

It was hard to swallow, and she took a moment to answer him. "You tell me."

"I haven't the faintest idea what you're talking about."

She couldn't see his face, but she could hear his voice. She could swear he sounded genuinely confused. Taking a deep breath, she said unsteadily, "You came back to the Pennyfoot the night Ian died."

The pause that followed terrified her. Dan's voice sounded strange when he answered her. "Yes, I came to see you."

"I know, but you came back again later. It must have been after nine o'clock."

Again the pause. "Yes, it was. I told you, I came back to see you."

A tiny flicker of hope caught fire. "I didn't see you."

"I know."

Now he sounded cold, and the hope fluttered out. "I don't understand."

"Gertie, the first time I came to see you that evening, it was to give you and the twins your Christmas presents. I left them in the motorcar so you could help me carry them in. But you were so upset over Ian I decided it wasn't a good time. So I came back later. You weren't there. I went looking for you and you were having some kind of argument in the library with one of the maids. So I gave up. I decided to wait until Christmas Eve in the hopes you'd be in a better mood, and I left."

She almost choked on a sob of relief. Before she could say anything, however, Dan spoke again, in a harsh voice that frightened her.

"You thought I'd killed Ian."

"No, I—"

"Am I that hard to trust? Don't you know me at all? I

thought we had an understanding. Obviously I was wrong."

Now she let the sob out. "I'm sorry, Dan, but when I found out about the fight you had with Ian, and then you lied about having an accident with the motorcar—"

"I did have an accident with the motorcar. It was my fault. I was still fuming about Ian and wasn't paying attention. I didn't tell you that or about the fight in case you blamed yourself. I didn't want to upset you."

She held out a trembling hand to him. "Dan, I'm sorry. I didn't know."

"I didn't lie to you, Gertie. I might have left something out, but I didn't lie to you. I thought you knew me better than that."

"I do, but—"

"I think it's time I left." He turned and started up the stairs.

"Dan!"

Pausing at the top, he looked back at her. His face was lost in the shadows, but there was no mistaking the hurt and resentment in his voice. "You need to have more faith in the people you know. I never once doubted you, even though just about everyone thinks you killed Ian Rossiter."

Her cry of anguish was smothered by the slamming of the door. Sinking onto the bottom step, she buried her face in her apron and sobbed.

CHAPTER

18

Cecily had spent most of the midday meal wrestling with her thoughts, and Baxter was noticeably put out as they left the dining room.

"I understand your eagerness to find out who killed Ian Rossiter," he said, as they approached the stairs. "But I simply must object to the quest taking up your complete attention. I thoroughly dislike having to eat in total silence while watching you dissect every piece of information you might have come across. You used to discuss your thoughts with me. Am I no longer worthy of an opinion?"

Instantly filled with remorse, Cecily tucked her hand in his elbow. "I'm sorry, darling. Really. You're right. I have been far too introspective with this dratted business. I'll be happy to discuss it all with you once we reach the privacy of our suite."

To her relief, Baxter seemed immediately pacified. Squeezing her arm, he murmured, "Once we reach the privacy of our suite I can think of something I'd much rather be doing with you."

She uttered a little gasp of mock horror. "Mr. Baxter, are you suggesting what I think you are suggesting?"

Instead of answering, he looked beyond her, with an odd expression on his face.

Turning her head, she saw one of her most prestigious guests hovering at her side and quite obviously within earshot.

Embarrassed, Cecily withdrew her hand from her husband's arm. "Good afternoon, Lady Roslyn! Is there something we can do for you?"

The woman's cheeks were pink as she glanced from Cecily to Baxter then back again. "I . . . ah . . . I'm sorry to interrupt you, but I would like a quick word with you, Mrs. Baxter, if you could spare the time?"

"Of course!" Cecily looked up at Baxter, disconcerted to see his eyes twinkling with humor. "Go on up, dear. I'll join you in a moment."

Baxter nodded, gave Lady Roslyn a slight bow of his head, then quickly climbed the stairs, out of sight.

Cecily smiled at her uneasy guest. "Would you like to come to my office?"

"Oh, no." Lady Roslyn dug into her handbag for a handkerchief and delicately dabbed her forehead. "I won't keep you but a moment. I didn't want to say anything until I was certain, but there's no doubt in my mind, so I thought I should report it at once."

With growing concern, Cecily drew the woman away from the stairs and closer to the Christmas tree in the corner. She had a nasty feeling she wasn't going to like what her guest had to say. "What is it you need to report? Is something wrong with your room?"

"Oh, no, not at all." Lady Roslyn shook her head to emphasize her words. "The room is lovely, quite exquisite. I just adore the eiderdown. Such a lovely shade of pink."

It was obvious the woman was having trouble saying what she needed to say. Cecily frowned. "What could be the problem then?"

Lady Roslyn glanced around the foyer, to where a group of people stood chatting at the foot of the stairs. Then she leaned forward and whispered, "I'm afraid you have a thief in the Pennyfoot."

"What?" Startled, Cecily had spoken louder than she intended.

Several of the guests turned their heads to look at her.

"Oh, dear," Lady Roslyn murmured. "I did so want to avoid causing a panic."

"It's all right. I don't think they heard what you said." Cecily waved and nodded at the group, some of whom waved back, then resumed their conversation. "What do you mean, a thief? Have you had something stolen?"

"An extremely expensive diamond pendant and a string of valuable pink pearls."

"Oh, my." Cecily clutched her throat, then quickly dropped

her hand as someone from the group glanced at her. "When was the last time you saw them?"

"When my maid unpacked my luggage. They were in my jewelry case in the top drawer of my dresser." Lady Roslyn shook her head. "I should have asked to put them in the safe, but we were too tired to bother that night and I didn't think of it again until I looked for my pearls a little while ago." She sighed. "Now I wish we hadn't been so lazy."

"I really am terribly sorry." Cecily glanced at the clock. "I can assure you, every effort will be made to find your jewelry and apprehend the thief."

To her surprise, Lady Roslyn touched her arm with a sympathetic hand. "Please don't upset yourself, Mrs. Baxter. I know it was no fault of yours. My husband never locks the door when we leave the room. He is a very trusting soul." She made a face. "I think he will try to be a little more careful from now on."

"Well, I can't abide the thought of a thief in the Pennyfoot. I shall certainly look into it and I hope we can return your jewels to you shortly."

"Thank you, Mrs. Baxter. I knew I could rely on you to do what is right." With a gracious nod of her head, Lady Roslyn glided away, exchanging a word or two with the group before ascending the stairs.

Cecily waited until the woman had reached the first landing before approaching the stairs herself. One of the men detached himself from the group and stood in front of her, preventing her from moving forward.

"Mrs. Baxter! Is there any news about who killed Ian Rossiter?"

His words had carried across the room and now the entire group of guests turned and stared at her.

Gritting her teeth, Cecily gave Archie Parker a stern look that she hoped conveyed her displeasure. "Not as yet, Mr. Parker. We are waiting for the return of Constable North-cott, which won't be until after the New Year. So I hope we can all try to forget this unfortunate business and enjoy the Christmas season. All of us at the Pennyfoot Country Club will do our utmost to see that you all have the very best opportunity to do so."

She had addressed the majority of her remarks to the group of guests, and was rewarded with uneasy smiles and nods from all of them. They moved away, leaving her standing with Archie Parker, who still blocked her way to the stairs.

He gave her a sly glance as she made to step forward, but refused to budge to let her pass. "I heard rumors that it could be that young maid, Gertie McBride," he said, lifting his hand to shield his mouth. "I can understand why you wouldn't want to say anything to them." He nodded his head at the stairs.

Cecily glared at him. "Well, you heard wrong. My chief housemaid was not responsible for the unfortunate demise of that young man."

"Oh, really. Then perhaps it was his other wife. Ah . . . Gloria I think her name is. She's staying here, isn't she?"

Cecily narrowed her eyes. "Mr. Parker, you seem to be inordinately interested in this murder case. I have to wonder why."

"Ah." Archie lifted his chin and stared at the chandelier

for a moment or two before looking at her again. "A little hobby of mine, Mrs. B. That's all. I read a lot of detective novels. Sherlock Holmes—my favorite. Cunning man, that, what?"

"Indeed." She suppressed a shudder. The obnoxious little man made her feel as if he knew every single thing about her. As he did everyone else. An idea occurred to her, and she leaned forward. "By the way, Mr. Parker, as long as I have your attention, I would like you to suggest a remedy for my husband's gout. It has been bothering him a lot lately."

Archie looked confused. "G-gout?"

"Yes." She gave him a determined smile. "It's a common complaint. You do have a remedy, don't you?"

"Oh, of course." Archie nodded, his nose twitching furiously. "Of course. Yes, indeed. I . . . ah . . . I'll give it to you the next time I see you."

"Oh, that's all right. I wouldn't want to inconvenience you. I'll come with you now to your room, and you can give it to me now."

"Oh, well, ah . . ." Archie ran a finger around the inside of his collar. "Actually, I don't carry my remedies with me while I'm on vacation."

"Oh, I thought you said you would give it to me."

"Ah, yes, I did. I forgot." He coughed. "If you will excuse me—"

"You are not in the business of selling remedies, are you, Mr. Parker."

Archie sent a hunted look over his shoulder. "Mrs. B., I assure you—"

"One more thing." She paused just long enough to make

sure no one else was within earshot. The group near the stairs had dispersed, most likely having retired to their rooms. "I'm curious to know how you knew that the murder weapon was a candlestick, and taken from the hallstand."

All the air seemed to rush out of Archie's lungs. He stared at her, his face set in stone, with not even a quiver from his nose. A subtle change seemed to come over him. He actually seemed taller, formidable, and just a little threatening.

It suddenly occurred to Cecily that she was in a vulnerable position. There was no one in the foyer now. Even Philip had disappeared from behind the desk, no doubt enjoying a late lunch. Most of the guests would now be taking an afternoon siesta in their rooms, or perhaps finishing off their Christmas shopping.

She was alone with a potential killer, and completely at his mercy.

Still huddled on the steps, Gertie raised her head as laughter echoed along the cellar's damp walls. Her arms felt stiff with cold, and she stretched out her legs, wincing as a cramp knotted her calf.

It was only then that she realized she still had Dan's coat around her shoulders. A tiny stab of hope lifted her chin. She would have to see him at least one more time. Maybe she could set things straight with him after all. Maybe her Christmas wouldn't have to be the heartache she'd envisioned.

Slowly she got to her feet and stamped them to get the circulation going again. Dan must be freezing out there without his coat. Then again, he could still be in the kitchen, waiting for her to come back in before he went home.

Galvanized into action, she grabbed the lamp from the wall, turned down the wick, and leapt up the stairs in the dark. Hitting the door with her shoulder, she shoved it open, then hung the lamp on its hook.

The mist was rolling in again from the sea as she crossed the yard, and she hugged the coat closer to her. Dan had to be waiting for her in the kitchen. He just had to be.

She was almost at the kitchen door when someone stepped out in front of her, frightening her out of her wits. In that first instant her heart leapt in the hopes it was Dan, but it was Sid Barrett who stood there grinning at her.

In no mood for his nonsense, she shoved him aside, but he held out his arms, blocking her way.

"What's yer hurry, beautiful?"

Outraged, she tried to push him aside. "Out of my way, you rotten sod, or I'll tell madam what a bully you are. She doesn't like bullies and nor do I."

"I just want to talk to you a minute, that's all." He lowered his arms but held his ground. "I know you must be missing a man's attention, now that your husband is gone."

She stared at him, disturbed by the gleam in his eyes. "No I don't, so there. I told you I have a boyfriend."

"Oh, you do, do you. Does he spoil you, then? Give you jewels and things?"

She tried to tug her arm free but he held on. "That's none of your business what he does."

"I bet your husband spoiled you, didn't he. I bet he gave you lots of pretty things."

"You leave Ross out of this. You have no business talking to me about him."

Sid shook his head. "I'm not talking about him. I meant your dead husband, Ian Rossiter."

Gertie puffed out her breath. "I keep telling you, he was never my husband. Go and ask his real wife if you want to know anything about him."

An odd expression crossed Sid's face. "I thought you were his real wife."

He let go of her and stepped back. Rubbing her arm, she glared at him. "I told you, I never was his wife. His real wife is Gloria Johnson. She's staying right here at the Pennyfoot. Why don't you bleeding ask her about flipping Ian Rossiter?"

Sid's eyes opened wide, and his mouth dropped open. He started to speak, but never got the chance to say anything. A burly arm wrapped around his throat, dragging him backward. With a choking cry he staggered back, scrabbling to stay on his feet.

"Is this little rat bothering you?" Clive asked, his voice deceptively calm.

Still rubbing her arm, Gertie looked anxiously at Clive's face. His jaw was set at a dangerous angle, and his eyes glowered with fury.

Visions of him holding a candlestick aloft shot into her mind. He was capable of killing. Looking at him at that moment, she had no doubt of that. Afraid for him, for what he might do, she shook her head. "It's all right, Clive. Really. Sid was just leaving, weren't you, Sid."

Held fast in Clive's powerful grip, Sid's face was pinched

with fear. His voice hoarse and high-pitched, he gasped out, "I wasn't going to hurt her, honest. I just wanted to talk to her, that's all. I was just going. I swear I was."

For answer, Clive gave him a hefty shove, sending him sprawling on the wet pavement. "Well, next time you talk to a lady, be a little more polite about it, or you'll have to answer to me."

Scrambling to his feet, Sid pulled his collar away from his neck. He looked about to say something, but Clive beat him to it.

"You've got exactly five seconds to get out of my sight, before I lose my temper and give you the thrashing you deserve. One, two . . ."

Sid opened his mouth, and Clive took a threatening step toward him. That was enough for Sid. He leapt for the gate, dragged it open, and fled through it, leaving it swinging behind him.

Gertie gave Clive a grateful smile as he moved toward her. "Thank you, Clive. You're always coming to my rescue lately. I wish there was something I could do for you in return."

The big man hesitated, as if there were something he desperately wanted to say. Apparently thinking better of it, he shook his head instead. "No need, miss. I'm glad to be of help."

She reached out and touched his arm. "Call me Gertie. Everybody does."

He glanced down at the spot she'd touched, then smiled. "All right, Gertie."

She suddenly remembered why she'd been in such a

hurry. "I've got to go. Thank you, Clive!" Without waiting for him to respond, she turned and ran for the kitchen door.

Bursting inside, she came to a halt, disappointment draining all her energy. The room was empty. Dan hadn't waited for her after all.

Sighing, she crossed the room to the hallway door. He'd have to come back for his coat. She still had that to hang on to, and if he didn't, she'd take it to him. What she had to say to him could wait until then.

CHAPTER
✿ 19 ✿

Standing in the hallway, Cecily considered her options. Simply running away didn't seem like a good idea; neither did yelling for help. After all, if she was wrong about Archibald Parker, and she seemed to be wrong about a lot of people lately, either action would seem pretty ridiculous.

Deciding that her best chance was to keep Archie talking in the hopes someone would come along, Cecily said quickly, "As a matter of fact, you were quite right about the murder weapon. It was a candlestick taken from the hallstand."

Archie's steady gaze never left her face. "You have it in your possession, I assume."

"Ah . . . not in my possession, no. It is safely in the hands of the proper authorities."

He looked at her as if he didn't believe her. "I see. And what have you deduced from that?"

She did her best to look innocent. "Absolutely nothing, Mr. Parker. It isn't my position to chase after a murderer. I prefer to leave that dangerous job to the constabulary."

"Very wise, Mrs. B. Very wise."

There was no doubt in her mind that his words were a subtle threat. Out of the corner of her eye Cecily saw with relief one of the footmen rush in through the front door. It was Sid Barrett, and he appeared to have been running, since he was gasping for breath.

He pulled up with a start when he saw Cecily and Archie Parker. "Oh, excuse me, m'm. I was just coming in to see if you needed me for anything. I'll be taking my two hours off in a few minutes."

Cecily had the distinct impression that Sid's hurried entrance was due to something far more personal than any desire to offer his services. She was vastly relieved to see him, however, whatever the reason for his haste.

"As a matter of fact, Sidney," she said, giving him a bright smile, "I do have an errand for you." She turned back to Archie Parker, who once more looked like the fussy little man with whom she was accustomed. "If you will excuse me, Mr. Parker, I have to take care of some business matters."

"By all means, Mrs. B. Good day to you." Nose twitching and shoulders hunched, he clambered up the stairs.

Cecily turned back to Sid, just in time to see resentment burning his face.

His expression quickly smoothed out when she looked at him. "What can I do for you, m'm?"

DECKED WITH FOLLY

Cecily shook her head. "Oh, that's all right, Sidney. It's a small matter and I can take care of it myself. Go on and enjoy your afternoon."

"Yes, m'm. Thank you, m'm." He touched his forehead with his fingers, but instead of leaving again by the front door, he headed for the kitchen stairs.

Cecily frowned, wondering for the first time why he hadn't used the tradesmen's entrance through the kitchen when he came in.

She had far more worries on her mind, however, and now she was in a hurry. She couldn't wait to get to her suite and discuss the latest developments with her husband.

Baxter looked up as Cecily threw open the door of their suite a few minutes later. "That was a long moment." He narrowed his gaze, peering at her over the top of his newspaper. "Is something wrong?"

"Everything." She crossed the room and flung herself onto her favorite chair. "Lady Roslyn informed me that someone has stolen jewelry from her room, and I have just had a most disturbing discussion with Archie Parker."

Baxter's newspaper rustled as he slapped it down on his lap. "Stolen? Are you telling me there's a thief here in the Pennyfoot?"

"I'm afraid so." Cecily sighed. "Worse, I think it's one of our staff."

"Good Lord. Why do you think so?"

"Mrs. Chubb told me that she'd also lost a ring. She thought it had fallen down the kitchen sink, but I'm wondering now if it was stolen. It's not like her to be so careless."

Baxter groaned. "That's all we need. A murderer and a

thief running around the Pennyfoot. This place is fast becoming a den of iniquity. I think it's high time we moved back to London."

She gave him an unhappy look. "You think that London is free from crime?"

"Of course not. But if we're living in a decent neighborhood there's much less chance of it being committed right under our noses."

Cecily stretched out her legs and regarded the toes of her shoes peeking out from under her skirt. "I used to be so good at solving these puzzles. I must be getting old. I don't seem to be getting anywhere with Ian's murder, and now we have something else to worry about."

"We'll have to make sure that everyone locks their doors." Baxter folded his newspaper and stood up. "I'll arrange for a thorough search of the staff rooms."

Cecily looked up in alarm. "Oh, I really don't want to do that. Besides, it could be any of the staff who don't live in. We hire all this extra help at Christmas and we really don't know any of them very well. Take that Sidney Barrett, for instance. There's something about him I just don't like."

"Barrett? What about him?"

"I don't know." Cecily thought about it. "For one thing, he thinks he's a lady's man. I've seen him pestering one of the maids, and Gertie has complained about him. I warned him to leave the girls alone. I'd get rid of him if we weren't so busy."

"Well, he won't be here for much longer. Only until the guests leave after New Year's Day."

"Then there's Mabel." Cecily shook her head. "I feel sorry

for that girl but she's really not a very good worker. I won't be sorry to see her leave, either."

"She'll be gone in a week or two. Then you won't have to worry about her anymore."

"Not only that, I found out that Gloria lied about the night Ian was killed, and I need to talk to her about that. I just can't seem to make any headway on this dratted murder."

Baxter walked over to her and took her hand. "Poor Cecily. This is turning out to be a trying time for you. I meant what I said, you know. Maybe it's time we started thinking about going back to London."

She looked up at him. "You know how I feel about that. The Pennyfoot is our home, the staff is our family. With my sons abroad I have no other family here. I'll be too lonely in London. We tried it once and I was miserable."

Baxter sighed and lifted her fingers to his lips. "Yes, I suppose you were. But all the upheaval and misadventures are not exactly making you happy, either."

She smiled. "They are keeping me alive. In London I was merely existing. Besides, in spite of everything, I do enjoy the challenge."

He let go of her hand and walked back to his chair. Sitting down, he murmured, "I confess, Cecily, there are times when I just don't understand you."

"Perhaps that's just as well."

He raised his eyebrows. "What does that mean?"

She laughed. "Only that it makes things interesting, don't you think?"

He grunted a reply, then retreated behind his newspaper.

Cecily remained silent for a moment, wondering if she

should tell him about her encounter with Archie Parker. The more she talked to that odd little man, the more strangely he acted. If it wasn't for a complete lack of motive, she might have suspected him of killing Ian.

Impatient with herself, she shook her head. She had reached the point where she suspected everyone she met of being a murderer. Yet none of her suspects had convinced her that any one of them was a killer. Perhaps she hadn't, yet, met the real murderer. It could be someone totally unconnected to the Pennyfoot. One of Ian's unsavory companions, perhaps.

Still there was the matter of the candlestick, taken from the hallstand and left in Gertie's room. That suggested an intimate knowledge of the country club.

What she really needed to do, she decided, was find out if anyone else in the Pennyfoot had a motive to attack Ian. How she would go about it would take some thought, and judging from the silence from behind her husband's newspaper, she had plenty of time to do that.

"What's the matter with you? You look like you've swallowed a bowl of lemons."

Gertie lifted her head and frowned at Mrs. Chubb. The housekeeper stood on the other side of the kitchen table, busily kneading pastry for the Cornish pasties.

Wary of Michel stirring his vegetable soup at the stove, Gertie murmured, "I was just wondering if I should tell madam something, that's all."

"Tell her what?"

DECKED WITH FOLLY

Gertie went on folding the serviette, fitted it into a silver holder, then laid it on top of the neat pile on the tray at her side. "Tell her about Sid Barrett."

Knowing she had aroused Mrs. Chubb's curiosity, Gertie waited.

Sure enough, after a long pause, the housekeeper raised her voice. "Gertie, I'm going to need some more lard from the pantry."

"Right away, Mrs. Chubb." Gertie dropped the next serviette and headed for the pantry.

Seconds later, Mrs. Chubb appeared in the doorway. "What's taking you so long?" she demanded loudly, then stepped inside and closed the door. Lowering her voice, she muttered, "All right, now what's all this about Sid Barrett?"

Rapidly Gertie relayed most of what Sid had said to her earlier. "Then Clive came along and chased the bugger off," she said, when she was done. "That man always manages to turn up at the right time."

"Doesn't he, though." Mrs. Chubb shook her head. "I don't like the sound of this at all, Gertie. I never did like that Sid. Always hanging around the women he is, and now he's making a real nuisance of himself. I think we should tell madam about it. I'll run up and have a word with her just as soon as I finish rolling out the pastry for Michel."

"Which," Michel said from the doorway, "I hope will be in the next moment or two, so I still have the time to bake the pasties for supper."

Gertie jumped, and Mrs. Chubb looked guilty. "I'll be right there," she said, and gave Gertie a warning glance before hurrying out of the pantry.

Gertie didn't need the warning. The golden rule in the Pennyfoot was to keep one's mouth shut. She knew better than to spread gossip about someone on the staff, or worse, a guest. It was one thing madam was stern about. But something still worried her about the incident. Something she hadn't told Mrs. Chubb. She shouldn't have told Sid about Gloria, because now he was probably going to pester her, too.

Gertie rubbed her forehead. Maybe she should warn Gloria, since it was her fault Sid found out about her.

Thinking about her run-in with Sid reminded her of how Clive had looked when he'd dragged Sid back by his throat.

She hadn't mentioned that to Mrs. Chubb, either. It frightened her to think of Clive being capable of murder. She'd always thought of him as a gentle giant. Her and the twins' protector. Yet that glimpse of him that afternoon had revealed another side of him.

It wasn't the first time. She'd seen him wrestle with Ian once before, when Ian had tried to kidnap Lillian. For a few minutes Clive had turned into someone she didn't know. Could he have fought with Ian again, and killed him this time? If so, he had done so to protect her. She was sure of that.

On the other hand, that would mean that he was the one that put the candlestick under her bed to make it look like she did it. No, she couldn't believe that. She *wouldn't* believe that. She'd already done that with Dan, suspected him for all the wrong reasons. She wasn't going to make that mistake again.

Returning to her task, she put her problems out of her mind for the time being. She had too much to think about, what with fretting about Dan, getting supper out for the guests, and seeing to her twins. She'd worry about Gloria later.

The next hour or so passed in a rush as Gertie and the rest of the maids scrambled to serve supper to the hungry guests. It was the night before Christmas Eve, and everyone was in a merry mood. The dining room rang with laughter and noisy chatter, and there was more than one guest who enjoyed one too many glasses of sherry and had to be guided out the door.

By the time all the dishes were collected and sent back to the kitchen, and the tablecloths changed and the floors swept, Gertie felt a hundred years old. All she wanted to do was go back to her room and rest her aching feet.

She went back to the kitchen for the last time to help put the clean dishes away. She was surprised to see Mrs. Chubb sitting at the table. Usually the housekeeper retired for the night once supper was served.

"I waited for you," she said, when Gertie walked up to her. "I've got something to tell you."

Gertie glanced at the maids giggling at the sink. "In the pantry?"

"All right." Mrs. Chubb got up and led the way. Once inside the tiny, cold room she closed the door until just a sliver of light shone through. "I had a word with madam," she said. "It looks as if we have a jewel thief in the Pennyfoot. Madam told me that one of the guests had some jewelry stolen from her room."

Gertie gasped. "Does she know who took it?"

"No, she doesn't. But whoever it was could have taken my ring as well."

"Wait a minute." Gertie clutched her throat as an idea came to her. "What guest was it who was robbed?"

Mrs. Chubb hesitated. "I'm not supposed to say, but madam did say it was room eleven, and that's Lady Roslyn's room."

"Oh, blimey."

"What's the matter?"

Gertie sighed. "Well, I don't know if this has anything to do with it, but I saw Mabel coming out of there this morning. I couldn't think what she was doing up there, but she said you sent her up there to change the pillows in Lady Roslyn's room so I didn't think no more of it."

Mrs. Chubb sounded grim when she answered. "I didn't send her up there. She was lying about that. I think we need to talk to that young lady. It's too late now, she's already gone home, but first thing in the morning I will find out what's going on with her."

"I don't want to get her into trouble or anything."

"If she didn't take the jewels then she's got nothing to worry about." Mrs. Chubb reached for the door handle. "I was going to ask Clive to take off the pipe underneath the sink to see if he could find my ring, but now I think I'll wait until I talk to Mabel."

Gertie gulped. "You think she took it?"

"I don't know what to think. This is all very upsetting, coming so soon after all the upset over Ian. I suppose we'll find out more in the morning." The housekeeper pushed the door open. "It's Christmas Eve tomorrow. I hate the thought of all this trouble right on Christmas."

"We could be mistaken," Gertie said hopefully. "Mabel

could have had a really good reason to be up there, and just didn't want to tell me."

Mrs. Chubb tightened her lips. "Perhaps, but whatever she was doing up there, I'm going to find out about it."

Gertie followed her out into the kitchen, feeling sorry for the young maid. She hadn't really liked Mabel all that much, but the girl walked around as if she carried the troubles of the world on her shoulders, and Gertie felt sort of responsible for her. She just hoped that it was all a mistake and she wouldn't have to worry what happened to the poor thing over Christmas.

It took another hour for her to put all the dishes away and get the kitchen cleaned up. Mrs. Chubb had sent the maids home, so she was all alone when she finally hung the tea towels over the stove to dry.

A quick glance at the clock told her it was time to go back to her room and relieve Daisy. The twins would hopefully be asleep, so she could just go to bed and drift off herself. Though somehow she knew that with Dan on her mind, as well as all the trouble with thieves and worrying about Clive being a murderer, it would take a long time for her to go to sleep.

Perhaps tomorrow, she thought, as she trudged down the hallway. Perhaps tomorrow they'd find out that Ian was the thief and not Mabel, that someone else and not Clive killed Ian, and that Dan would come to the carol singing like he'd promised and they could make up. That was what she hoped for most of all.

CHAPTER
❁ 20 ❁

"I told you that Mabel was up to no good." Gertie pointed to the clock on the kitchen mantelpiece. "I had a feeling when I got up this morning that something was going to go wrong. It's seven o'clock and she's still not here."

Mrs. Chubb sighed. "That's all we need. The busiest days of the Christmas season and we're short a maid. Well, you and Pansy will just have to work a bit harder, that's all." She wiped her hands on her apron. "I'll go and tell madam that Mabel's not here."

"Well, now you can't ask her what she was doing in Lady Roslyn's room." Gertie slapped a handful of polished forks onto the tray in front of her. "So we still don't know for sure if she took the jewels or not."

"You just can't trust anyone these days, and that's a fact.

You'd better get upstairs and help Pansy with the serving." Still grumbling to herself, Mrs. Chubb swung open the door and left.

Standing with Pansy at the dumbwaiter a few minutes later, Gertie waited for the load of dishes to arrive, her mind more on the coming evening than on the food waiting to be served. The day stretched before her like an endless ocean, hours to go before she had any hope of seeing Dan. He'd promised to come to the carol singing, and after that, she was supposed to help him distribute the toys to the orphanage.

She had no way of knowing if he would turn up, or if he would want her to help him with the toys. In fact, she didn't even know if she would see him again, after the way he left her last night.

A sharp nudge in her side made her jump. Pansy was staring at her, her head to one side.

"What?" Gertie swiped a strand of hair out of her eyes. "Did I grow another nose or something?"

Pansy grinned. "I was just wondering what you were thinking. That Sid Barrett walked right past you and you never even blinked an eye."

"Don't talk to me about Sid Barrett." Gertie leaned into the waiter and peered down the shaft. At the bottom someone was loading dishes, and she pulled back. "He's a shifty one. Up to no good, if you ask me."

"Go on." Pansy laughed. "He's all right. I've been thinking about going out with him. He was really nice to me this morning and asked me to go out with him, so I just might do that."

Gertie gave her a dark look. "If I were you, Pansy Watson, I'd stay far away from him. There's something nasty about him, you mark my words."

Pansy shrugged. "You're just jealous, that's all."

Gertie's derisive laugh echoed down the hallway. "Jealous? Of that smarmy snake? I wouldn't trust him farther than my little finger. He's always snooping around, listening to what everyone is saying. Remember when he was listening to us in the dining room? We didn't even know he was there."

Pansy frowned. "Yeah, I do remember. You know, I always thought that was really strange."

Gertie looked at her. "What was strange?"

"Well, you know, how Sid knew Ian's last name. When we were standing there talking about Ian dying and everything, we never said his last name. But then Sid came in and called him Ian Rossiter, like he already knew him."

Gertie stared at her a moment longer. Just then a loud rattle stole her attention and she turned to see the dishes sitting in the dumbwaiter. "Well, we'd better get a move on and get this food served up before it gets cold."

She grabbed a tray and headed for the dining room. She didn't want to think about Ian or Sid Barrett. She didn't even want to think about Dan, because when she did she got an awful ache in her stomach just thinking about what she'd do if he didn't turn up for the carol singing.

Cecily had risen early that morning, eager to get the day started. The first order of business was to talk to Gloria, and the best way to catch the woman was to wait for her in the hallway outside the dining room.

Baxter was a little put out when Cecily informed him she would meet him at the breakfast table, instead of going down together as they usually did, but when she explained why, he reluctantly agreed.

She was halfway down the stairs when she met Mrs. Chubb panting and puffing on her way up them. The housekeeper looked agitated, and Cecily felt a pang of apprehension, sensing more trouble.

"It's Mabel," Mrs. Chubb said, gasping for breath. "She didn't come in this morning. What's more, we think she's the jewel thief."

Cecily grasped the handrail a little tighter. "Mabel? That's ridiculous."

"Well . . ." Mrs. Chubb paused, her hand on her chest while she fought to steady her breathing. "Gertie saw Mabel up on the landing. She was coming out of Lady Roslyn's room. She told Gertie I sent her up there to change the pillows, but I never did. So what was she doing in there, that's what I'd like to know? She had to be the one that took the jewels. She must have known we were on to her and that's why she didn't come in this morning."

"Oh, dear." Cecily glanced down the stairs, relieved to see they were quite alone. "I'm sorry, Altheda. Manage as best you can without her and in the meantime I'll do my best to find her and bring her back here."

"Yes, m'm." The housekeeper clicked her tongue. "She seemed such a quiet little thing. Who would have thought she was a thief." She turned and clambered back down the stairs, while Cecily followed more slowly.

She had to agree, Mabel certainly didn't fit her idea of a jewel thief. She was a sad little thing, not too bright and certainly not very industrious. Not at all the kind of person one would think of as a criminal. Cecily shook her head. How could she have been so gullible? She should have better judgement when hiring her staff.

Stationed outside the dining room at the first clang of the breakfast bell, Cecily tried to shake off her melancholy as she greeted each guest as they arrived.

Gloria was one of the last to appear, and she didn't look at all happy, which was not really surprising considering she had just lost her husband.

Cecily stepped in front of her as she reached the door and gently took her arm. "I won't keep you more than a minute or two," she murmured, as she led the surprised woman away from the dining room. "I would like to have a word with you in my office."

Gloria offered no resistance, but meekly allowed herself to be ushered into Cecily's office and onto a chair.

"Now," Cecily said, as she sat down opposite her, "I want to talk to you about the last time you saw your husband."

Gloria's expression grew wary. "What about it? I told you all I know."

"I don't think you have." Cecily leaned forward, fastening her gaze on the other woman's face. "You told me you went to bed after Ian left the house that night, and that you never saw him again."

Gloria started fidgeting on her chair, but didn't answer.

Cecily tried again. "According to Bernard McPherson, the owner of the George and Dragon, you went to the public house to find your husband, isn't that so?"

Gloria stared down at her feet and mumbled, "Yes."

"Why didn't you tell me that?"

"I dunno."

Cecily sighed. "One more thing, how did you know Ian was fighting and received a black eye if you didn't see him again?"

Gloria jutted her lower lip. "Someone told me."

"I don't think so, Gloria. I think you saw Ian later that night, after the fight."

Gloria shrugged, but remained silent.

Cecily softened her tone. "I want to help you, but you need to tell me everything. What really happened that night?"

Tears squeezed out of Gloria's eyes and drifted down her cheeks. "It's all my fault. If I hadn't been so horrible to him he might have come home with me and then he would still be alive."

"Why don't you tell me what happened?"

Gloria lifted her chin, misery dulling her eyes. "When they told me Robert had left the pub, I guessed he'd come here. He wanted to see his children and Gertie wouldn't let him. So when I heard that he'd been fighting I knew he was in a really bad mood and that he'd probably try to bully Gertie into letting him see the twins."

"Well, you were right about that." Cecily leaned back on her chair. "Ian did come here to see Gertie."

A fierce light glowed in Gloria's eyes for a moment. "I know. I came here to find him. I came in the back way and I heard him arguing with Gertie. Then I saw her lock him in the coal shed. I waited until she was gone then I went to let him out. She'd taken the key with her, so I had to open a window and Ian climbed out."

"Ah, so it was you who helped him get out."

Gloria nodded. "He was spitting mad. So was I. I told him I knew he was trying to get back with Gertie, even though deep down I knew he only wanted his children. We had a terrible argument, and I kept asking him to come home with me, but he wouldn't. He said he was going to see the twins and nobody was going to stop him."

She shuddered, and fell silent.

"And that was the last time you saw him?"

After a moment Gloria spoke again, her voice thick with pain. "He stormed off toward the door, and I went the other way, to go home, without him. I never saw him again."

Cecily waited a moment or two for her to regain her composure. "Why didn't you tell me all this in the very beginning?"

"I thought I might get blamed for killing him." Gloria rubbed her upper arms, as if she were cold. "We were arguing, really loudly. I didn't know if someone might have heard us, and everyone would think I was the one that hit him."

"I see." Cecily clasped her hands in front of her. "Did you see anyone else in the yard that night?"

"No, m'm. Only Gertie and Ian."

"Is there anything else you can tell me? Something you might have forgotten? Something that Ian said that might help us figure out who killed him?"

Gloria lifted her shoulders and let them drop. "Nothing. I wish I did know something, but I don't."

"Very well." Cecily got to her feet. "Thank you, Gloria, for telling me the truth."

"Yes, m'm. I should have done it before, I know, but I was scared I'd be blamed."

"That's all right. It's understandable, under the circumstances." Cecily moved to the door and opened it. "But I hope you know that if you are in trouble, or need to talk to someone, you can always come to me. I'm very good at keeping confidences."

A thin smile washed across the other woman's face. "Thank you, m'm. You're very kind. I'll remember that in future."

Cecily gave her a few minutes to reach the dining room before following her. Going over their conversation, and what she knew so far, she could now piece together the events of that night.

Ian had come to the kitchen door demanding to see the twins. Gertie had refused. Clive had arrived on the scene and removed Ian, who had then gone down the pub. Dan had come to see Gertie a little later, learned of the quarrel, and gone down the pub to have it out with Ian.

After they'd fought, Ian had returned to the Pennyfoot, followed by Gloria. Ian had met Gertie by the coal shed and she'd locked him in. Gloria had then let him out, quarreled with him, and gone home without him. Gertie had given Clive the key, but by the time Clive got to the coal shed, Ian had gone.

Where? Who had really been the last one to see Ian alive? Ian must have met up with someone else after Gloria had left. Was it Dan, come back to finish the fight? Had Clive lied about Ian being gone when he got back to the coal shed? Or was Gloria not telling the truth when she said she'd left Ian alive and well?

Cecily sighed. Her head ached with the questions, theories, and possible scenarios. All these people involved with that night, all of them with a motive. This had to be the most puzzling murder she'd ever come across.

"Mrs. B.!"

Snatched out of her thoughts, Cecily came to an abrupt halt. Archie Parker stood before her, his nose quivering. "Yes, Mr. Parker. Is there something I can do for you?"

"I'd like a quick word with you, if I may?" Archie looked over his shoulder. "I won't keep you a minute."

Cecily looked longingly at the dining room door, so close and yet so far. By now Baxter would be seated and impatiently waiting for her. "Very well, Mr. Parker, but it will have to be just a minute or two. I have an urgent appointment."

"Yes, yes. I swear I won't take long." He looked down the empty corridor and beckoned to her. "Perhaps if we move down here no one will hear us."

Immediately on guard, Cecily reluctantly followed him down the hallway.

Archie paused in front of the broom closet, and gave her a toothy smile. "I was just wondering . . . ah . . . how many extra people did you hire for the Christmas season?"

Cecily straightened her back. "What concern is that of yours, may I ask?"

"I'm not at liberty to say." Archie's face once again took

on that strange transformation. "Just answer the question, please."

Taken aback, Cecily glared at him. "I must say, I do not appreciate your tone, Mr. Parker. In fact, if anyone should be asking questions, I should be the one asking you."

Archie drew himself up and squared his shoulders. His entire personality seemed to change from a nervous little weakling to a decisive and somewhat intimidating superior. "Ask ahead, Mrs. B. I'll be happy to answer."

Nervous now, she fought to keep her voice calm and unemotional. "What exactly is your interest in my staff?"

Archie glanced once more down the hallway, then lowered his voice. "I must ask you to promise that anything I say to you will not be repeated. To anyone. Is that clear?"

Cecily hesitated, reluctant to make a promise she knew she couldn't keep.

"It is the only way you will get answers to your questions, and what I have to say may benefit us both."

That was just too promising to ignore. "I'll do my best to keep whatever you say to myself."

For a moment Archie's keen gaze raked her face, then he nodded. "Very well. I'm not a salesman. I have no knowledge of medical remedies whatsoever."

Deflated, Cecily frowned. "I knew that already."

"Yes, but you don't know what I really am." He looked both ways, leaned toward her and muttered, "I'm a private investigator."

Cecily felt her jaw slacken. "A what?"

"Private investigator. Somewhat like yourself, I suspect, only I do it for a living."

"Oh, my." Cecily stepped back and leaned against the wall. "I had no idea."

"Of course you didn't. I'm good at my job."

"Are you investigating Mr. Rossiter's murder? I thought that was a matter for the constabulary."

"Well, I have a certain vested interest in the case." Archie patted his vest pocket, then pulled out a packet of cigarettes. Extracting one, he stuck it between his lips and went on talking. "Actually I'd been keeping an eye on Rossiter for some time in London. I knew he was fencing stolen goods, you see."

Cecily uttered a shocked gasp. "Ian? Are you quite certain?"

"Oh, yes." Archie pulled out a box of matches from his trousers pocket and opened it. Taking one out, he struck it and held the flame to his cigarette. "About a month ago, a robbery took place at a distinguished client's mansion. I'm not at liberty to divulge the name of the client, but I can tell you he is a prominent citizen of London."

Cecily, still grappling with the idea of Ian being a professional criminal, waited for him to go on.

Archie puffed on his cigarette, then waved the match in the air until the flame went out. "There had been a string of robberies in the vicinity, and the police hadn't had any luck finding the culprits, so this client hired me to find the thieves and return his jewels if possible."

"I see," Cecily said faintly. "And you think Ian was part of the gang?"

"Not sure about that part. He might have been working independently as a fence." Archie looked around for somewhere to deposit the spent match. "In any case, when I heard from one of my sources that Rossiter had attempted to fence a large haul of jewelry, I suspected he might be connected to the thieves. So I made the acquaintance of Mrs. Gloria Johnson, as a salesman of medicinal remedies. Luckily for me, she suffers from headaches, and I was able to convince her that my special elixir would cure them." He smiled, preening a little. "It's amazing what the power of the mind can do to heal ailments."

Cecily thought of Madeline, then dismissed the thought. There was a world of difference between Madeline's special powers and this imposter's fake cures.

"Anyway," Archie said, still waving the burned out match in the air, "Mrs. Johnson and I became familiar enough that she let slip a few things. Such as the fact that they were moving down here to Badgers End, and that her husband used to work at the Pennyfoot when it was a hotel."

Spotting a large potted aspidistra, he walked over, dropped the match into the pot, and sauntered back to Cecily. "Now where was I? Ah yes. Well, according to my source, the stolen jewels that Rossiter had tried to fence were too hot to get rid of safely, so he was advised to hang on to them until things cooled down. When his wife told me they were moving, I guessed he'd decided to keep the jewels for himself, and was leaving town so that the gang couldn't find him and get them back."

Cecily grasped her throat. "Ian was running away from a gang of criminals?"

"That's what I believe." He winked at Cecily. "What better place to sell off really valuable jewelry than to the guests of the Pennyfoot Country Club? It has quite a remarkable reputation in London, you know."

"Yes," Cecily said, her voice still faint with shock. "I had heard."

"Yes, well, it's well known that many aristocrats enjoy a visit to the country club, and I believe that Rossiter decided there would be opportunities for him to get rid of the jewels. Besides, it was a good place to hide."

"But he was working in the butcher's shop and living in the flat above. Why would he do that if he had all that money?"

"Ah." Archie nodded. "It's my belief that he left London with nothing but the jewels. That way it would take longer for the thieves to realize he was gone. He had to live somewhere until he could sell the loot, so he took the job at the butcher's to tide him over."

Cecily passed a hand over her forehead. "I'm still having trouble believing all this. Did Gloria know her husband was involved in all this criminal activity?"

"I don't believe so." Archie frowned. "Hard to tell. Anyway, it's my belief that the gang found out where he was, and sent someone to get their goods back."

"Do you think this someone killed him?"

"It's possible, I suppose, which is why I'd like to know who did it. It could lead me back to the gang. My main concern is finding the jewels and getting them back."

"Ian could have hidden them. I doubt he carried them around with him all the time."

"My thoughts exactly." Archie puffed on his cigarette. "I

searched his flat, of course. Nothing there." He gave her a sly look. "I don't suppose you have any ideas where they might be?"

"None at all." She hesitated. "I can tell you that someone here in the Pennyfoot is stealing jewelry. One of my guests reported some missing, as well as one of my staff."

Archie frowned. "Interesting. Any ideas who it might be?"

A vision of Mabel's sad face popped into Cecily's mind. "I'm afraid not. We have only just found out about it."

"So the robberies happened after Rossiter was killed?"

"Yes, we believe so."

"Hmm." Archie puffed smoke into the air. "In that case, I'd say our thief hasn't found Rossiter's jewels yet, and is still here, looking for them."

"Oh, dear. I should probably warn the guests."

"I wouldn't do that, Mrs. B. Give him a free hand, that's what I say. We're more likely to catch him in the act."

Cecily wasn't at all comfortable with that idea. She could only hope the detective knew what he was doing.

"In the meantime," Archie said, "I'll have to see what Mrs. Johnson can tell me. She still thinks I'm a salesman. I told her I decided to try the Pennyfoot after she told me about it, but I think she's suspicious of me anyway."

"Well, I certainly hope you find the jewels soon, and the thief."

"So do I, Mrs. B. So do I." He turned to leave, then paused, looking back at her. "Have you considered the possibility that your chief housemaid might have killed Rossiter? I heard her threatening him the night he died. As I told the constable, anyone making threats like that was capable of carrying them out. She's a strong lady, I don't doubt she could have killed him. I told the constable that, too."

Cecily stared at him. "So you were the one who told P.C. Northcott about Gertie's threats."

Archie nodded. "I certainly did. I let him in on what I was doing here, just in case there were any repercussions later. It's always best to come clean with the law."

"How did you happen to hear Gertie threaten Ian?"

Archie laid a finger against his nose. "I was out in the yard, wasn't I. Watching Rossiter. I thought he might be trying to unload the loot, but he was picking a fight with the housemaid."

"I see. So you overheard them inside the kitchen shouting at each other."

"Loud and clear. Got a voice on her, that woman." Archie took the cigarette out of his mouth and stuck it behind his ear. "Got to run, Mrs. B. Glad we had this little chat, and remember, not a word to anyone."

Still bemused by the unexpected revelation, she watched him stride down the hallway until he reached the end, where he once more adopted the slouch that hid his true bearing.

She had to admit, she was more than a little intrigued. Not that she particularly liked him any better, but Archie Parker was so much more than she'd realized, and she would have liked to talk with him about his experiences. Perhaps later, when all this upheaval was over and the dust had settled.

In the meantime, she had to decide what to do about the jewel thief. The temptation to warn all of her guests was strong, but she understood that Archie would have a better chance of catching the thief red-handed if he had no idea he was under suspicion.

That's if it was a man. She couldn't ignore Mrs. Chubb's suspicions about Mabel. The girl had been seen coming out of Lady Roslyn's room with no good reason for being there.

She should have mentioned it to Archie Parker, but she didn't want to make trouble for the girl without at least talking to her and getting her story.

Right after breakfast, she promised herself. She had Mabel's address in her files, she would pay the girl a visit and find out exactly what was going on.

"Cecily! Where the devil have you been?"

Hearing her husband's voice, Cecily felt a stab of guilt. Baxter was striding toward her, his eyes sparkling with temper. "I've been waiting for over half an hour for you. I'm about to faint from starvation."

"Oh, darling, I'm so sorry." She linked her arm in his and drew him back toward the dining room. "I've been delayed by a small problem with one of our guests, but it's all taken care of now."

He gave her a suspicious look. "Not anything to do with this murder business, I hope?"

"Of course not, darling." She smiled up at him and walked with him into the dining room, where the aroma of bacon and sausage tempted her appetite.

It would be really nice, she thought wistfully, if all these problems were cleared up before the evening. Tonight the carol singing ceremony would be held in the library. It was her favorite part of the Christmas celebrations and it would be so much nicer if Ian's killer was apprehended and Archie Parker departed with his recovered jewels. Nevertheless, no matter what happened, she told herself, she would not allow anything to spoil her enjoyment of the ceremony. As for right now, she would put aside all her worries and enjoy a nice breakfast with her husband.

"I'm going into Wellercombe for an hour or two," Baxter announced, as he walked with Cecily down the hallway to the lobby. "I still have some Christmas shopping to do."

Cecily felt a stab of relief. She could visit Mabel while her husband was gone. It would save a great deal of explanation. "Just like a man," she said lightly, "leaving everything until the last minute."

Baxter leaned over and pecked her cheek. "I don't get in the mood for shopping until the last minute. It's not one of my favorite pastimes."

"I know. Which makes it all the more special." She glanced at the clock. "I have plenty to do to keep me busy while you are gone."

"I'm sure you do. Don't wear yourself out." He strode off toward the door, and she watched him leave, thinking how fortunate she was to have married such a thoughtful, generous man.

Turning toward the stairs, she was unsettled to see Sid Barrett hovering close by. She hurried over to him, wondering if he was lying in wait to pounce on yet another of the maids.

Sid seemed uneasy as she approached, and looked as if he

might leave. She called out to him before he could do so. "What are you doing here? Aren't you supposed to be in the stables, helping Samuel groom the horses?"

"I needed to have a word with someone first, m'm."

"A word with whom? One of our guests?"

"No, m'm. It doesn't matter. I can take care of it later." Touching his forehead, he turned and hurried across the lobby, almost colliding with Archie Parker, who had just entered through the front door.

Shaking her head, Cecily was just about to mount the stairs when two childish voices called out from behind her. Smiling, she turned to greet her two godchildren.

Lillian and James rushed across the carpet toward her, arms outstretched for a hug, while Daisy followed at a more leisurely pace.

Cecily crouched down as two small bodies hurled themselves at her. Holding a child in each arm, she kissed them both on the cheek. "How are you, my little darlings?"

Daisy reached her, and straightened the scarf holding down her hat. "They are beside themselves with excitement, m'm. I can't keep them down, so I thought I'd take them for a walk."

Lillian looked up at her. "Is the elf coming, too?"

Daisy rolled her eyes at the ceiling.

Cecily tilted her head to one side. "Elf? What do you mean?"

Daisy clicked her tongue. "For the past three or four days she's been talking about this elf." She frowned at the child. "I keep telling you Lillian, there isn't any elf. It's all in your imagination."

"It's not! It's not!" Lillian tugged on Cecily's sleeve. "I saw him just now. I did! I did!"

"Shut *up*, Lillian!" James gave her a shove.

Cecily straightened, and patted Lillian's head. "It's all right, my precious. If you say you saw an elf, then I believe you." She smiled at Daisy. "Lots of children have imaginary friends. I don't think it will do any harm."

"He's not a friend." Lillian sounded belligerent. "He's a Christmas elf and he brought us a present."

At that moment a small group of guests entered the lobby, their voices raised in laughter. Cecily bent over to hear the child better just as James gave Lillian another shove, sending her into Cecily. "You promised you wouldn't tell anyone. Now Father Christmas won't come!"

"James!" Daisy stepped forward and grabbed the boy by the collar of his coat. "How many times do I have to tell you? Do not push your sister like that. You'll hurt her."

Lillian began to whimper, and Cecily pulled her close. "Daisy's quite right, James. It isn't nice to be so rough with your sister. Now tell her you're sorry."

James kicked the carpet and mumbled, "Sorry."

"There." Cecily gave Lillian a little push away from her. "You see? James is sorry."

For answer, Lillian gave her brother a hefty shove, and received an ear-splitting howl of protest. Heads turned, and Daisy hastily grabbed the hands of her charges. "I think it's time we got out in the cold fresh air."

"Good idea." Cecily hugged each of the children again. "Have a good walk, my dears. You need to be really tired so that you can go to sleep early before Father Christmas comes."

DECKED WITH FOLLY

"*If* he comes," James muttered.

"He will. I promise." Cecily watched them leave, thinking wistfully of how magical Christmas was to children. How wonderful it would be if everyone, young or old, could feel that same magic.

It was a little hard, she thought as she climbed the stairs, to keep up the Christmas spirit with so much on her mind. If only she could get everything resolved before the end of the day. That didn't seem very likely at present.

In fact, she was really beginning to worry about Gertie. If something didn't turn up in the murder case soon, her chief housemaid might very well find herself escorted down to the police station under suspicion. Somehow she had to find out what happened, before the last hours ran out.

CHAPTER

❈ 21 ❈

Kept busy with the extra work, the next hour flew by after all for Gertie. After helping Pansy make the beds, she dusted all the rooms while Pansy swept the carpets.

She was in such a rush for the day to go by, she actually finished her chores early, and decided to sneak a few minutes with the twins before she had to start getting everything ready for the midday meal.

As she reached the bottom of the stairs, however, Clive ambled toward her, his cap in his hands. "I was hoping to catch you," he said, as she paused in front of him. "There's something I'd like to show you, if you have a moment or two."

Slightly irritated at losing the chance to see her children, she glanced at the clock. "I only have about ten minutes."

"I'll be as quick as I can." He paused, then added, "It's rather important."

Curious now, she nodded. "All right. What is it?"

"It's outside." He gave her an anxious look. "You'll need your shawl."

She shook her head. "Nah, I don't have time to get it. I'll be all right. Where outside?"

"I'll show you." He led the way to the door, and, thoroughly intrigued, she followed him.

She couldn't imagine what it was he wanted to show her. It hadn't snowed in the last four days, so it couldn't be a snowman. Which was just as well, since she wasn't too fond of snowmen.

Stepping out onto the porch, she shivered. The wind was blowing directly off the ocean, bringing a salty chill she could feel in her bones. Before she could take another step, she felt a warm weight on her shoulders.

Taken by surprise, she hugged Clive's jacket to her. It covered her knees, and still held the warmth of his body. "Thank you!" She looked up at him, concerned to see him in shirtsleeves. "But now you'll be cold."

"I'm used to it. Come." He beckoned her to follow him and she obeyed, trudging behind him as he strode ahead around the corner of the building and across the lawns.

He kept up such a pace she was out of breath by the time they reached the edge of the woods. The dark skies made the shadows even deeper among the trees, and a damp mist cloaked the trail.

Gertie had kept expecting Clive to halt long before they reached the woods. Instead, he kept up the steady pace, charging ahead through the trees. She followed more slowly, doubts beginning to creep in. She couldn't imagine why he'd brought her all this way to show her something. Only then did she remember about Ian.

She remembered Clive that night, skulking across the yard long after he was supposed to have left for home, and soaking wet, like he'd been out in the rain. If Clive had killed Ian, then he had been the one to leave that candlestick under her bed in the hopes she'd be blamed for the crime.

A pang of fear dried her mouth. What if he was going to arrange some kind of accident to get rid of her? Then no one would know for sure that she hadn't killed Ian, and Clive would be in the clear.

She thought back, trying to remember if anyone saw her leave the building with him. Philip must have been behind the reception desk, but that didn't mean he'd seen her. It was Christmas. No one was coming or going, and Philip would sit on a chair and read when it was quiet.

Gertie gulped. She'd been pretty stupid to trust Clive so completely. He could have lied about Ian being gone when he got to the coal shed. He could easily have bashed Ian on the head and shoved him in the pond, then brought the key back with no one the wiser.

Heart pounding, Gertie came to a halt. She was too far from the club for anyone to hear her, and she had no doubt that Clive could easily outrun her.

From up ahead Clive's voice drifted back to her, muffled and strangely high-pitched. "Here it is! Over here!"

Torn with indecision, Gertie hesitated. Clive had protected her so many times. She found it hard to believe he would hurt her now. Then again, if she was wrong about him, she could be making the biggest mistake of her life.

Nevertheless, she felt compelled to find out what it was he was so anxious to show her. Praying that she wasn't walking into a trap, she started forward to the clearing where Clive waited for her.

Seated in her office, Cecily glanced at the clock. Another two hours before the midday meal would be served. Plenty of time to go into town and back. By now Samuel would have the carriage ready for her. With luck she would be back long before Baxter returned.

Several minutes later she was on her way down the Esplanade. Mabel lived in a boarding house on the edge of town, and Cecily felt a stab of apprehension as Samuel brought the carriage to a halt outside the drab looking house. Until now she hadn't considered the possibility that Mabel might have an accomplice, in which case, her meeting with the maid might be a little more dangerous than she had anticipated.

"Perhaps you'd better come with me," she told Samuel, as he opened the door of the carriage. "I think I might need your protection."

Samuel looked alarmed. "I thought you were just going to visit Mabel."

Cecily sighed. "I am. I should have told you all this before. There's a possibility that Mabel has been stealing from the guest rooms and I don't know if she has an accomplice."

Samuel's eyebrows shot up. "Don't you think it might have been better to let the constable handle this?"

"P.C. Northcott isn't here, Samuel, and I really don't want to call in the inspector or the Wellercombe police."

Samuel looked as if he would like to turn the horse around and leave as fast as possible. "Very well, m'm. Lead the way. I'll be right behind you."

Cecily smiled. Samuel could always be relied upon to help her in an emergency. "Come, then. I'm sure I'm worrying about nothing, but it doesn't hurt to lean on the side of prudence."

The gray-haired woman who greeted them at the door seemed surprised to see them. "Mabel?" she said, when Cecily asked for the maid. "I haven't seen her this morning. I thought she'd gone to work. She might be up in her room. It's the first one on the right, at the top of the stairs."

Thanking her, Cecily hurried over to the stairs and climbed them, grateful for Samuel's presence behind her. She tapped on the door of Mabel's room and waited several moments before knocking again, louder this time. "Mabel? Are you there? It's Mrs. Baxter. I would like to talk to you."

Still no answer.

"She's probably scarpered," Samuel said, looking worried. "Why don't we let the constable take care of her."

"I think she's in there." Cecily put her ear closer to the door. "I heard movement." She rapped again. "Mabel? I only want to help you. Let me in and we'll talk about what happened."

Another long moment of silence.

"It's no good, m'm," Samuel began, but just then a loud click turned both their heads.

Slowly the door opened, and Mabel's pallid face appeared in the crack.

Cecily smiled. "Are you alone?"

Mabel nodded, and Cecily heard Samuel breathe a sigh of relief. "Will you let us in?"

For another anxious moment or two the maid hesitated, then she stood back and opened the door.

Quickly Cecily slipped inside the room before the girl could change her mind. Samuel stepped in behind her and closed the door.

The room was tiny but cozy, with a small window overlooking the street. Although the furnishings were shabby, everything was neat and tidy—the bed was made and there were no clothes or shoes lying around.

Mabel pointed to the single chair in the room. "Please sit down, m'm."

She waited for Cecily to sit before seating herself on the edge of the bed. Samuel stood by the door, anxiety still creasing his face.

Cecily came straight to the point, as usual. "Mabel, it has come to my attention that one of our guests is missing some jewelry. I was wondering if you could help me find out where it is."

A dark flush crept over Mabel's cheeks. Tears welled in her eyes and spilled down her cheeks, and she dashed at them with the back of her hand. "He made me do it," she whispered.

With a leap of triumph, Cecily leaned forward. "Who made you do what?"

Mabel gulped and rubbed her nose. Samuel stepped forward and gallantly offered her his handkerchief. She took it and blew her nose hard, then crumpled the handkerchief in her hands. "I saw Mrs. Chubb's ring on the windowsill," she said, sniffing in between her words. "It looked so pretty. I've never seen a ring like that before and I wondered what it would look like on my finger. So I tried it on." She sniffed harder and more tears ran down her cheeks.

"It's all right, Mabel." Cecily reached out and patted her knee. "Just take your time."

"Well, then Mrs. Chubb came into the kitchen and I was afraid she'd see it so I ran upstairs, but I couldn't get the ring off and then *he* came along."

"Who, dear? Who came along?"

Mabel sniffed again. "Sid Barrett. He saw me tugging at the ring and he helped me. It hurt, but he did get it off. He said he'd put the ring back in the kitchen. But then he told me I had to take some jewels from one of the guest rooms to thank him, or he'd tell Mrs. Chubb I stole the ring."

She started crying in earnest. "I didn't want to, but he said I would go to p-prison and I got scared so I took them, but then I was afraid to go back there in case he made me do it again."

"Oh, dear." Cecily sat back. "Well, Mabel, I think you have been rather foolish. You should have told someone instead of doing what Sidney Barrett asked you to do."

"I didn't think anyone would believe me." Mabel dabbed at her eyes with Samuel's handkerchief.

Cecily got up from the chair. "I would like you to come

back to the Pennyfoot with me now, and we'll get all this sorted out."

Mabel looked frightened. "I don't want to go back. He frightens me."

Cecily took her arm. "I promise you, he will not bother you again. But I need you to come back with me now so you can tell your story to a gentleman who will take care of Sidney Barrett, and then you will never have to see him again."

Mabel still hung back, her face drawn with anxiety. "But what about the jewels? Will I have to go to prison?"

"I think we can settle things with Lady Roslyn, once she hears what really happened. As for Mrs. Chubb's ring, Sidney stole that, not you. The best thing for you to do is come back with me and get all this sorted out."

Finally the maid nodded.

Cecily waited while she fetched her coat from the wardrobe and then led the way down the stairs to the entrance.

The woman who had let them in came forward as they approached the front door. Apparently noticing the maid's tear-stained face, she asked anxiously, "Is everything all right, Mabel?"

"Quite all right, Mrs. Thomas. Thank you." Mabel managed a frail smile. "I'll be going to work now."

The woman still looked doubtful, but stood back to let them pass.

Once outside, Cecily felt that she could breathe again. Mabel still looked frightened, and Cecily tried to reassure her as they traveled back along the Esplanade.

"I'm sure Lady Roslyn will be understanding once we explain everything to her." She tucked her scarf more securely around her neck against the chill wind. "Rest assured I won't let you go to prison."

Mabel sat hunched on the seat, and seemed unconvinced by Cecily's remarks.

She would have to talk to Archie Parker the moment they got back, Cecily told herself. The sooner they got this matter settled, the better.

The walls of the Pennyfoot came into view as they rounded the curve, resplendent in the weak morning sun. The mist was gradually disappearing, allowing a blue sky to emerge above the ocean. It was going to be a lovely evening for the carol singing ceremony. As they approached the country club, Cecily caught sight of two figures leaving through the back gates. She recognized Sid Barrett at once, then smothered a gasp when she saw his companion.

He was leading the young woman by the hand, and as she turned her face to the street Cecily saw her quite clearly. It was Gloria Johnson.

Closer and closer Gertie crept, her gaze firmly fixed on the shadowy figure of the man waiting for her, her muscles tensed to make a dash for it at the slightest hint of danger.

"There it is! What do you think?" Clive pointed up into the branches above his head, but Gertie never took her eyes off him.

She was closer now, close enough to see his face. He was smiling, his eyes sparkling, his voice eager as she drew even nearer.

DECKED WITH FOLLY

"It took me a few evenings to finish it. I had to work in the rain to get it done. I was worried it wouldn't be finished in time, but I made it."

In spite of herself, she glanced up, wondering what the heck he was talking about. And then she saw it.

It was beautiful—sturdy and picturesque, with a roof and a window and a railing to hold onto—every child's dream. The most perfect structure she had ever seen. Now she understood. Now she knew why he was late that night and why he was soaking wet. He had come out here in the woods, in the cold snow and rain, to build her children a tree house.

"It's a Christmas present for the twins." He looked at her, his voice anxious now. "Do you think they'll like it?"

Once more an unfamiliar tear slid down her cheek. Dan wasn't the only man who could make her cry. "They will love it," she said, her voice breaking. "They will bloody love it." In a rush of gratitude, she reached up and planted a kiss on his cheek. "You're a good man, Clive Russell. Thank you."

She stepped back, digging in her apron pocket for her handkerchief. When she looked at Clive again his cheeks burned, and he avoided her gaze.

He looked down at his feet instead, and cleared his throat. "You'd better be getting back inside. I don't want to get you in trouble."

"Right." She slid his jacket from her shoulders and handed it to him. "Here, I won't need this now. I'll run back."

He nodded, still without looking at her, and took the coat.

She started back the way they'd come, but after a few steps, she paused and looked back. "Happy Christmas, Clive."

His smile lit up his face. "Happy Christmas, Gertie."

Flashing him a grin, she turned and ran down the trail. What a bloody fool she'd been to suspect him of killing Ian. She should have known he wouldn't hurt a fly. Just wait until the twins saw that tree house. They were going to go crazy, that's what. Grinning, she broke into a fast trot and headed for the club.

Seated in her office, Cecily tried to make sense of what she had learned that morning. She wasn't really surprised to learn that Sidney Barrett was behind the theft from Lady Roslyn's room. What she didn't know was if that was simply a coincidence, or if he was also the man sent to find the jewels that Ian had taken from the gang in London. If so, then he was quite possibly Ian's killer. In which case, what was Gloria doing with him and where were they going?

Cecily leaned her chin in her hands. Something kept niggling at her brain, insistent and urgent. Something she knew, yet did not recognize. It had happened to her before, more than once and always just before she had solved whatever was puzzling her.

Think. Carefully she went over everything she knew, or didn't know. There were so many questions unanswered. So many possibilities, and yet . . . something told her she already knew the answer.

Resting her chin in her hands, she tried to listen to what her subconscious mind was trying to tell her. For some reason, her thoughts kept going back to the twins. Something Lillian had said. Cecily shook her head. All she could remember was something about an elf. With a sigh of exasperation she got up from her chair and wandered over to the window.

From there she could see the yard below, leading out to the back gate. The weather, capricious as ever, had changed again. A gray sea now threw angry waves at the shore. It looked as if a storm might be brewing.

What was Gloria doing with Sidney Barrett? Somehow it just didn't make sense. Cecily thought hard.

What was it that kept tugging at her mind? Something important. Something the twins had told her. What had they talked about? Father Christmas and elves.

Suddenly, it all fell into place. Of course. She needed to talk to the twins. Right away.

CHAPTER
❁ 22 ❁

Cecily reached the kitchen just as Gertie burst through the back door. The housemaid started to say something, but Mrs. Chubb, having just pulled a tray of coconut tarts from the oven, jumped in first.

"Gertie McBride! Is that any way to behave? Look at your cap. It's hanging on by one pin. It's a wonder you didn't lose it."

From across the room, Gertie glanced at Cecily. "Sorry, m'm." Hastily she tugged her cap straight and tucked the stray hair back underneath it.

Mrs. Chubb swung around, her face creased in dismay. "Oh, I didn't see you there, m'm. What can we do for you?"

"I need to speak to Gertie right away." Cecily checked

herself. "At least, I need to talk to the twins and I'd like Gertie to be there."

Gertie looked surprised, as did the housekeeper. "Well, get along, Gertie. Take madam to see the twins."

Rubbing her arms, Gertie walked cautiously toward her.

Unable to contain herself, Mrs. Chubb demanded, "Where have you been, out in the cold without your coat?"

"In the woods."

"What the blazes were you doing in the woods?"

Gertie smiled. "Looking at a tree house."

The housekeeper clicked her tongue in annoyance. "You're not making any sense."

"Clive built it." Gertie turned to Cecily. "You should see it, m'm. It's beautiful. Clive was out there every night in the snow and rain building it. The twins are going to love it. He did it for a Christmas present for them."

Mrs. Chubb gasped. "Fancy that! That was really good of him."

So that was what Clive didn't want to tell her, Cecily thought. He wanted to keep it a secret until he'd shown Gertie what he'd done.

"It was a lovely surprise." Gertie rubbed her arms again. "And to think I thought he might have been the one that killed Ian."

Cecily started. "Gertie . . . I need to talk to the twins. Now."

"Yes, m'm." Looking worried, Gertie barged through the door.

Cecily followed her, hurrying to catch up as she rushed down the hallway.

They reached the door together, and Gertie gave her an anxious look. "I hope they didn't do nothing to get into trouble, m'm. I know they're a bit overexcited and all, but Daisy's been keeping an eye on them—"

Cecily held up her hand to halt the gush of words. "It's all right, Gertie. They haven't done anything. I just need to talk to them, that's all."

Gertie still looked apprehensive as she opened the door.

Daisy looked up from her perch on the bed, then jumped to her feet when she saw Cecily. "Good morning, m'm."

"Hello, Daisy." Cecily smiled at Lillian and James, who sat on the floor playing with building blocks. At least, James was playing, while Lillian watched. "I just want a word with the twins."

Lillian scrambled to her feet, obviously delighted at the interruption. "Are we going for another walk?"

"Not now, precious." Cecily bent down until her face was level with the little girl's. "I want you to tell me about your elf."

James's chin shot up and he looked sternly at his sister. "She made him up," he said, sounding cross.

"Did not." Lillian pouted. "You saw him, too."

James's face turned red. "He said not to tell."

Cecily turned to the little boy. "Who told you not to tell?"

James looked down at the carefully built blocks and then, with a swoop of his hand, knocked them all flying. "He said if we tell, Father Christmas won't come." He glared at his sister. "Now look what you've done! Now we won't get any toys."

Lillian started to whimper, and Cecily put an arm around

her. "It's all right, little one. I promise you, Father Christmas is coming tonight."

Lillian sniffled. "How do you know?"

"Because he told me." Cecily crossed her fingers briefly, hoping she'd be forgiven the white lie.

Gertie, looking worried, bent over her son. "James, you tell me the truth right now. What did you really see?"

James jutted out his lip. "He was a big elf."

"Where did you see him?"

"He came in here."

Gertie gasped in horror, her hand over her mouth.

Daisy uttered a shocked cry. "James! He couldn't have done. I haven't seen anyone in here and I'm in here all the time."

"The other night," Gertie said, her voice hoarse with fear. "I went to the kitchen to get some milk and something to eat. I was only gone about five minutes, but . . ." She swallowed. "I thought Lillian had been playing with my things. That's when he must have come in and left the candlestick."

Lillian nodded. "It was the elf. He said Father Christmas had sent him with a present for us and he put it under your bed. He said we weren't to touch it until Christmas morning." She shot James a look of accusation. "James said it would be all right if we just looked at it and then put it back. But then Mama came in and took it away."

Gertie dropped to her knees and pulled both children into her arms. "I'll never leave you alone again," she said fiercely. "I swear to God."

"Then you saw the elf again, didn't you, Lillian." Cecily bent down again. "In the lobby this morning?"

Lillian nodded.

Gertie stared at her, while Daisy uttered another muffled cry. "Who was it?"

"Sid Barrett." Cecily straightened. "He was leaving the lobby when you brought the twins in to see me. I don't have time to explain everything now. Gertie, find Archie Parker. Tell him to meet me at the flat over Abbitson's, the butcher's shop. Tell him to come right away."

Gertie scrambled to her feet. "Isn't that where Gloria was living?"

"Yes. I believe Sidney Barrett is taking her there. He probably thinks Ian has hidden something he wants in the flat and could be forcing Gloria to find it for him."

Gertie gasped. "Then he did know Ian before. Pansy was right."

"If I'm right, then Gloria might be in danger, so please, hurry, Gertie."

"It's all my fault. I told him about Gloria. He didn't know about her until I told him. If he hurts her—"

"Gertie . . . please. Find Archie Parker."

"Yes, m'm. Right away." Dropping a flustered curtsey, Gertie lunged for the door. "What about Mr. Baxter? Won't he want to know where you're going?"

"Mr. Baxter isn't here. If he does come back before I return tell him I'll be back as soon as I can."

"Yes, m'm." Gertie dragged open the door and fled out into the hallway.

Daisy looked frightened as she gathered the children close. "What shall I do?"

DECKED WITH FOLLY

Cecily smiled at the twins, both of whom were staring at her with fear on their faces. "Just stay here and make sure the twins have plenty to keep them occupied. We want them to be tired so they'll sleep tonight."

Lillian's eyes lit up with hope. "Father Christmas is really coming tonight?"

"Yes, he is." Cecily moved to the door. "And I happen to know that he has a very special surprise for both of you."

She could hear their squeals of excitement as she hurried up the hallway to the stairs and thanked the power of Christmas magic.

Out in the lobby she cornered a footman and ordered him to have Samuel ready the carriage once more. Then she hurried upstairs to fetch her coat and scarf.

A few people were wandering in and out of the lobby when she rushed down again, but she could see no sign of Gertie or Archie Parker. She would just have to leave and hope that he caught up with her.

Baxter had not yet returned, and she left a message with Philip to tell him she'd be back shortly. Then she hurried out to the stables, where Samuel was almost finished harnessing the horse.

"Has Mr. Parker been out here yet?" she asked, as Samuel cinched the last strap of the bridle.

"No, m'm. Was he supposed to meet you?"

"I'm sure he's on his way." She lifted her skirts to climb into the carriage. "Tell one of the footmen to get the trap ready for Mr. Parker. He'll be following me into town."

"Yes, m'm." Samuel disappeared into the stables, then a

short time later hurried out again. Opening the carriage door, he stuck his head inside. "I couldn't find Sid, so I told Lawrence to drive Mr. Parker into town."

Settling back, she nodded. "Very well. Thank you, Samuel."

"Yes, m'm."

She felt the carriage sway as he climbed up onto his seat and gathered the reins. It was just as well she had Samuel with her, she thought, as they trundled across the yard and through the gate. Waiting for him to close the gate behind them, Cecily thought about what she might do once she reached the flat. She really hadn't thought much about it until now.

The best thing to do would be to wait for Archie Parker to arrive. If Sidney was a killer, it wouldn't be wise to tackle him, even with Samuel by her side. On the other hand, Gloria could be in danger. She wasn't holding Sidney's hand after all. He'd been leading her out onto the street. Probably against her will. In which case, time was of the essence.

The carriage jerked as Samuel nudged the gray forward. Cecily felt a stab of apprehension. She could only hope that Gertie had managed to find Archie Parker and that he was right behind her.

The sound of church bells, as they entered the town, reminded her that it was Christmas Eve. The carriage rattled up the High Street, scattering busy last-minute shoppers, until they pulled up outside Abbitson's, the butcher's shop.

The name had been changed twice in recent years, but to Cecily, it would always remain Abbitson's. The shop was crowded with anxious customers, all jostling for the best last-minute bargains. Geese hung upside down in the window, alongside turkeys and chickens, all of them looking pale and forlorn without their feathers.

Cecily hastily looked the other way. She had trouble equating a steaming, golden roast turkey with the live variety strutting around a farmyard.

The door opened and Samuel poked his head through the gap. "Did you want to wait for Mr. Parker, m'm?"

"Yes, I think we should." She peered anxiously out the window. "Do you see any sign of him?"

Samuel withdrew his head, then looked in again. "Not yet, m'm."

"Very well, we'll give him a few minutes." She settled back on her seat to wait.

Across the street a gentleman hovered outside a hat shop, obviously trying to decide on a Christmas gift for his lady. Next door at the toy shop, people hurried in and out, loaded up with packages for some lucky children.

Everyone seemed to be in a hurry, frantically trying to get everything purchased and transported home in time to enjoy the celebrations.

While here she was, stuck in the carriage, waiting for help to come. What was happening to Gloria? What if she knew Sid had killed her husband and Sid thought she had to be silenced? Was Sid Barrett evil enough to kill in cold blood? Considering he was a member of a London gang of thieves, it seemed likely.

Cecily sat forward. She could no longer sit there contemplating the possibilities. Gloria's life could depend on her. She had to act now.

Urgently she rapped on the window. Once more the door flew open and Samuel peered in.

"Yes, m'm?"

"Samuel, we must go up to the flat and rescue Gloria this minute."

Samuel looked as if he had been punched in the stomach. "Rescue who?"

"Gloria. Ian Rossiter's wife." Realizing her stable manager had no idea what she was talking about, Cecily scrambled down from the carriage. "Come with me, Samuel. And bring your whip. We might be in dire need of a weapon." Ignoring Samuel's grunt of apprehension, she marched purposefully toward the butcher's shop.

Gertie muttered to herself as she tumbled up the stairs in her haste to reach the top. Why was it that whenever she had to find someone in a hurry, their room was always on the top floor?

Gasping for breath, she rushed down the hallway to Archie Parker's room. Silence greeted her knock, and she tried again, bruising her knuckles as she pounded on the door.

The door next to her opened instead and a wary face looked out at her. "I say there, is something wrong?"

Gertie forced a smile. "No, sir. Sorry, sir. I was just looking for Mr. Archibald Parker. I don't suppose you've seen him anywhere?"

The gentleman frowned. "That Parker chap? Bit of a bounder if you ask me. Unsociable fellow. Can't imagine what he's doing down here on his own. Doesn't even answer when spoken to, and always skulking about in the corners."

"Yes, sir." Gertie was backing away, nodding and smiling. "Well, thank you, sir. I'll find him."

Relieved to see the door close, she turned tail and ran back to the stairs. If Mr. Parker wasn't in his room, he could be anywhere. Grumbling under her breath, she charged down the stairs a good bit quicker than she'd come up them.

All she could think about was Gloria in the hands of that sleazy sod, Sid Barrett. Not that she and Gloria were on the best of terms, but she didn't like to think of anyone at Sid's mercy.

She'd seen the look in his eyes when he'd cornered her out in the yard. He'd frightened her, and she didn't scare easily. That was a mean one, all right, and she could well believe he'd coshed Ian over the head with the candlestick.

Maybe he hadn't meant to kill him, but Ian was dead anyhow, and now Gloria was a widow and all alone.

Gertie reached the lobby and paused to get her breath. She still had trouble understanding why Gloria had stayed with her husband after she'd found out he'd gone through a mock wedding with another woman. Or why Ian hadn't had any children with her.

Still, none of that mattered now. What mattered was finding that drippy Mr. Parker and getting him to the butcher's shop. Though, that was something else she didn't understand. Why would madam want someone like that silly clod to help her with Sid? It didn't make sense. Then again, nothing much made sense these days. Like her row with Dan.

Gertie started down the hallway to the bar. She should never have suspected Dan of killing Ian. No wonder he was upset. Still, how was she to know what he was doing skulking around the Pennyfoot late at night without telling her he was there?

Misery engulfed her again as she remembered him walking out on her. If he left her, the kids would miss him dreadfully. So would she. The last time he'd left she had been miserable for months thinking about him and wondering what he was doing.

She reached the bar door and peered inside. Several men sat at the tables and at the long counter, but none of them was Archie Parker.

Her next stop was the dining room. Although it was over an hour until lunchtime, she thought he might be in there having a late cup of coffee or something. The room was empty, however, and she suppressed a wave of panic.

What would she do if she couldn't find him? Madam was waiting for him, and Gloria was with Sid, who might do heaven knows what to her, and there'd be no one coming to help her. It didn't look as if Mr. Baxter was back yet. What was she going to do?

Gertie swung around, gathering herself to dash down to the library. Just as she was about to launch herself forward, however, a figure stepped out of the shadows, right in front of her.

Gertie shrieked. He'd come up on her so silently she hadn't heard a thing. Heart pounding, she glared at Archie Parker. "What the bloody hell do you think you're doing?"

"Following you. Someone said you were looking for me."

DECKED WITH FOLLY

Gertie peered at him, puzzled by the transformation in him. He seemed taller, somehow, and not at all drippy. Even his voice had changed. For a moment she wondered if she'd mistaken him for someone else, but then he spoke again, his voice urgent and crisp.

"Why were you asking for me?"

"Madam told me to tell you to meet her at Abbitson's, the butcher's shop, sir."

He frowned. "Butcher's shop? Where is that?"

"It's in the High Street, sir." It was strange, but before when she'd talked to him, she'd resented having to call him sir. Now it seemed the right thing to do.

"Did she say why she wanted to meet me there?"

"Yes, sir. She thinks Sid Barrett killed my . . . killed Ian Rossiter. He's taken Gloria . . . Ian's widow to the flat over the butcher's shop because—"

"All right, wait." Archie held up his hand. "You can tell me on the way there. Come on, we must get a carriage ready right away."

"Madam's already gone in the carriage, but you can take a trap, but . . ." He was walking away from her and she had to hurry to catch up with him. "I can't go with you, sir."

"Yes, you can. I don't know where the shop is and you must show me. Besides, I need to hear everything on the way down there."

"But I have to get ready for the midday meal."

"That can wait. I'm not so sure Mrs. Baxter and Mrs. Johnson can."

Gertie stared at him. "Right." They had reached the lobby and as she passed the reception desk she called out to Philip.

"Tell Mrs. Chubb I had to leave for a while. I'll be back as soon as I can."

She didn't wait to see Philip's reaction. It was unheard of for a housemaid to just get up and leave right before the midday rush. Chubby would have a pink fit.

Gertie puffed out her breath. She just hoped madam would understand she had no choice, or she could be in really bad trouble.

CHAPTER
🎔 23 🎔

With Samuel close on her heels, Cecily marched down the alleyway next to the butcher's shop and paused in front of a shabby entrance. Twisting the handle with her gloved hand, she pushed the door open and stepped inside the dark hallway.

A cat meowed and slunk past her, escaping into the daylight beyond. Behind her, Samuel growled deep in his throat. "What's that awful smell?"

Cecily wrinkled her nose. "I imagine it's animal waste."

"Ugh."

Her sentiments precisely. Nothing smelled quite as bad as a butcher's shop at the height of the Christmas rush. Holding her breath, she climbed the stairs to the flat above.

She had barely reached the landing when she heard a

shrill scream from inside the flat. Without wasting another moment, she raised her fist and pounded on the door. "Gloria? Open this door, please. It's Mrs. Baxter."

For a long moment she could hear no sound from within. Once more she pummeled the door and this time was rewarded by a muffled whimper. With a warning look at Samuel, she called out, "Open this door at once or we'll break it down."

A voice answered her, so full of menace she hardly recognized it as belonging to Sidney Barrett. "Get out of here, before someone gets hurt."

Cecily tightened her lips. She beckoned to Samuel once more and he came forward, his eyes wide with concern. "Don't you think we should ring for the constable first?"

"P.C. Northcott is in London," she muttered. "We don't have time to wait for a constable from Wellercombe. Besides, Mr. Parker should be on his way, and not too far behind. We just need to play for time until he gets here."

Samuel's eyes widened even more. "Parker? What's he got to do with anything?"

"He's a private investigator." Cecily shook her head. "We don't have time for explanations now, Samuel. We have to get inside that room."

Samuel eyed the door. He wasn't exactly a robust young man. In fact, he was rather on the skinny side, but Cecily had seen him in action plenty of times before, and knew he was stronger than he looked. Wrestling with horses all day strengthened his muscles. She wasn't so sure about his resolve.

DECKED WITH FOLLY

"Just throw your shoulder against it," she said, giving him an encouraging push toward the door. "It looks frail enough. It should give under your weight."

Sid must have heard her, as he yelled out, "You try coming in here and I'll make you sorry you ever laid eyes on me."

Gloria started to call out, too, but her words were cut off as if a hand had been shoved over her mouth.

Samuel sent one last pleading glance at Cecily.

"Now, Samuel." She patted his shoulder. "I'll be right behind you."

Looking even more worried at that assurance, Samuel pulled in a deep breath.

Cecily crossed her fingers and closed her eyes, praying that Archie Parker would get there soon.

A loud thud opened her eyes. Samuel stood in front of the closed door, rubbing his shoulder. "Looks like it's stronger than we thought."

Once more Sid yelled. "I'm warning you!"

Samuel frowned. "That twerp is beginning to get on my nerves." Lifting his foot, he drove his boot into the door, then threw his full weight against it. With an ear-shattering, splintering crash the door flew open and Samuel disappeared.

Before Cecily could draw breath she heard a thud and a grunt from inside the room, and then Gloria screamed. Cecily tore into the room and pulled up short to avoid tripping over Samuel's crumpled body on the floor. Sid stood over him, a heavy frying pan held in his hand, while Gloria cowered in a corner.

With a cry of dismay, Cecily dropped to her knees. Samuel's eyes were closed, and he lay motionless, except for the slight rise and fall of his chest. Thank the Lord he was still breathing.

She looked up at Sid, who still held the frying pan aloft as if he would strike again. Anger gave her courage and she glared at him. "Is that how you killed Ian Rossiter?"

His mouth curled into a sneer, though she could see the fear in his eyes. "I don't let anyone get in the way of what I want. Rossiter made a bad mistake when he stole from me."

"I can see that." Carefully, Cecily got to her feet and took a step toward Gloria.

Sid raised the frying pan. "Don't move! I'd hate to have to hit a lady."

Glancing over at the shivering woman in the corner, Cecily murmured, "You don't seem to have any trouble abusing Mrs. Johnson."

"She knows where her husband hid the jewels." Sid's fierce scowl distorted his face. "It's her own fault if she won't tell me where they are."

Gloria switched her terrified gaze to Cecily. "I keep telling him. I don't know nothing about any jewels. I never saw them. Ian never said anything to me about them. I swear on the Bible."

"Perhaps he didn't steal them from you after all," Cecily said, keeping an eye on Sid as she shifted one foot closer to Gloria.

Sid was staring at Gloria and didn't notice her transfer her weight and shift again. "She's a bloody liar. She knows where they are, she just won't tell me." He raised the pan higher. "Don't think you can keep them all for yourself, you rotten bitch."

Hearing a slight sound, Cecily glanced down at Samuel. He hadn't moved, but she thought she saw his eyelids flicker. Then she heard the sound again, and quickly coughed to cover it.

"Is it really worth inflicting all this pain for just a few jewels?" She edged over a little farther, so that Sid turned to face her, his back to the door. "I mean, how much can they be worth?"

Sid's grin was evil. "Wouldn't you like to know. They're worth a fortune, that's what. There's forty carats of diamonds in the set, all perfectly matched. The biggest haul we ever pulled off. Ian was my fence. He'd done a good job for me before, so I trusted the bugger to get rid of the diamonds for me. The bloody sod took off with them."

Cecily faked a look of sympathy. "That must have been upsetting. How did you know where to find him?"

A shadow moved outside in the hallway. Gloria whimpered and Cecily shot her a warning look. Sid was reliving his fury now and too angry to pay attention to her.

"He told me he used to work at the Pennyfoot and married the chief housemaid there. When I found out he'd left town I guessed he'd go running back to her." He glanced at Gloria. "He never told me about that one. If he had I would've had the jewels back by now."

Cecily shifted backward an inch or two. "So you applied for the job at the club to wait for Ian to make an appearance?"

"Yeah. I knew it wouldn't be long and sure enough, he showed up that night. I was going to follow him home, but when he went inside the club on his own, I met him in the lobby." He glared at Cecily. "What difference does it make, anyway? I'm not going to stand around here talking all day. Tell her to give me back the jewels. Then I'll get out of here and leave you all alone."

"I told you, I don't know nothing about them." Gloria burst into loud sobbing, and Sid rolled his eyes.

Raising the pan again, he took a step toward Cecily. "Tell me where they are or she gets it."

Gloria cried harder.

"You've already killed one man," Cecily said, backing away. "Isn't that enough for a few diamonds?"

"I didn't mean to kill him. I hit him too hard, that's all." Sid's expression grew desperate. "I was angry. I trusted that bugger and he betrayed me. Nobody does that to Sid Barrett. Nobody."

A movement in the doorway snatched Cecily's attention. She saw Archie Parker take a step forward and Sid begin to turn. Before either one of them could react, a whirlwind of fury in the shape of her chief housemaid hurtled past the detective, straight at Sid.

Gertie's hand was raised above her head and clutched in her fingers was a candlestick. With a howl of rage she brought it down on Sid's head. His look of shock was almost comical, then his eyes rolled up in his head and he crumpled to the floor.

"That," Gertie said, her voice high-pitched and shrill, "is for killing Ian, you rotten sod."

DECKED WITH FOLLY

"Good God, woman." Archie bent over the fallen jewel thief. "You could have killed him."

Gertie wasn't listening. She'd caught sight of Samuel lying on the floor, his eyes open and a dazed look on his face. "Crikey, Samuel." She dropped to the floor beside him. "What the bloody hell are you doing down there?"

"Resting." Samuel gave her a weak grin. "You've got a wicked right arm, there, Gertie. Ever thought of joining a cricket team?"

"Go on with you." She took hold of his hand and pulled him up to a sitting position. "I see you brought your whip with you. Why didn't you use it?"

"Didn't have time."

"Well, he gave you a pretty good crack on the head. You've got a bloody bump the size of an egg."

Samuel explored his head with his fingers and winced. "I didn't see that coming."

Archie picked up the cast iron frying pan from the floor. "This did almost as much damage as the candlestick."

Gertie looked at Sid, who had started to groan. "Well, at least I didn't kill him with it. More's the pity."

Cecily, who had moved over to Gloria the minute Sid hit the floor, had an arm around the trembling woman. "Did he hurt you?" she asked, her voice just a little shaky.

Gloria rubbed her arm. "A few bruises here and there but I'll be all right. Not like poor old Ian." She glared at Sid, who still lay on his back. "I can't believe that bugger killed him."

"And tried to put the blame on me," Gertie added, looking as if she'd hit him again at the slightest provocation.

"I hope that isn't the same candlestick that he used on Rossiter," Archie said, pulling a pair of handcuffs from his pocket. He bent over and snapped one end on Sid's wrist, then snapped the other end on his own arm.

"Nah. I grabbed this one off the hallstand on the way out." Gertie helped Samuel to his feet. He looked a little pale and not too steady on his feet, but he managed a wobbly smile. "Think of everything, don't you, luv."

"I do me best." Gertie looked anxiously at Cecily. "Mr. Parker insisted I come along with him, m'm. He didn't know where the shop was and I had to tell him everything that was going on. I know Mrs. Chubb is going to be after me for leaving like that, but I didn't have time to explain and—"

"It's all right, Gertie." Cecily dug in her pocket for her handkerchief and handed it to Gloria, who was still sniffling. "I'll explain to Mrs. Chubb."

"Thank you, m'm." Gertie tilted her head at Archie. "Did you know this bloke is a detective, like Sherlock Holmes?"

"Yes, I did actually." Cecily smiled at him. "Thank you for getting here so fast."

"My pleasure, m'm." He hauled Sid, who looked as if he would rather still be lying on the floor, to his feet. "Now, if you don't mind, I'll take this scoundrel into Wellercombe for charging. All right if I take the trap? The rest of you can go back in the carriage, right?"

"Oh, please." Cecily waved her arm at the door. "I don't want to see that man's face again if I can help it."

"Yes, well, you might have to say your piece at the trial." Archie shoved the sullen-faced Sid toward the door. "I wouldn't want him to slip through our fingers now that we got him for murder."

"It's not murder if I didn't mean to kill him," Sid protested.

"Well, we'll see what the judge has to say about that." The two of them disappeared down the stairs, with Sid arguing all the way down that he couldn't be charged with murder.

Cecily hurried over to Samuel, who still seemed a little dazed. "Are you all right? Should we take you to see Dr. Prestwick?"

Samuel shook his head, then winced. "No, m'm. I'll be fine. I just want to get everyone back home, that's all."

"I feel responsible, Samuel." Cecily felt a little queasy at the sight of the bump on his head. "I ordered you to bust open the door. I really didn't expect that dreadful man to hit you."

"It's all right, m'm. It was worth it to see him taken away in cuffs."

"Yes, I have to agree, I felt relieved about that. Now we'd best hurry back to the Pennyfoot. We are dreadfully late for the midday meal, and I have a few things to take care of before getting ready for the carol singing this evening."

Gertie made a little sound and Cecily turned to her. "Were you going to say something, Gertie?"

"No, m'm." Gertie's face looked a little strained, and no wonder, after everything that had happened. "I was just thinking about the carol singing, that's all."

"Ah, yes. I'm looking forward to it." Cecily glanced at Gloria, who seemed to be recovering nicely. "I hope you will join us this evening."

The young woman smiled. "I'd like that very much."

"Good, then that's settled." Cecily headed for the door. "Come, let us leave this place."

"Just one moment, m'm?"

Cecily paused, and looked back at Gloria. "Yes?"

"I have to get something first." She moved over to the fireplace and lifted up the coal scuttle. After setting it aside, she pried up four of the tiles from the hearth, then reached inside.

Cecily wasn't terribly surprised when Gloria held up a black velvet box.

Gertie, however, uttered a loud gasp. "The jewels! You swore on the Bible you didn't have them!"

Gloria sniffed. "I wasn't holding one at the time, though, was I."

"That don't make no difference." Gertie looked at Cecily for help.

Cecily gave her a slight shake of her head. "What matters is that the jewels are safe. We must see that they get back to the rightful owners."

"Do we have to?" Gloria clutched the box to her chest. "I was hoping to keep them. After all, I lost my husband because of these."

Gertie snorted. "Where do you go where you can wear a blinking fortune in jewelry?"

"I wasn't going to wear them." Gloria smiled. "I was going to sell them. What I'd get for these would set me up for life."

"What you'd get for those," Cecily said dryly, "would be a

few years in prison. That's stolen property, young lady, and highly recognizable. It has to be returned."

"Can I get a peek at them first?" Gertie held out her hand for the box. "I never saw real jewelry close up."

Gloria looked as if she would refuse, but Cecily took the box from her unwilling hands and opened it.

Light from the gas lamp on the wall set the jewels ablaze. Even Cecily gasped at the sparkle of brilliant color dancing in her hands. "These are magnificent," she said, her voice hushed with awe.

"Bloody hell." Gertie leaned in for a closer look. "I could fancy meself with those around my neck."

"I hate to intrude on the all the admiration," Samuel said faintly from across the room. "But I have one monster of a headache, and if you want me to drive you home I think we'd better go now."

"Oh, poor Samuel." Instantly contrite, Cecily snapped the lid of the jewelry box shut. "Come, let us get back to the Pennyfoot where the poor dear boy can rest. We want everyone to enjoy the carol singing this evening."

She smiled at Gertie, concerned to see the sour look on her housemaid's face. It was obvious Gertie was upset about something. She would have to ask her about it later, but for now her first priority was to get Samuel back to the club and off his feet. Right now he looked as if he was having trouble staying upright.

Holding the precious jewels tightly in her grasp, she led the way downstairs and out into the fresh air.

*　　*　　*

By the time they arrived back at the Pennyfoot, Samuel was looking very much the worse for wear. Cecily ordered him to his room, with a promise to look in on him later. She then followed Gertie to the kitchen, where Michel was crashing saucepans around in a high fit of temper.

Mrs. Chubb's face turned red at the sight of Gertie, but before she could open her mouth, Cecily hastily intervened.

"You must excuse Gertie," she said, as the housemaid scuttled over to the sink to give the maids a hand. "She had to come to my rescue and was extremely brave in attacking a rather nasty villain. I'm sure she'll tell you all about it later, but right now I have urgent business elsewhere."

Mrs. Chubb's face wore a look of astonishment. "Very well, m'm. By the way, Mr. Baxter was in here looking for you. He seemed upset about something."

"Oh, heavens." Leaving Mrs. Chubb to stare after her, Cecily flew through the door and down the hallway.

Arriving at her suite a few minutes later, out of breath and apprehensive, she paused to compose herself before entering.

Baxter was in his usual chair, his face hidden behind a newspaper. Without bothering to lower it he said quietly, "So there you are."

"I'm sorry, darling." She hurried over to him, anxious to make amends. "I'm afraid time got away from me."

"You know you missed the midday meal."

Suddenly realizing she was starving, she uttered a sigh. "So I did. I'll have Mrs. Chubb send up something a little later when things calm down in the kitchen."

The newspaper rattled as he lowered it. "Where were you?"

DECKED WITH FOLLY

"It's a long story, my love." She pulled off her scarf and hat and threw them on the sofa. Raising the jewel box, she added, "I found the jewels."

He frowned. "What jewels?"

"Oh, didn't I mention them to you?" Taking a seat, she began to tell him everything that had happened.

His face grew longer and more alarmed as she got to the part about breaking into the flat. Expecting a lecture from him, she was surprised when she finished her account of the afternoon's activities without any comment from him at all.

His silence made her more nervous then any amount of shouting would have. She peered at him, fearing the worst. Had she finally overstepped the boundaries? Had he given up on her entirely, and no longer cared what happened to her?

She waited for what seemed an eternity, then whispered, "Are you very angry with me? I had to go after Sid, don't you see? He'd killed Ian, and I was afraid he'd kill Gloria, too."

Baxter sighed and passed a hand across his forehead. "I don't think you realize how I feel when you disappear and I have no idea where you've gone. Given your penchant for attracting danger, I can only sit in fear for your safety, with no real assurance that I will ever see you again."

"I'm sorry, I—"

She broke off with a gasp as he surged to his feet and pulled her into his arms. "What would I do without you, my dearest? I ask myself that every time you engage in these precarious escapades. When will you ever give up such treacherous ventures? When you finally meet your match and lose

291

the game? Is that my destiny? To lose you to a clever and fiendish criminal?"

"No, my love, I pray not." She clung to him, full of remorse. "I do not expose myself to such dangers without considering the risks, or making certain I have some protection. Samuel was with me this afternoon, and Mr. Parker not far behind."

Baxter sighed and let her go. "Very well, I shall simply have to grow old before my time with the worry of it all."

She smiled. "You will always be young to me, my love. Now finish reading your newspaper while I put these jewels in a safe place. Then I'll order something to eat and we'll have a nice rest. I'm looking forward to singing carols with you tonight, and I want to look my best. At least now I'll be able to enjoy the evening knowing that Lady Roslyn and Mrs. Chubb have recovered their jewelry and once more justice has been served."

"At a cost to my good looks," Baxter muttered, getting in the last word as usual.

Gertie stood near the window of the library, with one eye on the street. Guests and staff alike had been invited to the ceremony, and the room was packed, with every chair taken and many people standing around the Christmas tree.

Madeline stood next to her husband, her bare toes peeking out from under the hem of her flowing cotton frock. Defying expectations that her attire would become more appropriate once she was the doctor's wife, Madeline continued to dress as she pleased, still raising eyebrows everywhere she went with her bohemian style of fashion. Gertie admired that. No one told Madeline Pengrath Prestwick what to do.

She glanced across the room to where Phoebe Carter-Holmes Fortescue stood hissing at her husband. The colonel's bushy white eyebrows shot up and down, and he kept tugging on his mustache, but otherwise appeared unaffected by his fussy little wife's reprimands. Gertie shook her head. Poor bugger. Nothing he ever did would please that woman.

Sighing, she glanced out the huge bay window again, hoping to see Dan's motorcar pull up outside.

The lamps were lit all along the Esplanade. The shops had closed, and nothing moved on the street. It all looked so peaceful outside, and she felt a sudden longing to be out there, hoping the cold wind from the ocean would blow away her melancholy.

She missed Dan. Her heart ached at the thought of being without him again. This time probably for good. The twins would miss him dreadfully, but in time they'd forget him. She didn't think she ever would.

All around her, voices were raised in a ragged but joyful rendition of "The Holly and the Ivy." Someone moved to her side, and she looked into the smiling face of Clive.

"You're not singing," he said, bringing his head closer to hers in order to be heard above the chorus.

She shook her head. "Can't sing, can I. What about you?"

He shrugged. "Not around anyone who can hear me."

She managed a grin. "We're in the same boat, then, aren't we."

He was smiling, too, but his eyes were serious when he looked at her. "Nice place to be, in the same boat as you."

Her smile faltered, uncertain how to take that. She was about to answer when another voice grabbed her attention.

"Hello, Gertie."

Turning, she felt a rush of relief and pleasure. "Dan! You came!"

His smile was all she needed. Warmth seemed to flood the room, and the lamps appeared to grow brighter. Flames leapt higher in the fireplace and the voices now seemed to sing in perfect harmony. Dan was there right in front of her, and it was finally Christmas.

She barely noticed Clive as he murmured a good night and melted away. Putting her hand in Dan's she said softly, "I've been waiting for you."

For answer he raised her hand to his lips. "Happy Christmas, love."

And it was.

Printed in the United States
by Baker & Taylor Publisher Services